I0694395

THE DEATH AND RESURRECTION OF BASEBALL

Echoes From A Distant Past

WILLIAM R. DOUGLAS

WOODBRIDGE
PUBLICATIONS

WOODBRIDGE
PUBLICATIONS

THE DEATH AND RESURRECTION OF BASEBALL:
  ECHOES FROM A DISTANT PAST

VFW name used with permission from Veterans of Foreign Wars.

Special thanks to the estates of Babe Ruth, Lou Gherig, and Jackie Robinson for permission to use their names.

Paperback ISBN-13: 979-8-9859591-0-9
Hardcover ISBN-13: 979-8-9859591-1-6 (dustjacket)
Hardcover ISBN-13: 979-8-9859591-3-0 (casewrap library edition)
Ebook ISBN-13:   979-8-9859591-2-3

Library of Congress Control Number: 2022905192

Woodbridge Publications • May 2022

Woodbridge Publications
McHenry, IL

For God, for Family, for all of us.
E Pluribus Unum,
and
to my wife Laurie,
my best friend and cheerleader,
and to my beloved family and The Hour Gang.

ACKNOWLEDGMENTS

I want to give special thanks to the initial editing and review team: Kylie, Maggie, Breanne, Glenn, Sue, and Jim. Additionally, I give thanks to Ashley Melander for the heavy lifting and much-needed deeper editing of the manuscript. Her expertise took my draft manuscript and the story, to the next level. She is truly talented in her craft. Also thanks to Ryan Forsythe for his expertise in formatting the book as well as the tedious work of the book cover first design. Also thanks to Brenda Drake Lesch, who designed the re-imagined cover of this revision. I found all three of these talents on upwork.com.

Follow the author at
www.authorwilliamrdouglas.com

"At what point then is the approach of danger to be expected? I answer, if it ever reach us, it must spring up amongst us. It cannot come from abroad. If destruction be our lot, we must ourselves be its author and finisher. As a nation of freemen, we must live through all time, or die by suicide."

**Abraham Lincoln, January 27th, 1838,
Springfield, IL**

"The one constant through all the years, Ray, has been baseball. America has rolled by like an army of steamrollers. It has been erased like a blackboard, rebuilt and erased again. But baseball has marked the time. This field, this game: it's a part of our past, Ray. It reminds us of all that once was good and that could be again."

**James Earl Jones as Terence Mann, 1989,
Field of Dreams Universal Pictures**

FOREWORD BY
DON WARDLOW

You will like the world William R. Douglas has created in this book.

In our current world, I have watched players' salaries and strikeouts rise while attendance falls in baseball parks around the country. Youth leagues continue to fold.

In our current world, even the most loving families in our world scatter to the four winds. Those same families are splintered by political differences that didn't seem to matter 40 years ago when I left home to go to college.

I am inviting you to William R. Douglas' world of a future United States. He pictures a world where baseball had to close up shop because America entered a second Civil War in 2061. His world is America, 2166 A.D., 100 years after the second Civil War ended. With 4 major cities in ruins, his world is the small Illinois town of McHenry.

Our protagonist is 12-year-old Joe Scott, who starts out with one of his buddies on a regular Saturday to explore, not sure of what they are looking for or what they might find. They find a relic. Like the tip of an iceberg, finding the relic is the beginning of a much bigger search and adventure.

It's easy to imagine baseball forgotten and our country nearly ruined by war. You just have to follow the current news and sports.

It takes a man of vision to imagine the game I love and a young boy's quest to try and restore it to a post-war American society.

William R. Douglas is such a man.

Don Wardlow *was the first blind professional baseball broadcaster, working with four teams between 1991 and 2002. His story is detailed in the documentary* **Miracle League: The Don Wardlow Story.** *After writing the blog* **Baseball As I See It** *from 2015-2019, Don now hosts* **The Baseball Lifer Podcast.**

PREFACE

The writing of my first novel was the culmination of several inputs, all important ingredients towards the story.

Those inputs came at different times in my life, and, in fact, were decades apart. I list them below, not in chronological order of their occurrences, but in an order that best illustrates what went into my thought processes that led to the germination of the idea behind the storyline for this debut novel.

In 1993, I read David Aikman's profoundly disturbing novel, *When the Almond Tree Blossoms*. In it, Aikman (who once worked as TIME Magazine's senior foreign correspondent), presents a scenario for a second American civil war, based on ideological lines (i.e., conservatives vs. liberals). The novel ends with a nuclear-powered ballistic missile submarine cruising up the Potomac River, flying the flag of the resistance.

At the time of publishing, in 1993, the Cold War had just ended a few years earlier, with the fall of the Soviet Union. Here on American soil, what was just beginning was the current era of political polarization between liberal and conservative ideologies, which has continued, in varying degrees of ferocity, to the current times and remains on a deadly trajectory.

Ten or so years ago, I came across an article about games that kids used to play, way back before the American Civil War of the 1860s. These old, "extinct" games had long been forgotten, due to the passage of time and the changing whims of what kids like to play.

For the bulk of my working career, I have worked in the Information Technology field. I spent most of that time working with servers. I was in the IT field when the Internet for the masses exploded onto the world stage in the 1990s. This newly interconnected world and the free flow of information has also been a temptation for nefarious individuals, criminal enterprises, and rogue states to engage in all manner of theft, large and small. From time to time, they've also engaged in the spreading of computer viruses for the sole purposes of destruction.

In 2011, I read William Forstchen's novel, *One Second After*. This New York Times bestseller tells the chilling tale of an EMP (electromagnetic pulse) attack against the United States that throws the entire country back into "horse and buggy" mode.

EMP attacks render all electronics, from the most complex to the most mundane, permanently destroyed. Since nearly every aspect of modern America has a printed circuit board as a critical functional component, the destruction of all of them at once, via an EMP attack, would be catastrophic, to say the least. In Forstchen's novel, 90% of the U.S. population is dead within several months.

One Second After caused quite a stir within the halls of the U.S. government, and in fact, the author sent a copy of the book to every member of Congress, hoping to stir action. To date, the entire nation's modern infrastructure remains gravely imperiled in the event of an EMP attack.

When I was a child, growing up in the 1960s, baseball was still king and was known as "America's Pastime." As my childhood went on, baseball changed. Money became a larger component at the professional level, with collective bargaining and free agency. Later, in my adult years, professional players went on strike (for more money). I expect that by 2030, at the very latest, we will all see baseball's first billion-dollar contract. A ten-year, $100 million-a-year contract to play ball. What effect will that have on the average fan struggling from paycheck to paycheck? What if it turns off huge numbers of fans?

Watching the game used to be easy (and free). Now, it's very hard to find a televised baseball game to watch, without paying someone for the privilege, and the funny thing is, you still have commercial breaks. Nowadays, not everyone can afford the top-of-the-line sports bundle to watch their favorite baseball team. Without free televised games, many potential fans are left by the wayside to pass their time watching something else, and in doing so, some have already lost interest in the game of baseball.

Meanwhile, in the youth realm, the shifting tastes of what games and sports kids want to play have been changing.

To be clear, youth are still playing football, but that is coming under increasing pressure because of concussions and other injuries. They are also still playing basketball. Of all the youth sports, "pickup games" of basketball bode well for the sport's continued long-term health and existence.

Kids are also still playing soccer, and in recent years, lacrosse, in increasing numbers.

Then there's baseball.

Sandlot ball, where kids gather and play the game without adult supervision, is all but dead.

In-house baseball leagues (i.e., non-travel baseball leagues) continue to see rapidly declining numbers, because of the popularity of travel-ball. The enormously more expensive travel-ball leagues have a built-in cut system. You have to try out for travel-ball, and if you don't make the cut, in many locales, you are out of luck. This is a recipe for disaster!

The number of travel-ball teams can never match the number of teams that an in-house league can accommodate. Thus, if the in-house leagues continue to shrink (or disappear altogether), that means fewer and fewer kids playing baseball (and softball), which eventually translates into fewer and fewer adult fans. What if that trend continues? What if it becomes no longer "cool" to even play baseball?

In 2016, the general storyline of the book had coalesced around the central theme of baseball having died. But how? The popularity of it waned, kids got interested in other things (like video games) and other sports (like soccer and lacrosse). Adults also lost interest. Financial woes enter the picture for some teams. A protracted labor strike also casts a pall over the game, at all levels of play.

But what else could so utterly eliminate a game from our culture? A proverbial "nail in the coffin," a second civil war, the likes of which are unparalleled in the histories of the nations of the world. This would be no *ordinary* civil war. If it were, recovery would be much faster. How do you take a super-power like the United States and knock it down so badly that it takes decades for the country, and the world, to get back up? Take a fratricidal war, that includes a limited nuclear exchange involving four large metro areas, and add in an EMP attack, along with the worst cyber-attack in modern times. That's how.

The war acts like a giant eraser. Erasing lives, geography, and parts of our culture. In the war's aftermath, it is this clawing back from the near-total devastation that is an important undercurrent in the storyline. At the beginning of our story, America has recovered, technologically, back to where it was at the war's out-break. Self-driving cars and trucks. AI equipped domestic robots. Vertical take-off and landing commercial aircraft. And much more. But there are still chunks of American culture missing, they just don't know it. One missing piece is baseball.

The rediscovery of a lost and forgotten part of America's pre-war past and culture is rich in symbolism. For baseball is as much a symbol of America itself as it is a game still enjoyed by millions.

So it was in Destin, Florida, during a family reunion trip in 2016, that I announced to my son, Joe, and brother, Scott, (both avid baseball fans) that I was going to write a novel and that the central character's name was a melding of their first names.

Enjoy the story!

THE DEATH

AND RESURRECTION OF

BASEBALL

Echoes From A Distant Past

PROLOGUE

The year is 2166. It has been over a hundred years since the end of the Second American Civil War, which began on April 12th, 2061.

The sport of baseball has been dead for well over a century. There is no living soul that personally remembers the game.

Before the Second American Civil War, the game of baseball (at a professional level) had succumbed to financial woes that were further exacerbated by a prolonged labor strike of three years. At the amateur level, the explosive growth of soccer and lacrosse, at all levels of play, combined with the pressures of other interests and other sports, caused the kids to simply lose interest in baseball, and it was no longer "cool" to play the game.

Baseball's last breath came as an unintended consequence of the Second American Civil War. Internationally, the sport died as well, because of the loss of its American sponsors.

The United States and the entire world survived this post-war period, but not without extreme costs to lives, culture, and history.

It has taken a century for the United States to recover from the three devastating blows suffered during the war.

The first blow was the loss of four major US cities: New York City, New York; Chicago, Illinois; Charlotte, North Carolina; and Atlanta, Georgia. The destruction of these four large, metropolitan areas was caused by a battlefield nuclear exchange that led to the single greatest loss of American lives on American soil in one day.

The second blow was a massive cyberattack launched half a world away. It used a weaponized computer virus that erased everything on every computer, public and private. Worldwide havoc ensued, because of the loss of all data and knowledge.

The third and final crippling blow was an EMP attack that plunged the United States and parts of Canada and Mexico into "horse and buggy" mode. The EMP attack destroyed the nation's electric grid, all electronic devices, all public and private transportation networks, and led to a breakdown in law and order brought on by a supply chain collapse.

When the maelstrom had ended, the developed world found itself not much better off than a third world country. As a result, the entire world was plunged into a severe and decades-long depression. With the rest of the nations of the world focused on caring for their own, there was no help to be found for a country the size of the United States.

Thus, an agonizingly prolonged period of survival mode ensued before reconstruction could begin. Reconstruction took several decades to return America and the industrialized world to some semblance of their former glory.

Now, with the sun rising on the reconstructed United States, McHenry, a town in northern Illinois, is home to an intrepid twelve-year-old boy named Joe Scott.

Joe has a knack for exploring and sets out one day with a buddy to see what is in the woods east of town, on the other side of the river, which has been labeled a "no-man's-land" since the end of the war.

While there, Joe discovers a century-old relic that sets him on a quest to learn its meaning. His journey leads to the rebirth of a game long since forgotten by time and the ravages of civil war.

CHAPTER ONE

It's in the Woods

Twelve-year-old Joe Scott was not amused by the comments from some of his friends that he was odd. So what if he didn't like to sit inside and waste hours at a time playing the latest metaverse immersion experience. Unlike the old MVI, which had been all the rage, this newer evolution of gaming introduced a level of sensory interaction that Joe found unpleasant. Joe had determined to set out on a different course, one that led him towards a great love of the outdoors and a quest for discovery.

At 5 feet 7 inches tall, young Joe was the second tallest kid in his 6th-grade class at Landmark Middle School in McHenry, Illinois. He was also stocky and the strongest kid in his class. An average student, Joe was well-liked by both his teachers and classmates. But, like most students, he lived for the weekends. Two full days of outdoor exploration and adventure.

So it was that this typical Saturday in September was not much different from the last one, except for the fact that he had raced to finish his obligatory weekly chores in record time. He had started on his chores on Friday night, just so that he could spend this first Saturday in September doing what he loved best, being outside with his friends and "exploring undiscovered country," his favorite phrase for his expeditions into the great outdoors. His gang included several other buddies who had caught the same exploration bug and decided they would much rather be outside than inside on most days.

On this day, however, it was just Joe and his buddy, Ted, that went on an expedition of discovery in the VFW Woods on the east side of town, across the Fox River.

Although McHenry had largely escaped the carnage and destruction of the Second American Civil War that had occurred 100 years earlier, she did not escape it totally.

The Battle of McHenry was fought on the east side of town and centered along a line that stretched from a small industrial park, just to the east of the old VFW hall, over to the east bank of the Fox River, where it turned south along River Road and then ran clear down to the Illinois Route 176 bridge.

For almost all of Joe's young life, tales of death, ghosts, and hauntings in those woods had kept him, and others, out of it. While some tales were surely exaggerated, others not so much. The size of the American Military Cemetery north of town gave stark and sobering testimony of the sheer depth and scale of the carnage that had happened in the battle over a century earlier.

But on this day, Joe and Ted had decided to defy the wishes of their parents and go exploring in the VFW Woods to see what relics and treasures lay there, just waiting to be discovered. Joe had heard, what he believed to be a reliable rumor, that the Army was about to give the "all clear" and that the woods were no longer a danger to life and limb. In spite of the old stories, Joe's thirst for exploring would not be quenched this day; no, this expedition would start a fire in him. Teddy, his partner for the day, was the perfect pal for this quest.

Fellow twelve-year-old, Ted Lee Banks, aka Teddy, was among Joe Scott's best friends. Ted and his family lived a few doors down from Joe, and he and Joe had been best friends since the first time they met, years earlier. A full hand-width taller than Joe, Ted was lanky, with glasses and rusty brown hair. Witty and quick to smile, Ted was the kind of friend that would light up a room when he walked into it.

Joe and Ted both attended McHenry's Landmark Middle School and were in the same 6th-grade class with Mrs. Meeghan. While Teddy was great at math, Joe's favorite subject was history. They would often get together and help each other out with their homework. Each of their respective favorite subjects was the other's weakness. Which worked out great, since they could do their homework together and help each other out.

On this particular day, the two of them had planned to meet up at the old war memorial park on Pearl Street, a few doors down from their homes.

"If we're gonna do this, we have to do it right. If we mess up and get caught, we'll be in so much trouble. We'll be grounded for a month," Joe said.

"A month! More like the rest of the summer for me," Teddy exclaimed. "Okay, but remember, the first snake I see, we're so out of there! I hate snakes!"

"Stop worrying," Joe said. "It's gonna be awesome! Did you bring a water bottle?"

"Yeah, and I brought some chips too, in case we get hungry," Teddy replied. "And I got a flashlight."

"Cool! I've got a pocketknife and some rope."

The late summer sun was high in the sky as the boys set out and walked the few blocks to the western shore of the Fox River. Over on the east shore of the river began the VFW Woods. The woods lined the entire riverbank, to the north and south, as far as the eye could see. The trees had even grown up on what had been the old Illinois State Route 120. To the east, the road was now destroyed, and nature had reclaimed the space. The Rt. 120

bridge was now useless to cars, since there were several bomb holes in the bridge deck, but it was still somewhat safe to walk across, if you were careful.

In that close-knit town, word traveled fast back to parents of kids seen getting into mischief, so Joe and Ted quietly slipped behind a pile of rubble, just north of the bridge. The old road dead-ended right there at the base of the rubble and the bombed-out bridge.

Joe raised his head, peered out over the edge of the rubble, and studied the old road and businesses to the west. Sensing the coast was clear, he motioned to Ted to follow him, and they made a mad dash toward the Rt. 120 bridge.

Before the war, the Fox River served as a dividing line of the town, separating the eastern part — half incorporated and half not — from the central business district and larger western portion of the city. Illinois Rt. 120 had been a major four-lane, east-west highway linking McHenry County to Lake County and Cook County in northern Illinois, both to the east and southeast.

The Rt. 120 bridge had been severely damaged during the battle. But, since it only led to the irradiated Lake County and Cook County, it was decided early in the post-war reconstruction period to abandon the bridge. Just five miles to the east began the uninhabitable zone that stretched to Lake Michigan, then down and around clear over to the Michigan state line.

As they made their way across the bridge, Teddy was the first one to start feeling a little nervous.

"Joe, you sure about this? What about the stories we've heard?"

"Relax, will ya? They're just stories! Nothing to 'em," Joe insisted.

A huge bomb crater lay at the base of the bridge on the east side, and they had to traverse busted concrete, twisted rebar metal, and weeds to slide down into it.

"I still don't get it," Joe sighed. "Why did they do it?"

"Do what?" Teddy asked.

"The war," Joe answered. "Why did they have to resort to shooting each other? It's crazy to think about. Like the chapter about the Battle of McHenry in our history book. Kids all over America read about our hometown and this battle and all the people that died right here."

"Yeah, I know what you mean," Teddy said. "My dad says it was over politics. My mom says it was over religion."

"I'm so glad it was such a long time ago and things are better now," Joe said.

"Me too," Teddy agreed. "Me too."

"Hey, my dad says there's even talk of fixing the bridge and rebuilding the old road to the east, where the wasteland is," Joe said, trying to steer the conversation to something a little less depressing. "He says some scientists may have figured out a way to make the places to the east livable again."

"Wow, that would be so cool!"

Emerging out of the crater, they were face to face with a tall forest of maple and oak trees. Adding to it was a thick growth of underbrush. Earlier, before they had set out for the day, they had both dressed in long pants and long sleeves, despite the late summer heat. Now they were both glad they did.

"Hey, that looks like a path or something," Teddy observed, pointing to an opening in the brush, about 20 yards to the left.

"Okay, let's check it out," Joe said.

They walked into the forest on what was, more than likely, a deer path. As they walked along, they heard the sounds of birds in the air and the crunch of leaves and sticks under their feet. After just a minute, the air became noticeably cooler, and the sunlight was much dimmer. The forest canopy was thick, and wildflowers that carpeted the sporadic open areas enhanced the forest smells.

Joe was the first one to spot the large pile of debris 50 yards ahead. "Hey, look. I think it's the ruins of the old marina. I read about this in history. During the battle, it was a field hospital and command post. When the front lines started moving closer to the river, they moved the field hospital further west. They also changed the command post to the old Justen Hotel on the other side of the river."

"Wow, so that's the pile of rubble and the memorial on the other side of the bridge where we started?" Ted asked.

"Yeah, that's all that's left," Joe replied. "There was also another bridge right by the marina. The Pearl Street Bridge. They blew it up as a defensive measure, as the other side was getting closer."

Ted looked at the rubble. "That must have been one hairy moment when all that went down."

"Right? I can't even imagine," Joe stated. "To make matters worse, after three days of fighting here, the battle blew up and turned into the huge battle of the Fox River Valley. There was fighting clear down past Elgin. That's something like 25 miles away.

"That's a lot of shooting," Ted said.

Joe paused, then looked at his buddy in the eyes. "And a lot of killing."

Turning their focus back towards the ground directly in front of them, Joe spotted something.

"Look! I found an old flashlight made of green metal. I think it's aluminum!" Joe shouted, as he picked up the beat-up soldier's flashlight and rubbed the dirt off.

After turning it this way and that, he put it into his back pocket, excited that he was the first to find a relic half-buried in the dirt. Ted was thrilled that they had found their first bit of treasure so soon into their adventure too, and he began looking ahead of them for more.

Seeing something tubular sticking up from the ground, Ted hurried over for a closer look. He reached down and gave it a yank. It barely budged. He could tell a large part of it was buried. After a few minutes of digging with his hands, he wrestled the relic up from out of the ground. With excitement, Ted yelled out, "Joe, look at this! It's an old rifle."

"Whoa!" Joe gasped.

"Looks like the barrel is all that's left," Teddy said, examining his find.

"Ya' gonna keep it?" Joe asked.

"Well, sure, why not?" Teddy answered. "I can swing it around and move the brush out of our way as we move along."

"That's a great idea," Joe conceded. "Hey, look, there's a tree limb laying over there. I'll grab that, and we can both swing away."

The deer path led onward towards the east. As the boys continued to walk, they passed burnt-out homes that had collapsed and had long ago become overgrown with vegetation. They occasionally stopped to pick through the rubble of a home for a short while, before moving along down the path, deeper into the woods.

About 30 minutes into their hike, they came upon a large building. Much larger than the ruined homes they had passed, but not as big as the marina.

"Hey, let's take a look in there," Joe said. "It's not totally collapsed, so we should be okay."

Stepping over debris and the vines that had invaded the building, they were excited by the prospect of finding some good relics inside the place. Of all the ruins they had seen so far on their venture into the woods, this building appeared the least damaged from the battle, time, and the elements.

"Hey, look at this. I think it's a sign," Ted said as he picked up an old, degraded piece of metal. Sure enough, there was a faint outline of letters and numbers.

"Can you make it out?" Joe asked.

"I think so," Ted muttered, squinting at the faded print. "Let me go over to the window and get a little more light on it so I can see it better."

Walking towards a south-facing window, Ted held the relic up to the opening, long bereft of glass. As the sunlight illuminated the sign, he read aloud.

"It says V - F - W Post Four - Six - Zero … I'm not sure, but I think the last number is a zero too."

"Wow, we're in the old VFW building!" Joe exclaimed. "This is where, during the battle, both sides ran out of ammunition and fought hand to hand until there were like only a few soldiers left. The VFW building was really important. Something like the Alamo. Towards the end, it came under mortar fire and took a direct hit. Did a lot of damage, but it wasn't totally destroyed."

"Obviously, since we're standing inside of it," Ted said. "What happened that they made this place off-limits for so long?"

"Well, there were lots of unexploded bombs and stuff. After the nukes, there was really no sense in keeping this area open. Making the no-man's-land start at the river just made a lot of sense to the military government at the time," Joe explained.

"Oh yeah, and then there's the story of Hezekiah Smith," Ted added.

"Hezekiah Smith!? You remember that story? I thought history was your worst subject?" Joe mused.

"Yeah, it is. But a story of a guy getting blown to bits over here on this side of the river, after stepping on an old mine, well, you don't easily forget that. That sticks with you, even for guys like me that don't like history," Ted replied. "Alright, that's enough history. C'mon professor, let's keep looking."

They lingered a few minutes looking for more artifacts but found none of any interest. Joe noticed another doorway on the east wall, and the two explorers passed through it and re-emerged outside.

On that side of the ruin, there was no path. Just old bomb craters filled with thick brush and trees. Heading eastward, Teddy, using his gun barrel turned makeshift sickle, and Joe, using the small tree limb, took turns swinging away to help knock down the brush so they could walk easier.

They had been slowly fighting through the undergrowth for about ten minutes when, just ahead, Joe noticed a gigantic wall of green ivy through the forest. It was unmistakable.

"Hey, you see that?" Joe asked. "Look how big it is!"

The wall of green towered over their heads.

"Whoa," Teddy breathed. "What is it?"

As they pushed their way through the thick brush, they came right up against it. It was thick with ivy, brush, and a tree here and there. The wall was high and curved up and out of sight. Looking to the south, they could see that the wall dropped dramatically and continued on a straight line to the south. Before moving down that way, Joe reached out his hand into the thick ivy to see what it was attached to. Sticking his hand in, he pulled away leaves and vines until he felt something metallic.

"It's a fence. Let's follow it that way," Joe said, as he pointed to the right.

As they made their way along the wall of ivy, south, Ted marveled at how big it was. "It's like a green monster."

The ivy and other vegetation had grown up next to and through the chain link, creating a massive walled carpet of green. Some parts of the fence were missing, but the vegetation had taken over, replacing the destroyed sections with their tentacles of ivy and branches, along a nearly straight line.

As Joe walked along, he noticed a patch of ivy with a small gap in it. He took a closer look and could make something out. "Hey, I think I see something here. I think it's a sign or something."

He cleared away the ivy from the tattered remains of an old sign attached to the fence. It was covered with dirt and moss. Getting one of the water bottles, he popped the cap open and splashed some water to wash it off as much as he could. He struggled to read the faint words of the sign out loud.

"The word 'No' is clear. Then I can see a P … an E … another P …" Joe rubbed at the remaining dirt. "Hold on, let me splash some more water on it." When he did, the rest of the faint lettering became more clear to read. "I got it!" he announced. "It says 'No Pepper.'"

Ted looked confused. "Huh? No Pepper? What's that mean?"

"Beats me," Joe shrugged. "Maybe this place was a restaurant?"

"Kinda weird for a restaurant to put up a sign up like that," Ted doubted. "No Pepper? What the heck?"

Joe was about to keep walking and leave the sign behind, when he felt a powerful urge to stop and take another look. He stared at it for a long time. "No Pepper," Joe whispered.

Joe took out his pocketknife and extracted the screwdriver bit from it and unscrewed the sign from the fence. He could not put his finger on it, but Joe felt in his gut this sign meant something. If he was wrong, no harm done. It would be just another relic to add to his collection.

The boys continued to walk south to a point where the fence dropped to around four feet in height. There, the brush, ivy, and woods were the thickest they had come across since entering the path down by the river. It was almost impenetrable. But, undeterred, the boys fought their way through to the end of the line, where the fence made a sharp turn away from them and curved slowly to the left, until the forest blocked their view of it.

Ted felt a little uneasy about going any further. "Joe, I think we've gone far enough. I really think we should go back home. I don't want to get near the radiation zone. Where exactly is that?"

Joe replied, "We're safe here, Ted. The radiation zone starts about 5 miles to the east of here."

"How big is it?" Ted asked.

"It's big, bro. It stretches all the way to Lake Michigan, then all the way south and around the bottom part of the lake clear over to the Michigan state line."

Ted shook his head in disbelief. As he did, he felt a slight shudder in his body. His mind was made up. "Let's go back home."

"Why? We're okay," Joe argued. "There might be something else over here."

"Nah, I'm done," Ted insisted. "Let's go back."

"Are you sure?" asked Joe.

"Yeah," Ted said. "Let's go back now."

"Well, okay, if you say so."

They started heading back, retracing the path they had made by clearing the brush. On the way back, Joe caught a glance of something large lying on the ground to his right, by a large oak tree. It was partially covered in vegetation. As he cleared it off, he could tell there were three words. The first one was Buss. The second word was mostly obliterated with a hole. "*Shrapnel maybe*," he thought. The third was only partially readable, and the letters F-I-E-L were barely visible.

"Buss blank Fiel. What does that mean?" Joe wondered out loud.

"The last word was probably field," Ted said. "As for what it means, I don't know, but we better keep heading back."

As they continued on, they stumbled across a few more relics, but none of any interest to them, so they left them there where they lay. All the while, on the way back, Joe could feel the cold metal of the "No Pepper" sign as it pressed against his side where he held it. The more he held it, the more glad he felt he had taken it down.

As Ted and Joe made their way back towards the Rt. 120 bridge, Joe wondered what other relics were in the thick forest beyond the fence that had, for now, stopped their advance.

"Teddy, we need to go back sometime soon. I got a feeling there's more cool stuff to find."

"Well, if you say so," Ted said. "But next time, let's bring the rest of the guys with us too."

"Yeah, why not," said Joe. "Maybe tomorrow, after church. This sign has me wondering."

Teddy glanced over at Joe, with a puzzled look on his face. "Yeah, right. No Pepper. I have no idea."

"Look, we gotta be clear about something," Joe stated. "We can't let our parents find out we were here. If they do, there's no way they'll let us ever come back!"

"Plus, we'll be grounded for who knows how long. Okay, my lips are sealed," Ted said. "I promise."

"You swear it?"

"On my mother's grave!"

"Huh?" Joe said, looking confused. "Your mom's alive."

"I heard my dad say that once, when he made a promise to our neighbor."

"Well, okay then."

Fifteen minutes later, they emerged back onto the Fox River bank as the sun was lowering toward dinner time. After again traversing the old, ruined state route bridge and making it back to their neighborhood, they parted company.

Joe walked into the garage. Seeing the back side of his dad, who was hunched over working on something, he quickly walked past and said hi. Just outside the door and out of sight of anyone around, he realized that, if his mom saw the sign, she might get suspicious. So, he tucked it up underneath his shirt and walked into the kitchen, where his mom was preparing supper. After giving a cheerful "hello," without stopping, he headed to his younger brother's room.

"Austin, promise not to tell anyone what I'm gonna tell ya."
"Ok, promise. What is it?"
"You won't believe what we found! It's in the woods."

CHAPTER TWO

Collateral Damage

Sam Scott had met and fallen in love with Mary Woodbridge during his junior year at McHenry High School. Mary was a sophomore that year. It was quite some time before he worked up enough courage to ask her to the Homecoming dance. She shyly accepted. But the night had been a comical disaster. Sam was late to pick her up, his car broke down, and he made several dumb comments because of an overwhelming nervousness.

A month later, after Mary had forgiven his missteps, Sam worked up the courage to ask her out again for a second date. He took her up to Lake Geneva, Wisconsin. They had an incredible evening aboard a dinner cruise. She knew, before the night was over, that she would marry Sam one day.

Two years later, upon Mary's graduation from high school, Sam convinced her that, rather than wait until college was finished, they could get married right away and still pursue their college degrees at Freedom University in Woodstock, Illinois.

After graduating from Freedom, the United States Department of Recovery and Reconstruction hired Sam as an accountant.

The department was housed in the giant, 110-story Eisenhower Federal office building on the south side of McHenry. The mammoth building housed 5,000 workers, all engaged in doing their part in the ongoing efforts to reconstruct the nation from the carnage of the past. The Department of Recovery and Reconstruction had similar facilities in three other regions, but theirs was second in size only to the headquarters' facility in Alexandria, Virginia, outside of Washington, D.C.

Mary also worked there, as Director of Human Resources. They would both often ride their bikes to work, since it was only a 20-minute bike ride from their home in midtown McHenry.

Now, they were the busy parents of five kids. Their first-born, Joseph, was a bundle of energy and occasional mischief. Second-born son, ten-year-old Austin, was a more cautious, reserved, and compliant child. The twin girls, Anne and Nellie, age eight, were rambunctious, but only to a level of unbelievable cuteness. Their fifth child, also a daughter, Lynn, had just turned three years old and had been a surprise addition to the family.

This particular Saturday, Mary Scott was at the three-quarter mark of what was turning out to be another typical, busy late summer day. Earlier, she had risen at 7 AM to eat breakfast with the family. Sam had long ago developed a love for cooking breakfast. That morning had been no exception, as he had arisen at 6 AM to cook up breakfast for his high school sweetheart turned bride of twelve years and their brood of five children.

After breakfast, the day had been partly filled with errands and chores, not only for Mary, but also for Sam and the kids. Joe had been the first to finish his chores and had been especially focused on getting through his list quickly to meet up with his buddy, Teddy, at 12:30 PM. Now, at suppertime, Mary was busy making an enormous meal as a thank-you for Sam's excellent breakfast and for the hard work the kids had put in earlier in the day.

As she was preparing supper, Joe noisily entered the back door of the house and bolted into the kitchen. He had a peculiar look on his face when he cheerfully said, "Hello," before darting up the stairs.

At the instant he said hello, Mary spotted something tucked underneath Joe's shirt. She played coy, while simultaneously fighting back the urge to either laugh or ask Joe what he had been up to. She decided to do neither and simply bring her motherly prowess to bear later, after supper time, as any good mother would.

One thing was for certain, her oldest child more than likely had been up to some sort of mischief. After all, kids would be kids, and Joe was more mischievous than most. Mary looked up at the clock and noted the time, 4:54.

A moment later, Sam came in from the garage smelling ripe of sweat, dirt, and grease.

This Saturday had been especially busy for Sam. While Mary had gone out to run a bunch of errands, he had been busy directing their brood of five kids in serious yard work on this warm September day. The kids finished their chores by 1 PM, after which he released them to go play. Joe had finished up ahead of his siblings, and was quick to run over to Teddy's house, not an abnormal occurrence for a Saturday afternoon.

After the yard work, Sam had focused on organizing his workbench. Full to overflowing with greasy tools and other odds and ends, he relished getting it all sorted out and cleaned up again, with tools back into their rightful places. While a desk job paid the bills, he enjoyed doing this kind of work when at home, and he found it therapeutic.

Finishing up, he strolled through the door that led into the kitchen. "Hey, hon, what's for supper?" he asked.

"Your favorite," Mary smiled. "Steak, baked potatoes, sweet corn, salad, and a special treat for dessert."

"Really? That sounds fantastic! I'll go upstairs and clean up. Where are the kids?"

"Joe is upstairs talking to Austin. The girls are in their room playing," Mary answered. "Hey, did you see Joe come home a minute ago? He was gone a long time with Teddy this afternoon."

"Yeah, he came in through the garage and said hi," Sam said, taking off his dirty shoes and placing them on the rack by the door. "Before I could turn around and say hi back, he was racing into the house. Why, what's up?"

"You too?" Mary responded. "He ran through here and went straight to Austin's room. He was acting weird, and I could tell he was hiding something underneath his shirt."

"Really? I wonder what it could be. You want me to go upstairs right now and find out?"

"No, let me check on it after supper. If it turns out to be more mischief than I thought, we'll have a three-way conversation with him."

"Oh boy, he loves those!"

Mary chuckled, "Alright, get cleaned up — and I mean cleaned up, stud muffin."

"You got it, love! Gimme 10 to 15 and I'll be back down for supper. I'm starving."

Suppertime was something that Sam and Mary had determined, early in their marriage, would be an important cog in the workings of their family life. Ages ago, before the war, it had slowly become the custom in the United States that eating dinner was a sort of every-person-for-themselves deal. This dissolution of family dinners had unintended consequences for the fabric of the family and had been rather significant in the run-up to the civil war.

Twenty years after the war, as the country slowly emerged from the wreckage, psychologists and sociologists attached to the president's Office of Reconstruction issued the findings from their research.

They had sought to understand key societal ailments that had contributed to the pre-war run-up. Their findings clarified that, for the nation to rebuild, families needed to grow stronger and more cohesive. One key suggestion was to revive the custom of families gathering around supper tables every night. It seemed silly at first, and while initially slow to catch on, eventually there was no turning back to the dysfunctional dinner customs of the pre-war era. Once the tradition caught on again, it spread like wildfire.

There was something to be said about families breaking bread together. Taking a timeout and sitting together around a dinner table. Touching base and sharing how one another's days had gone. Sharing the day's triumphs and, sometimes tragedies, however minor. Laughing together over a good meal. It was all so very cathartic.

At suppertime, the girls were the first ones down. Anne and Nellie had just celebrated their eighth birthdays the previous week. They both escorted three-year-old Lynn and helped put her in her highchair. It had been a busy day of chores, in stark contrast to the previous Sunday's big birthday bash held in the twins' honor.

"Hi Dad, hi Mom," Anne was first to quip.

Mary looked over at Anne first and then made eye contact with the rest of the girls. "Thanks, girls, for all your hard work today!"

"You're welcome, Mommy! Guess we can't have a big party every weekend," Nellie bellowed out and then laughed.

"Got that right, girl," Mary smiled. "That little birthday shindig set us back a bit. But I figure you're both worth it."

Just then, the boys exploded down the stairs, making all sorts of noise. Austin had beaten his brother in a race down the hall and down the stairs to the dinner table. Joe had come in second by a whisker.

Mary gave Sam "the look." He had seen that look many times and knew what it meant, and he was quick to assert some parental authority.

"Alright boys, simmer down and take a seat," Sam lightly scolded.

With that, the last of the brood was seated, and they all went quiet. As was the custom, they all extended their arms outward and linked hands, and then Sam said grace before they began eating.

Twice, Mary had to slow the boys down from eating too fast, in between the stories and laughter that peppered their family dinner time. The girls regaled them with a play-by-play of the game they had enjoyed together, after their chore time with Dad. Austin detailed the plot of the delightful book he had gotten lost in after his chore time had ended. While adventurous, he was nowhere near as adventurous as his brother, Joe.

Joe had been unusually quiet so far, and Mary decided that it was the perfect time to ask him how he had spent his afternoon, after he'd finished his list of chores in record time.

"Well, Joe, tell us about the rest of your day," she prompted.

"I hung out with Teddy this afternoon and went roaming around." As soon as the word "roaming" had left his lips, Joe instantly felt uneasy.

"Roaming around, huh?" Sam said, giving Mary a knowing look. "What type of roaming around, son?"

"Aww, just walking around outside," Joe answered vaguely, pushing his food around on his plate and trying to avoid eye contact.

"Outside is a pretty big place there, Joe," Mary chimed in. "Anywhere specific?"

"I don't know, Mom, we just hung around together."

Not wanting to make a scene, Sam and Mary both backed off, especially since they both caught Austin giving Joe an odd look when he said he had been "roaming around."

After dessert, the girls went outside to play with Austin. Joe started to tag along behind them, but then he stopped dead in his tracks and turned to his dad.

"Dad, what does 'No Pepper' mean?"

Sam looked up quizzically. "No Pepper? Not heard that expression before. Why, where did you hear it?"

"I didn't, I read it on the sign," Joe blurted out, without thinking. *Dang,* he thought to himself. *Now I'm really busted.*

"Sign? What sign, son?"

Mary quickly chimed in, "The one he had tucked under his shirt when he came home from 'roaming around' with Teddy."

Joe jerked his head around and looked at his mom. "Mom, I swear, you're the hardest person on the planet to keep a secret from!"

"That's what moms do, kid," she responded, trying to hide her smile. "That's what moms do."

"I want to see this sign," Sam said, in a tone that clearly meant the issue was not up for debate.

Joe, sensing his secret foray into the woods would soon be a secret no longer, hung his head and marched upstairs. In less than a minute, he returned with the old, rusty, rectangular sign and handed it to his dad.

Sam took it and stared at it for a long time. Turning it over and then back again, he broke the silence, "No Pepper. Well, I'll be. Son, where did you get this?"

The moment of truth had arrived. Joe stood silently and fidgeted with his hands, arms, and legs, not sure what to say. "Um, when I was out roaming around with Ted."

"I asked where, not when," Sam retorted. "The truth, now, young man."

"The VFW Woods," Joe admitted.

Mary yelled and turned a little pale. "Joseph! How many times have your father and I told you the woods are off-limits?!"

"I know, Ma, but we just wanted to explore," Joe whined. "Besides, nothing happened. We're okay."

"Son, that's not the point. Your mom and I didn't want any of you kids in those woods for a reason."

"Didn't it …" Mary trailed off, turning even paler.

Sam, calming down, said, "I just got word the other day. The Army finally issued their report on the VFW Woods part of the old battlefield. They're 100% positive there's no more unexploded ordnance or mines. It took them a few months to scan the entire area, but it's all clear. I was going to tell you the other night, Mary, but it was late, and you were already asleep when I got the email alert from the office."

Mary, though noticeably calmer, turned and looked at her son, but said nothing.

"I'm sorry, Mom," Joe pleaded.

Mary rose from her chair silently, turned, and left the room.

"You better have more to say to your mother before bedtime tonight and, by the way, you're grounded tomorrow," Sam said.

"I'm sorry, Dad. I'll talk to mom before bed, I promise."

"Good. Now, let's have another look at that sign. Where exactly did you find this in the woods?"

"Attached to an old fence behind the ruins of the old VFW hall."

"The VFW Hall!" Sam exclaimed. "You really were roaming around! Why don't we start from the beginning? Tell me about yours and Ted's most excellent roaming around adventure, from start to finish."

Sam listened, without interrupting, as Joe related to him all he and Teddy had experienced during their foray into the infamous VFW Woods earlier in the day. When he had finished,

Sam took a deep breath and put a hand on Joe's left shoulder. "How much do you know about the history of the Battle of McHenry and what actually happened in and around that old VFW hall?"

"Just what we learned in history class."

"I thought so," Sam replied. "Let me tell you what's not in your history book, and for good reason."

So, Sam sat down and had a long talk with his firstborn son. He told him of what had happened in the battle, and of course, the collateral damage that had played a huge part in the eventual ending of the war.

Sam knew that some details of what had happened in the battle were too graphic to include in the history book for middle school-aged kids, like his son. So, he relayed what he believed was age appropriate.

He told him how the battle had waged for three long days and debased into hand-to-hand combat in its last hours. Five hundred and seventy-five unarmed civilians were tending to over 4,000 wounded and dying, from both sides, and they were all killed in the crossfire of an artillery and mortar barrage. At the battle's end, there were only two soldiers left standing, one from each side. Each was caked in the blood and filth of battle, exhausted, and near delirious. They looked into each other's eyes and were struck with recognition. In disbelief, the father called out his son's name, and the son answered. They rushed toward one another and embraced and wept. The story of father and son Jackson and Deshawn King's battlefield reunion went down in the annals of the Second Civil War as a defining moment that would later set the wheels in motion for peace after the nuke exchange.

"After the war," Sam continued, "they declared the area a no-man's-land because of the minefields and explosives around the old hall. Not to mention the radiation zone a few miles away to the east. The final casualty count for the Battle of the Fox River Valley, which included the Battle of McHenry, was 250,000 dead, 20,000 missing, 50,000 wounded."

When Sam was done, he quietly and gently wiped the tears from his son's sun-freckled face and pulled him in close in a warm embrace.

"I love you very much, but you need to understand that when your mom and I put rules in place for you kids, it's for good reason. Oftentimes, it's to protect you kids. I know I've told you this before, son. Let's not have this discussion again. Okay?" Sam asked.

"Yes, dad," Joe said quietly.

Sam continued, "On Monday at work, I'll check in with the archivists and see if they have any clues about this 'No Pepper' sign. No promises, but I'll try to help you find the answer to this riddle. For now, you better get upstairs and talk to your mom."

CHAPTER THREE

The Relic

That Monday, Sam pedaled to work alone, as Mary had taken the day off to spend some quality time with the girls. After racking his bike, Sam strolled into the front door of the lobby, displayed his ID badge to the guards, and proceeded up the escalator to the second floor for the quick elevator ride up to his office.

As was his custom, as the escalator took him past the memorial that towered from the atrium floor to the ceiling of the second floor, some 70 ft up, he said a quick prayer for his fellow workers and himself. He thought again about the monumental work being done there on behalf of the nation and how it had all begun all those many years ago, before he had even been born.

They had built the Eisenhower Federal Building 25 years after the war, and it was home to the 250 military personnel assigned to the United States Army Corps of Engineers Radiological Health Physics National Command Center. The rest of the building's occupants were the civilian workforce, composed of federal workers and contractors. All of whom were working for either the United States Department of Recovery and Reconstruction or the National Science Foundation. Combined, 5,000 people were working tirelessly on reconstruction and decontamination efforts in the building named after the 34th president of the United States.

They had formed the United States Department of Recovery and Reconstruction five years after the Second Civil War had ended. Before its formation, it had become clear to the surviving leaders that no single agency of the federal government was up to the monumental task of trying to rebuild such a vast country. Brainpower and planning alone were enough of a daunting task, let alone the logistics of all the moving parts needed to rebuild a nation ravaged by war.

The federal government and all 55 state governments, at that time, were still operating under martial law. Congress had yet to reconvene, because four-fifths of its elected members had died during the war and its aftermath. Special election plans were still being worked out, but President James Jackson did not have the luxury of time. The nation was in ruins, and the survivors were desperate for civilian leadership to show the way toward recovery and reconstruction.

So, with the powers vested in him through and during martial law, President Jackson had formed this new cabinet-level position and ordered it to carry out three objectives. These objectives were, number one, to coordinate federal help to all the states requesting assistance in their respective recovery efforts. Number two, to come up with a master plan for the reconstruction of vital national infrastructure and to manage, coordinate, and implement that plan. And third, to plan, manage, and implement the National IT Data Recovery Project.

Despite the new federal agency's formation all those years ago, recovery efforts crawled along at a snail's pace for years, primarily because of a post-war period called the "dark ages." During this time, there was no electricity for 99% of the survivors, and there was a total collapse of both the air and ground transport systems. Add in the resultant famine and disease from the breakdown in the food supply chain, the collapse of the healthcare system, and the collapse of modern sanitation, and the "dark ages" became, in some ways, more horrific for the survivors than the actual civil war itself.

Sam's thoughts came back to the present as he entered the elevator. His office was on the 85th floor. It was almost a miracle that the building had even been completed, given the deficits of the nation twenty-five years after the war had ended, especially the lack of computers. It was decided, back then, to use the existing paper archival blueprints for the destroyed Empire State Building in New York City. The two-hundred-plus-year-old blueprints were discovered in a secret vault, maintained by the NSA, deep inside a mountain bunker in the Shenandoah Valley of Virginia.

After the quick ride up, Sam exited and headed straight for Eduardo Chavez's office.

Eduardo was the Midwest director for the National IT Data Recovery team. He and his team had been working for decades to scan or manually enter the data from hard copies of every book, magazine, document, and newspaper that had survived the war. The material came from all over the country, from public, private, and government sources.

During the war, the Black Hole virus had wiped out every bit of data on all storage media worldwide and then had erased itself. With no carcass to examine, the surviving computer security gurus could only offer theories. There had, long ago, developed an international consensus that the instigators of the virus were more than likely disillusioned cyber-intel agents who had become anarchists and planned to destroy all data.

There were various theories as to the motive. The one that intrigued Eduardo and Sam the most was the theory that the perpetrators wanted to "roll back the clock." They wanted to see if the world would take a different direction than the one it had been on at the time of the release of the virus. By wiping all data, computers worldwide became nothing more than silent hulks of silicon, plastic, and metal. They had no power or usefulness without data and code. With the global erasure of data, and the ensuing blow to the global exchange of information, the playing field was leveled between the developed world and the third world.

Eduardo's role covered the non-news recovery efforts, which included books, magazines, and periodicals. The books were fiction and nonfiction alike.

His group had recently been tasked with processing another large allotment of resources from the United States Library of Congress. The large shipment, which had arrived two months prior, contained hundreds of cartons of books on entertainment, hobbies, and sports. Eduardo and his team were indexing every resource and then running each page through a 10K hi-def scanner that would then archive the page onto the newly developed ultra-high encryption electron condenser media. The information was then auto duplicated to 12 different sites around the world, including Site Yankee at Cheyenne Mountain, outside of Colorado Springs, Colorado.

Site Yankee was the largest and most secure data storage system on the planet, bar none. All this replication was to ensure nothing could ever wipe out the world's data ever again.

"Good morning, Sam! How was your weekend?"

"Busy as always," Sam answered. "Busy as always. How was yours?"

"Great! Rosita and I took the kids out to Rockford for the big hot-air balloon fest. They ran us ragged."

Sam chuckled, fully relating. "Yeah, we were going to go to that too, but our chores list got a little behind from the twins' birthday party the last weekend, so Saturday we ran ourselves ragged playing catch up," he commiserated. "Say, Eduardo, I got something here in my knapsack. I need you to look at it when you have time."

"Sure, whatcha got?"

Sam slung the knapsack from his back and set it on Eduardo's large desk, which was full of stacks of books. He unzipped it and pulled out the rusted sign Joe had found. "My son found this."

"Wow, that's an old relic, for sure," Eduardo said. "Where did he find it?"

"The old VFW Woods, back somewhere past the ruins of the hall."

"The VFW hall! Wow, he was walking around in there?" Eduardo exclaimed. "Thank God they cleared out the last of the unexploded ordnance last month. It surprised the Army that there was still some stuff in the area around there."

"Tell me about it," Sam said. "I just got an email the other day giving the all-clear. Anyway, Joe and his buddy Ted were exploring, and they found this old sign on what was left of a fence. It's hard to read, but you can make out the words 'No Pepper.' It has Joe's curiosity up, and I told him I would look into it here and try to help solve the riddle. Can you help?"

"Sure, let me take a quick scan of it and see what I can dig up. I'll get back to you by Friday."

"Thanks, Eduardo. Say, how's work going these days for your group?"

"Well, it's coming along, but even with the high-speed scanners, it's very time-consuming to scan all this stuff. The old books are a challenge, especially. We're trying to keep the bindings from falling apart. Six or seven times out of ten, we're successful. The rest of the time, the repair shop is quite busy repairing book bindings."

"Wow, sounds tedious," Sam said. "Hey, let's have lunch

today. My treat and payment in advance for the info."

"Sure, sounds great," Eduardo agreed. "But I can't promise you anything yet."

"Ah, I'm not worried. I can't imagine this sign is all that big of a deal, anyway. See you at noon in the lobby."

CHAPTER FOUR

It's in the Attic

"Brian, are you going to pick up the phone or pick your nose? Which is it?"

"I got it, Josephine, I got it." Grandpa Moses picked up the phone after being startled awake from a great mid-afternoon nap. "Hello?"

"Hi Dad, it's me," Mary said, on the other end of line.

"Well, hello Me," Grandpa Moses joked. "How are you?"

"Good, and you, Dad?"

"Well, you know, sweetie, not too bad today, not too bad at all. I just woke up from a fabulous nap. Was dreaming of your mom again, God rest her soul."

"Aww, that's so sweet," Mary sighed. "Especially after all these years."

"Still seems like yesterday, sweetie. Hard to believe it was 25 years ago last month."

"I know, Dad. I miss her and think of her every day. Every day," Mary said. "Listen, the reason I called was to see if you'd like to have the boys come over and stay the weekend after next. Sam and I have plans to take the girls away for some serious daddy-daughter and mommy-daughter time."

"Sweetie, you know my standing rule. You guys are always welcome here anytime, even on short notice. Heck, even with no notice!"

"Thanks, Dad. I'll have Sam make the flight arrangements. How are things in Dyersville?"

"They're good," Grandpa Moses answered. "Seems like the National Recovery Act has finally hit these parts too. Say, how goes the work for Sam?"

"Oh, he's been extremely busy. He just found out the other day that the Army did a sweep of the old battlefield in the VFW Woods. They finally gave the all-clear."

"Really? You don't say. Well, I'm sure the boys can fill me in. I'll pick them up in the old truck. They always seem to get a kick out of old Betsy."

"Dad, are you kidding me? Why are you still driving? And you mean to tell me you still drive that 200-year-old truck!?"

"I most certainly do! She runs like a top. Found me an old treasure trove of parts too! Paid a small fortune for the lot of 'em!"

"Lord, have mercy," Mary groaned. "Ok. Listen, I gotta go. I'll call you in a day or so with the flight information. Bye, love you!"

"Love you too, sweetie. Always have, always will."

Grandpa Moses's real name was Brian Albert Woodbridge. Brian's five-foot ten-inch frame was stocky but not overweight. At 85 years old, he still had a full head of hair, albeit white as snow. While many of his peers had slowed down (or died), Brian was determined to go out with his shoes on, doing something fun.

Brian had been born during the "dark ages" of the post-civil-war era. His generation was especially respected because of all that they had endured just surviving, not to mention crawling out of the ash heap of the war. In fact, his generation was often referred to as the Crucible Generation.

As the father of Mary Woodbridge — now Mary Scott — he was so accustomed to being called Grandpa Moses that whenever someone called him by his real name, it would take a moment to register in his aged, though still sharp, mind. His live-in RN caregiver and housekeeper, Mrs. Josephine Murphy, did just that, calling him Brian from time to time, just to keep him on his toes.

The nickname "Grandpa Moses" came about from his old friend Wesley Wainwright. Wesley had been going through a tough time many years earlier. Brian's deep Christian faith and wisdom had been instrumental in helping Wesley through it all. So, one day, while Brian was imparting some sound advice, Wesley said, "I'm gonna start calling you Grandpa Moses."

The name stuck and was quickly picked up by friends and family alike. In fact, Brian had taken such a liking to the nickname, that, when he would introduce himself, he would add, "You can call me Grandpa Moses."

Grandpa Moses was a local celebrity in Dyersville, Iowa. After spending the better part of his working life in Illinois, as an airplane mechanic at Rockford International Airport, he started retirement in the small town of Ridott, IL, out west of Rockford.

After several forays camping and fishing west of the Mississippi, he got lost on one trip and wound up in Dyersville, Iowa. He fell in love with the town and set his sights on a beautiful farm, northeast of town, as his final retirement haven.

The local celebrity status came about due to him running for the United States Congress at age 65 and winning. When his term limit of four years was up, he resumed his retirement on the farm in Dyersville.

Not long after he moved in, he got the shock of his life when he found out the farm he had purchased once belonged to his third paternal grandfather. He was a feed corn farmer in those days and was the third generation of the family to live-in the old farmhouse, which had been built in the 1860s. They had added on another bedroom and bathroom, in the late 1940s, to accommodate a larger family. The farmhouse was then rehabilitated and modernized three more times: in the early 2000s, then in 2030, and then again about 2140, when Grandpa Moses had bought the place.

The west-facing porch was timeless and had served as an informal gathering place for family, friends, and neighbors, not only for Brian, but for every family that had ever lived and entertained here. The stunning sunsets of the area were best enjoyed from that very porch and were of particular delight when the corn was high and tasseled out.

Grandpa Moses was a self-proclaimed "mild hoarder." With stern instructions from his daughter, Mary, Nurse Josephine had kept his hoarding stashes strictly confined to the third bay of the garage and a portion of the attic. The barns, of course, were unrestricted "man cave" land.

Moses loved to go up into the attic and gaze at what he affectionately called his "artifacts." Every time he did, he would see the ancient trunk over in the far corner.

He had tried to open the trunk decades earlier, when he first spotted it after purchasing the old farmhouse but couldn't. One time, he had gone to the garage and fetched a hammer and was ready to hammer the lock off, when he paused and thought to himself, *"Why do that? Why not just leave it alone and let my imagination wonder what's in there, but not actually find out. If I leave it a mystery, my imagination wins."*

So, he did. He left it alone, vowing he would open it one day, but only when he knew and felt that the time was right.

The flight carrying Joe and Austin had arrived on time at Dubuque International Airport. Grandpa Moses met the boys at the gate, escorted them downstairs to get their luggage, and headed out to the parking lot. The boys always got a thrill when they saw the old truck that Grandpa had owned all their young lives. They hopped in with glee and enjoyed the ride back to Dyersville, along U.S. Route 20.

The grandkids were in a great mood and were full of superlatives over Grandpa's ancient 1959 Chevrolet Apache turquoise pickup truck. Despite the age and the noise, old Betsy dutifully got them back to the farm, safe and sound.

"Okay boys, flex those muscles and take your luggage up to your room. You remember where?"

"Sure do, Grandpa, second room on the right, past the washroom," Austin answered.

"Excellent memory!" Grandpa Moses praised. "Once you both get settled, come and meet me on the porch for a lemonade."

Before following Austin down the hallway, Joe turned and said, "Sounds great, Grandpa. It's so cool to be here again!"

"I like cool! See you both in a bit."

The boys were quick to get upstairs and put their clothes away. As was their custom, they both flung themselves onto their respective beds to take in the pillow top mattresses. Once they did, it was over, as Grandpa knew well. They closed their eyes for what they thought was a moment, only to wake up an hour later.

Once awake from their unplanned naps, the boys meandered down into the kitchen and hugged Nurse Josephine. After exchanging pleasantries, she gave them each a glass of homemade, fresh-squeezed lemonade.

Austin, a lemonade fanatic, announced, "Wow, Miss Josephine, this is the best lemonade I've ever had in my whole life!"

Josephine was caught by surprise by the compliment. "Well,

Austin, I'm mighty glad you like it so much. I'll have plenty more the whole time you and your brother are here."

Joe, not usually quick with compliments, just smiled at Josephine and took a big gulp. "Where's Grandpa?" he asked.

Josephine motioned to the door and said, "He's out on the front porch waiting for you both."

With that, the boys headed out to the front porch, and to no one's surprise, there was Grandpa in his wicker rocking chair, napping.

"Grandpa, wake up!" Joe exclaimed.

With his eyes still closed, Moses answered, "Who says I'm asleep? I was saying a prayer for our time together."

"Really?" Austin asked.

"Well, I might have gotten a wink or two after the prayer."

The boys laughed as they sat down on the wooden Adirondack chairs and took some more sips of lemonade. Josephine had already put a glass next to Moses while he was asleep. He took a nice, big first gulp, looked over at the boys, and smiled. "So, tell me about the VFW Woods."

Joe was so surprised to hear the question from Grandpa that he choked a bit on the ice-cold drink. After regaining his composure, he slid down from the chair, onto the deck of the porch. Putting his hands behind him on the gray, weathered floor, he told his grandpa of his adventures into the VFW Woods and the mysterious relic he had found.

When Joe finished, Grandpa sat for a long time without saying a word. He looked off into the distance for what seemed like an eternity. The boys, good and rested, sat passively staring at their beloved grandpa.

After a long while, Moses finally broke the silence. "Say, quite an adventure you had. You're a lucky young man you didn't accidentally step on a mine. The Army already gave the all-clear, but you didn't know that yet. So next time, mind your mom and dad. Your mom was pretty upset you went in there against her and your dad's orders."

"I know," Joe said, his eyes downcast. "I'm really sorry, and I told Mom and Dad that."

"One day, you'll be a dad, and you and your wife will understand and want to protect your kids from harm, just like your mom and dad do. Never forget that, boys."

"We won't," echoed both boys.

"So, let's talk about this sign you found," Moses said, finished with his obligatory talking-to. "Your dad find out anything from the archivist at his work yet?"

"No, not yet. His friend, Eduardo, is looking into it," Joe said.

"Hmmm, is that right?" Immediately after the words left Moses's lips, the thought came to him, *Now is the time to open the trunk.*"

Grandpa Moses was taken aback by the thought, especially the intensity of it. Just yesterday, he had gazed at the trunk and imagined it had long ago been the property of a pirate, filled with gold and priceless gems. A ridiculous thought, but he reminded himself that imagining was the fun part and helped fuel his desire to leave the trunk alone. Now, however, he recalled the vow he had made to himself that "when the time was right" it would be opened.

He gazed out again over the tops of the tasseled corn along the horizon. His mind recalled the past, both the good and the bad. Then, resolutely, he turned to his grandsons. "Boys, go into the garage and fetch me a hammer."

The boys jumped up and started an impromptu race to the toolbox in the garage. Joe got there first and grabbed the biggest hammer in sight. They both ran back to the porch and jumped over the two front steps, landing within feet of their grandpa. Moses let out a belly laugh and headed back into the farmhouse. After climbing the long stairs into the attic, he led the boys over to where the trunk was, over in the far corner.

He told them about the trunk and how he had been keeping it for such a time as this. He thought for a moment about letting the boys give the lock a whack, but he decided, no, he wanted to do this himself.

Turning to Joe, he said, "Young man, hand me that hammer in your hands."

Joe handed his grandpa the mini sledgehammer he'd carried from the garage.

Moses lifted it high and let it come swiftly down on the lock. With a loud bang, the lock flung open violently. He sat there for just a moment and thought to himself, *"Wow, this is the day."* He removed the broken lock, raised the latch, and then lifted the lid for the very first time.

A myriad of distinct scents instantly filled the room. The smell of wool and cotton, along with the unmistakable scents of cedar and leather.

It was a little dark in the attic's corner, and the three pairs of eyes strained to see what was inside. As their eyes adjusted to the low light, Grandpa Moses reached inside and pulled out the first item.

It was a uniform of some kind. It had pants and a matching shirt. The shirt buttoned down the middle and had narrow pin-stripes. It was faded white. He turned the shirt around to see the name on the back, Woodbridge. Joe saw a look of astonishment on his grandpa's face. Moses reached in again. Next out was a leather item. It was big and had lacing and an opening for a hand and grossly oversized fingers. Grandpa had worn many types of work gloves in his long career and on the farm, but never had he seen a glove as big as the one now in his hand. He turned it this way and that, surveying it. He tried it on his left hand and wondered where the matching glove was for the other hand.

Austin couldn't help himself and reached into the trunk for the third item. It was a hat. "Why does it have a big capital 'B' on it?" he wondered, as he put it on. To his surprise, it fit his head perfectly.

Joe would not sit by and let those two have all the fun. He reached in and pulled out a long piece of wood that had a round barrel and a tapered handle at one end. Joe then spotted a pair of shoes with rubber spikes on the bottom and took them out as well. They reminded him of soccer shoes, but they were different. Moses then lifted out some sort of padded thing that looked to be something to cover a person's chest. Austin grabbed another type of leather glove that was very much different from the first one Moses had taken out. It was much bigger than the one on his grandpa's hand. Next, Joe grabbed some sort of helmet that had covers for the ears. He had seen football helmets, but this looked nothing like that. Austin lifted out another helmet with metal bars in the front, while Joe spotted a small, white, hard leather ball with red laces in a strange pattern.

There were several more balls that the boys grabbed and added to the growing pile on the attic floor. Finally, they took the remaining items and a book out of the aged treasure chest.

Thinking the chest was now empty, Moses had started to close the lid, when Joe spotted a yellowed envelope in the near right corner. Its yellowed paper had blended in with the brown and yellow cedarwood that lined the inside of the chest.

Joe reached down and picked it up ever so gently. He could tell the paper was a bit brittle, but not so brittle it would fall apart. He handed it over to his grandpa, who lifted it close to his eyes. In the dim light, Moses could make out some writing on the cover of the envelope. It was one word, in all capital letters: BASEBALL. Upon reading it, he gasped and dropped the envelope.

After a long moment, he picked the envelope back up and looked at Joe. "Let's go down to the porch. I want you to read this letter out loud to us."

With that, they went back down the stairs and out the front door to the porch. On the way, Grandpa yelled for Nurse Josephine to come quickly. She had been in the kitchen preparing supper. They all gathered on the porch and took a seat.

"Go ahead, Joe. Open it up."

Joe was nervous. Even at his age, he knew something extraordinary was happening, but he didn't know what or why. He stuck his finger underneath the flap and opened the envelope. Then he removed the pages and read:

June 15, 2064.

To the reader of this letter:
First, please forgive the length of this letter. The contents of it are so important, I could not willfully try to squeeze this all into one page.

I thank God that human eyes are now gazing at my words. It probably means a couple of things. One, that the United States of America has survived this second, and far more costly, civil war. Two, that a treasured part of our national heritage may yet be reborn.

I am a veteran of the United States Army, having served in the Middle East in 2025, as well as in the North African War of 2027.

When the Second Civil War broke out three years ago, in April of 2061, I found myself sickened by the thought of bearing arms against my countrymen. So, I took a vow of neutrality.

Last night I wept at the news of the latest casualty reports. We've now lost over a million citizens, and I feel the worst is yet to come. As I write, several Smithsonian facilities are burning. Our National Archives building is also on fire, along with many other museums in major cities. The Washington

Monument, Lincoln Memorial, and Jefferson Memorial have all been blown up. The face of Mt. Rushmore was just destroyed by a cruise missile yesterday. Vast quantities of our history, heritage, and culture are literally going up in flames in this madness.

Thus, I, along with several like-minded veterans, hatched a plan to preserve important cultural elements of our nation, in the event this current catastrophe worsens and obliterates large parts of our culture. It was also hoped that one day in the future, the finder of this letter and these artifacts would be instrumental in seeing these cultural treasures of our nation resurrected.

As I write, America's once glorious pastime, baseball, has died. The reasons are varied. The explosive growth of soccer and lacrosse certainly did not help, and neither did the lure of video games. Nor did the 3-year strike at the professional level or the unrelenting financial troubles of the professional and semi-pro teams. The kids, and even the adults, just don't have any interest in the game anymore, either. The game's last breath has come from this horrible war raging from coast to coast.

Our national anger and divisions have driven us into the abyss! We are, at present, in free fall, but I am not surprised. The seeds of this war were planted decades ago and were hiding in plain sight for all to see. The art of political compromise died several decades prior to the first shots. Our American psyche had become far too polluted by narcissism, avarice, meanness, and a total inability to conduct the affairs of state with reasonable civility and dialogue.

I expect that, as you read this, I will have long since gone to my eternal rest. I pray that this awful war will now be a distant event and an important lesson in your history books. Much like the First American Civil War was an important lesson in my history books, when I was a boy in school, here in Dyersville, Iowa.

As I write, people in Chicago and New York are extremely on edge. There have been rumors, on both sides, of the deployment of battlefield nukes. Also, there are rumors that Charlotte and Atlanta are targets as well.

God only knows what's next. My nerves are frayed to the edges. But enough of this sad tale. Now for the hopeful part of this letter.

My buddies and I drew lots to see which cultural preservation task each of us would have the responsibility to preserve for some future discoverer. The lot for baseball fell to me.

So it is that you are now the bearer of an important mission to further the cultural recovery of the United States of America. The Resurrection of Baseball.

The chest you have found contains equipment for the game of baseball, which I collected for your mission. But there is more, much more, for you to uncover. My instructions were to have the artifacts collected and placed into three vaults.

Vault number one is the trunk you have discovered in the attic of my old farmhouse, here in Dyersville, Iowa.

I buried vault number two out behind the barn, here on the farm.

In the event my farmhouse does not survive the war, I have placed an identical letter in the second vault. I am trusting and praying my house survives the war, along with the trunk in the attic. I have included exact coordinates for the buried vault, just in case the barn is no longer standing.

Vault number three is buried below vault number two. Vault number three has a lead covering separating it and vault number two.

Vault number two is quite large and contains a

large cache of baseball equipment, uniforms, rule books, and game balls.

Vault number three is smaller and contains sealed, vintage electronics, along with vintage storage media containing all things baseball. There are thousands of hours of movies and instructional videos that you can use to study the game and learn and teach it again.

Vault number three was the costliest to assemble and the most important. The logic behind it is the thought that an EMP attack (God forbid) would destroy every single piece of electronic equipment in the nation. That, along with a computer virus, could 'erase' all electronic archives of everything, including the history of baseball.

Now, for the most important part of my letter. I hope you are a young person, athletic, and full of energy. In the event you are not, I ask you to find such a person and shepherd them in this endeavor.

Your mission is three-fold. Number one, recover vaults number two and three. Second, study the rules and instructional videos in vault three and teach the game of baseball to your family, friends, and neighbors. Teach the game to all who wish to learn it and give the game back to America, so they can resurrect it to new life during America's rebirth. Finally, play ball! There is no better way to learn baseball than by getting out there and playing a game, as often as you can.

It does my heart good to contemplate that some future, young Americans will one day read this and be instrumental in the resurrection of this game that was, in times past, such an important part of our nation's culture. Oh, how I loved this game in my youth.

I wish you Godspeed in this effort!
Sincerely,
William Richard Woodbridge III

Joe lowered the yellowed papers and was silent. They all were.

A golden glow lit the sky, as the setting sun was just touching the corn tassels. It was a sight to behold. Grandpa Moses always loved sitting in his rocker at that time of day, especially at that time of the year.

He had sat quietly while Joe read his ancestor's century-old letter, indulging himself with his evening smoke on the 100-year-old pipe that had belonged to his great-great-grandfather, William Richard Woodbridge III.

Moses put the pipe down and looked out at the sunset and the fertile fields of corn gently waving in the September breeze. The boys and Nurse Josephine sat for several minutes without saying a word. Joe looked intently into his grandpa's eyes. They were glistening in the sunlight. Joe was certain he detected a tear in those beloved eyes. Joe also had a distinct feeling that what he had just read was big. Very big, indeed.

After rubbing his eyes and clearing his throat, Grandpa Moses finally broke the silence. "Boys, we'd better get to bed early tonight after supper. We've got quite the day ahead of us tomorrow. Josephine, we need a big breakfast tomorrow. 'The Works,' please! Understood?"

Josephine looked pleasantly surprised and nodded. "Moses, you haven't ordered 'The Works' for breakfast in a long time. Boys, you're in for a special treat!"

"Great! But what's for dinner tonight?" Austin quipped.

CHAPTER FIVE

It's in the Dugout

The next morning, the sun rose at 6:41 AM, but Josephine was in the kitchen by 6:30 to start cooking "The Works" while Moses and the boys were still asleep. It was always the coffee brewing that aroused Moses from a good night's sleep, and that day was no different. As the smell wafted upstairs into his room, the aroma of it grabbed his attention and pulled him awake. He always enjoyed that first whiff of it. The other scents of bacon, eggs, hash browns, French toast, and pancakes were all jumbled in there too. It offered an irresistible pull to rise and get moving.

As was his custom, Grandpa Moses rose and took just two steps to the rocker where he spent time reading his Bible. When he was finished, he said a prayer for the day, stood up and walked out of his bedroom, and headed over to the grandkids' room. The boys were still fast asleep when Moses walked up to their beds and gently shook them both. Austin was the first to crack his eyes open. Joe, still snoring, was a little harder to rouse.

"Time to wake up. We've got a big day ahead of us," Moses encouraged. "Josephine's got breakfast almost ready. Get ready and meet me downstairs." With that, Moses stepped out and headed back to his bedroom for a moment, but he emerged soon afterward and headed downstairs.

Austin turned to his brother and asked, "Whatcha thinking?"

"This is gonna be one long, fun day," Joe answered, a huge grin on face.

"I wonder how we're going to dig this thing up?"

"I guess we'll find out. I hope we're not digging it all out by hand," Joe worried.

"Me too!"

The boys got ready and hurried down the stairs to the breakfast table. There, they were met by Grandpa Moses, already seated and taking his first sip of black coffee. Nurse Josephine was also there to greet the boys with a good morning hug and hello.

Josephine had been Grandpa Moses's live-in nurse and caregiver for the last 30 years. He paid her well, and she was happy. She knew her job, performed it well, and was considered part of the family.

Josephine Parker had been a nurse longer than anybody could remember. Nursing was in her family, going back at least three generations.

Her great-great-grandmother, Maxine, had served as a nurse during the Second Civil War and had been outside of Atlanta during the battlefield exchange of nukes.

That horrible event was the single largest loss of human life in warfare in one day. Though she never met her great-great-grandmother, Maxine's stories of the long days tending to the dying and the wounded, along with those suffering from radiation sickness, were handed down orally to her at a young age. The stories of Maxine's wartime heroics had inspired Josephine to become a nurse.

Upon graduating from nursing school, the internationally acclaimed Rockford Clinic, located in Rockford, Illinois, hired Josephine on, and that was where she met and fell in love with a young intern named Tyrone.

They married a month later and lived a happy 30 years together, before he died of influenza during the epidemic of 2135. They never had children, and Josephine remained single. In 2136, she met Grandpa Moses during his rehab stay at the hospital in Dubuque. Josephine had taken up a position at that hospital soon after her husband's passing.

Moses was looking for a live-in caregiver/nurse/housekeeper and offered her a handsome salary. She had lived at the farm ever since and had grown quite fond of the grandkids.

⚾ ⚾ ⚾

To start their day, the four of them sat down for "The Works," as Grandpa fondly referred to this special breakfast. Joe and Austin had enjoyed partaking in this breakfast feast at Grandpa's several times before. That morning, however, they were a little more excited. Everything just seemed to have a special air about it.

The boys sat down in their customary seats, across from Grandpa Moses, and quietly waited. Once Josephine took her seat, they all locked hands and bowed their heads while Moses said grace.

After shoveling the first bite of pancakes into his mouth, Joe asked, "So, Grandpa, what's the game plan for today?"

"Well, I think we'll use the small Case backhoe today. Once we hit the vault, you boys can pile in with the shovels and have at it."

Joe looked at Austin and grimaced slightly, "Sounds good. How long do you figure it will take us?"

"Oh, I don't know. It all depends," Moses mused, as he took a sip of coffee. "Is the vault intact? What if the lid is broken? How fast can you two dig? We'll just have to wait and see."

Josephine was quick to add, "You boys be careful today. It's supposed to be a high of 85 degrees. I'll bring some lemonade out around ten o'clock or so. I figure you'll be ready for a break around then."

"Yes! I love your lemonade!" Austin exclaimed. "Can you bring cookies out too?"

"You bet! Fresh-made, crunchy chocolate chip cookies. I'm going to start on them right after I clean up the kitchen from breakfast."

"Say, Josephine, sometimes you remind me of my mother, but that's a good thing!" Moses bellowed out and laughed.

Josephine, always quick with a reply, quipped, "Your mom had her hands full, of that I am certain, young man."

"Aw, I know I'm special, but not as special as these two boys. Boys, finish up and help clear the table. I'm headed out to the barn to fire up Ol' Cat."

With that, Moses slipped out of the kitchen, went out the back door, and headed towards the barn. Moses was nationally recognized as an expert on the restoration, care, and maintenance of centuries-old farm equipment. He had the largest collection in the Midwest and, at least once a week, took a call from another restorer who needed his technical guidance.

Moses opened the barn door and headed straight over to Ol' Cat, as he affectionately called his 1959 Case backhoe. That tractor had been the very first piece in his collection, which he started over 50 years ago. The nickname came very early on in his ownership of the Case tractor. It was born when his old cat, Bucyrus, took a liking to the large tractor seat and spent hours napping up there, while Moses was busy bringing the old tractor back to life.

Bucyrus would sleep soundly, even through the clanging and banging of Moses's restoration efforts.

As Moses climbed up and took a seat, he cracked a smile, thinking of his old feline friend from all those years ago. Looking down, Moses pulled the choke, gave her some gas, and turned the key. Ol' Cat turned over one time and fired right up. It had been a few months since she last ran, so she belched out a cloud of smoke as she "cleared her throat" and rumbled to life.

Just then, the boys came running into the barn, all excited to see Ol' Cat running. Moses had taken both of them for a ride in it the previous spring. They always got a thrill whenever Grandpa fired up one of his antique tractors.

Grandpa motioned for the boys to stand back, as he shifted into gear and lurched forward. Proceeding out the barn entrance, Moses swung wide and headed toward the rear of the barn. Once stationed, he extended the bucket way out and drove it down into the ground with a loud thud. Ol' Cat's front end heaved upward somewhat, because of the force of the bucket driving down into the hard ground. After breaking through and filling the bucket, he raised the arm and swung it over towards the back and deposited it.

Thirty minutes later, another scoop was met with a loud thud. Moses completed the motion and swung the arm away to dump the load off to the side. He then shut off the engine and clambered down from the tractor. Using a ladder, he climbed down into the hole to inspect what he'd hit. Sure enough, as he cleared some dirt, he could tell it was concrete. Moses climbed out and ordered the boys into the hole with their shovels to start digging.

Despite the boys' apprehension about digging the thing out by hand, there they were sweating and digging and loving every minute. They didn't care that it was hot, and their excitement grew as more and more of the vault came into view because of their efforts.

Fifteen minutes in, as they took a short water break, Austin looked at his grandpa with a puzzled expression. "Grandpa, I don't get it. Who would bury this thing here and why?"

"Well, you heard what our ancestor wrote. He buried this stuff in the hopes some good folks would find it one day and help restore something that was once very important to our nation. Seems to me he was pretty smart. You do remember what happened during the war, don't you?" Moses asked.

"Of course I do," Austin answered.

"Ok, pop quiz," Moses said. "Tell me what happened. Let's see how good you remember your history lesson on the war."

"Aw, do I have to?" Austin whined. "Joe's better at history than me. Always has been."

"I know that, Austin. But I'm asking you."

"Alright, well—"

Joe interrupted, "You don't remember, do you?"

"Yes, I do!" Austin insisted. "The Second Civil War started in April 2061, outside of Chicago. The Black Hole virus hit America on June 13th, 2062, or 3, I think?"

"You think? Or do you know?" Moses waited for the reply.

"I don't remember," Austin admitted. "I'm sorry."

"Austin, I want you and your brother to study up on this again, you hear? It is the duty of every American to know this history, so that it never, ever, ever happens again. Clear?"

"Yes, Grandpa. Are you mad at me?"

"Mad at you? Of course not! Don't mistake my sternness for anger. I'm not angry," Moses reassured him. "I just want to make sure that when you boys have grown up into men, the America you live in will figure out how to resolve differences of opinion without resorting to a shooting war on American soil ever again. That war was the ultimate failure of the adults to get along with one another, even if they did not agree with each other, understand?"

Both boys, in unison, replied, "Yes, Grandpa."

"Well, good then. So, I'm going to fill in the blanks on our war history. This time next year, I expect you both to recall it from memory, clear?"

"Yes, Grandpa," they again replied in unison.

"Well, okay then, here goes. The Second American Civil War started on April 12th, 2061. The nuke exchange occurred during the third year of the war and took place on June 17th, 2064. The nukes killed 75 million people immediately, and another 35 million died from radiation poisoning over the following weeks and months. On June 20th, 2064, the Black Hole virus entered key command-and-control systems for the U.S. military, all rebel-held systems, the electric grid, other key infrastructure, and every computer on the planet connected to the Internet. Twenty-four hours later, all data on all systems had been destroyed. On August 1st, 2064, an unknown state or group launched an EMP attack against the United States from a ship or submarine in the Gulf of Mexico. They launched three nukes at us. The ship's computers were disconnected from the Internet and, therefore, escaped infection from the Black Hole virus.

"The nukes were air burst at an altitude of 248 miles over Colorado Springs, Colorado; Louisville, Kentucky; and Virginia Beach, Virginia.

"The electromagnetic pulse fried every electronic device from coast to coast. All of America, parts of Canada, and Mexico were plunged into horse and buggy mode.

"Within 12 months of the EMP attack, another 300 million Americans had died because of disease, starvation, and the resultant anarchy from the breakdown of law and order and the food, fuel, and medical supply chains.

"In the decades that followed, millions more died from disease and starvation. After the Great Influenza Epidemic, the decline in the United States population finally stabilized at 8.2 million citizens."

No matter how many times Grandpa Moses recited the history of that era, there was always the same reaction: a stunned silence, followed by a deep and overwhelming sense of mourning for the horror of it all.

Joe seemed to detect a tear welling up in Grandpa's eyes again.

Before he could be sure, though, Grandpa grunted and blurted out, "Break's over, boys. Back into the hole, and let's get this thing uncovered."

Austin and Joe jumped back down into the hole and finished digging the dirt off the entire top of the lid of the vault in another 20 minutes. They were soaking wet from sweat, but it was done.

Moses looked and saw that both ends of the vault had large eye hooks embedded into the cement. After sending the boys back into the barn to get chains, he had them hook the chains up to all four of the eye hooks and began raising the arm of the backhoe. It was unclear, for a moment, if the lid was raising or the whole vault was. A few seconds later, he could tell the entire vault was being raised by his actions in the backhoe.

Clear of its burial hole, Moses crept the tractor arm and the vault away from the hole, after he'd made sure the boys were well clear of it. After lowering the vault, several feet away from the hole, there was a final thud as the weight of the vault met the hard ground.

Turning off Ol' Cat, Moses clambered down and inspected the vault to see how the lid was secured. After a close look, he discovered a series of bolts covered in tar. He also discovered a thick layer of tar and some other sealant around the seam of the lid.

As he pondered on how to break the seal, Joe suggested, "How about a torch to burn off the tar?"

"Good idea," Moses praised. "Go to the barn and get the torch."

An hour later, Moses had burned off all the tar. He then showed the boys how to use an air ratchet. He had two airlines out, so they could each work on one side of the lid, undoing the nuts. It took the boys another half an hour to get all the nuts off. Once that was done, Grandpa Moses attacked the seal with a crowbar. It soon, however, became apparent that he would need help. After telling Joe to go get two more crowbars, he had Joe and Austin each work a side, after showing them the technique he was using.

They had just finished when Josephine showed up with lemonade. It was another welcome break.

"Well, boys, you all look hot, sweaty, and mighty determined," Josephine said, inspecting their work. "How goes it?"

"Well, it's been hard work, but you're just in time. We finally broke the seal on the seam of the lid, and we're ready to lift it off," Moses announced.

"Yeah, we had to dig hard to get this sucker uncovered!" Austin exclaimed.

"You boys did good, real good," Moses praised. "Hey, Josephine, stick around for the unveiling."

"Ok, but I can't stay too long."

First, Moses measured the vault, with Joe's help. It was ten feet long, six feet wide, and five feet tall. The lid itself was three inches thick.

"Why are we measuring it, Grandpa?" Austin asked.

"Because I can guarantee someone is going to ask how big the vault was."

After measuring it, Moses climbed back up into Ol' Cat, fired her up, and swung the bucket around. With the finesse of a seasoned equipment operator, he brought the edge of the bucket up and slowly brought the strong hydraulic power of the arm to bear against the several-hundred-pound lid. After a few hard pushes, the lid finally gave up its century-old hold and moved. Joe was the first to smell leather — a lot of leather.

Grandpa lowered the bucket back down to the ground and turned off Ol' Cat. He clambered down again, only this time with an enormous smile on his face.

He, Josephine, Joe, and Austin all walked up, gazed into the open vault, and were astonished at the sight. Moses's great-great Grandpa Woodbridge's hard work at sealing the lid had paid off. The contents were in pristine condition, with not even a hint of water having seeped in over the century. It was miraculous.

What lay before their eyes was a sight that took their breath away.

Boxes filled the entire vault. Each labeled. Uniforms, socks, gloves, bats, and many boxes of balls, just like the ones in the attic. There were numerous boxes of everything that they had earlier found in the attic trunk.

They all stood there in stunned silence, surveying the sight.

Finally, Josephine spoke, "Boys, what in the world have you all unearthed?"

Moses paused before answering, "History, my dear, history."

Joe turned and looked at Austin, then at his grandpa. "Grandpa, what are we gonna do with all this stuff?"

"Well," Moses pondered. "First, we better get it into the barn. Boys, I need each of you to go back into the barn and fire up an old riding lawn mower. Ones with trailers hitched up to the tractor already. We'll use them to load this stuff up and bring it in.

So, they spent another hour hauling all the items from the vault and neatly stacking them into piles along one complete wall of the big barn.

Once they had finished, Moses hooked the chains back up and lifted out the smaller, third vault, which was now visible at the bottom of the hole. At least, he thought that was what he was doing.

Once he began lifting, however, he realized that what he was actually lifting was a lead covering. The vault was, in fact, still in its burial place.

The large vault, that had been buried on top, had thoroughly protected this smaller vault.

The kids attached the chains to the smaller vault, and Moses finally lifted it out and swung it over to the opposite side of the hole from the larger vault.

The smaller vault measured 8 feet by 4 feet by 4 feet. It had a similar seal along the lid, which the boys spent another hour breaking.

When they were done, Moses again used the bucket of Ol' Cat to pry the lid off. It came off and made a thud as it hit the hard ground. Moses turned off the engine and climbed down.

Whatever was inside had been packed with extraordinary care. First, there were layers of burlap sacks, an inch thick. Then some plastic sheeting. Once that was removed, the boys found individual boxes, triple wrapped in plastic.

Joe lifted the first one out of the vault and took it out of its wrappings. In big letters were the words "Magnavox DVD Player." Joe had barely finished reading the name before Austin grabbed another box and opened it to read "Magnavox LED TV." Moses was in on the action now, too. His box contained a Magnavox VHS VCR. There were three each of the TV, DVD player, and VHS videotape player.

There were also boxes and boxes of books. *The Encyclopedia of Baseball, The History of Baseball, Baseball Rules, Teaching Baseball,* and many, many more.

Next, they lifted out several more boxes filled with silver, round discs. Joe looked at one and noted the label. "Grandpa, what's a DVD?" he asked, puzzled.

Austin was looking at another box of strange items. "Yeah, Grandpa, and what about these black, plastic rectangles that say VHS? What are they? I've never seen anything like these before."

Moses looked at the boys and laughed. "History, boys! That's history. And it was all dug out of the ground too, right here in good ol' Dyersville, Iowa, in my own backyard!"

Austin whispered to his brother, "Looks like we're in for another long history lesson. Maybe we better break for lunch."

It took a few hours after lunch to re-sort everything they had brought into the barn earlier, as they had been so excited that they had not taken the time to stack things into any kind of cohesive order. This time, Moses was right there supervising the boys and directing them on where to put what.

Once they were done, Moses grabbed one of the electronic boxes marked DVD and had the boys bring a vintage TV into the house. After reading the instructions for the DVD player, he hooked it up to the power cord. Next, he plugged the cable into the flat-screen television. Meanwhile, he had tasked Joe with going through the stacks of silver discs and picking one out. Some had no printed labels, just titles written in black marker. Others were released by the old movie studios.

Joe was sorting through them all, when a title caught his eye. "*The Sandlot.* Hey, this one is from 1993. Let's try this one."

"Wow, 1993, that's ancient!" Moses marveled. "Ok, hold on a minute."

Grandpa was reading the yellowed paper on how to operate the strange device. Once he finished, he hit the power button. The machine made some quiet noises, and the front panel blinked. Next, he hit the button the manual listed as "eject." A narrow, rectangular door opened, and a square tray slid out from the insides of the machine.

"Ok, Joe, put the silver disc on the tray," Moses instructed.

Joe placed the silver disc onto the square black tray, Moses hit another button, and the disc disappeared into the belly of the machine. Joe hit the "play" button. Again, there was a quiet noise, this one like a whirring sound. All three stood gazing at the dark screen. Then, it lit up with the words "20th Century Fox."

For the next hour and a half, they watched and said nothing, alternately smiling, laughing, and focusing intently as the movie played. Finally, the credits rolled.

Joe looked over at his younger brother and broke the silence. "Baseball. Huh. It looks like fun."

Austin spoke, "Grandpa, is that what America was like before the war?"

"I don't know, son. I'd hate to make a hasty determination. We have a lot more of these videos to watch. Boys, how'd you like to stay for the rest of the week?"

"Cool!" Austin shouted, immediately after Moses finished asking the question.

But Joe was quick to add, "Mom and Dad are expecting us though, plus we got school."

"Don't you worry, boys. I'll call your mom tonight, after you both go to bed. I don't expect this to be a problem at all. You can remote into school and e-learn from here for the week."

CHAPTER SIX

Home Sweet Home

Rockford International Airport was one of the busiest airports in the nation. Although it had served solely as a military base during the war, they had converted King Air Force Base back to a dual role of civilian and military use after the war. Since Chicago O'Hare and Chicago Midway were lost during the war, Rockford became a major air hub for domestic and international travel. In the last several years, it had increased in size, with double the number of gates and a total of eight active runways.

With their girls in the trusted hands of a babysitter, Sam and Mary arrived at the airport early and decided to have lunch in Terminal One at Rock's Steakhouse. It had been over a week since they'd seen the boys, and they were missing them. Sam had good news to share with Joe. Mary just wanted to hug them both and tousle their hair.

American Shuttle Flight 1959 from Dubuque Regional Airport would, under normal circumstances, be a 25-minute flight, but there was a long, narrow, two hundred-mile no-fly zone that started north of Platteville, Wisconsin. From there, it continued south to Pittsfield, Illinois, south of Interstate 72, near the Mississippi River.

The no-fly zone resulted in the creation of an east-west air route further north, near Platteville, Wisconsin, which formed a giant northward arc from Dubuque up to Platteville and then down to Rockford. All of this added another 30 minutes of flight time before descending into Rockford International. Sam had found out that the no-fly zone was temporarily in place for an Air Force trial run of some secrecy. Mary and Sam took advantage of the extra flight time and opted for a steak lunch at the locally famous steakhouse.

They were enjoying filet mignons with a glass of red wine and great conversation, when Mary remembered Joe's sign and inquired about it. "So, what did Eduardo find out about Joe's relic?"

"Seems our son has found a link to an old game called baseball. The sign was a notice to players of the game not to play a kind of warm-up exercise called pepper."

"Really?" Mary said. "Tell me more."

"Baseball hasn't been played since before the war. It's a dead sport. Back when it was popular, some players would play a kind of warm-up activity called pepper. They used a thick wooden stick called a bat and a small, round leather ball. One player would hit the ball along the ground or in the air, straight at a group of players with big leather gloves, who were standing roughly twenty feet away. The players would catch the ball then throw it back to the batter, who would hit the ball again to the next player. They did this in a kind of rapid-fire way to sharpen hand-eye coordination.

"Pepper had become somewhat popular again with the professional players in the waning days of the sport. Many places banned pepper on youth fields, though. Hence the word 'No' in the sign."

Confused, Mary asked, "Ok, but why would they post a sign to not play it if it was supposed to be something beneficial?"

"Not sure," Sam shrugged. "Maybe because they were so close, and they were prone to get hurt too easily."

Mary paused for a bite of her steak. "Huh. Sounds boring, actually. What else do you know about baseball?"

"Nothing. I'm so buried at work, studying some dead pre-war game is low on my radar."

"I know that feeling!" Mary laughed.

Just then, both their comms alerted. Flight 1959 had touched down and would be at Gate 22 in a few minutes. After finishing up their meal, Sam paid the bill. Then they took their leftovers and headed down the Terminal One concourse for Gate 22.

They arrived at the gate just as the boys were exiting the jetway.

Joe and Austin raced the 20 yards to see who would reach Mom first and give her a bear hug. Joe won by a nose, but Mary was quick to embrace both her boys, while Sam looked on and smiled.

"Mom, we missed you so much. I'm glad we're home," Joe shouted.

"I missed you guys, too. I'm so glad to hug you both. Did you have a good time with Grandpa?"

Austin jumped up and down. "Did we ever! We found so many cool treasures and relics, you won't believe it!"

"Yeah, and they were all about some old game called baseball!" Joe exclaimed.

The word gave Sam a jolt. "Wow, you don't say. Hey, you know that old sign you found? That's about baseball too."

"No way! Are you serious, dad?! What does it mean? Tell me — tell me!" Joe yelled.

"Settle down, son. Let's get your luggage, and I'll tell you what Eduardo found out about it, on the ride home."

With that, Sam led Mary and their sons down the concourse and downstairs to the baggage claim.

Mary's comm alerted again. She gazed down and saw a message from her dad. *"Bringing a truck with treasures from our find. Should be at your home in two days. Make room."*

Mary showed the message to Sam. He read it, winked, and gave Mary a slight smirk, to which she gave him a light, playful slap on the back of the head.

But Joe caught their exchange. "Hey, what's that all about?" he demanded.

"You'll find out soon enough," Sam smiled. "Let's get your luggage and get you boys and us back to home-sweet-home."

On the hour ride home, the boys listened to their dad explain Eduardo's findings about the old, rusted metal sign Joe had found.

Joe was thrilled that the sign had a connection to all the baseball stuff they had found back at Grandpa's, and he excitedly began sharing with his mom and dad all that Austin, Grandpa, and he had accomplished on their trip. Joe even recalled one movie they had watched that contained a one-minute clip of some players playing pepper before they played an actual game of baseball.

Sam and Mary kept making eye contact, smiling, and adding the occasional remark, as Joe animatedly retold every detail he could recall of their ten-day trip. Now and then, when Joe would pause to catch his breath, Austin would add colorful commentary. They all had a grand time, as the family hovercraft whisked them silently home, down the four-lane highway.

Once they cleared Glacial Ridge on Illinois State Rt. 120, they glided eastward into the Fox River Valley and the sprawling environs of the city of McHenry.

Sam would always take time to gaze out as they came over the crest of the ridge. She had grown much in the last 25 years, as the National Recovery Act paid off huge dividends to cities like McHenry.

It was understandable that, in the early years of recovery, the scant funds available had to be spent on key cities, like Washington, D.C. Philadelphia, Boston, and a bunch more, before they could spend money on the smaller cities and towns across the vast, but very scarred, American landscape.

It had thrilled Sam to be a part of the previous week's ribbon-cutting ceremony for the brand-new high-speed rail line that connected the Great Northern route to Seattle, Washington. The new Union Station, built on the south side of McHenry, had proven to be a tremendous boon to the city and surrounding areas. This neck of Illinois was experiencing full employment for the first time in over 100 years. It felt good, very good indeed.

The hovercraft slowed and entered the driveway of their home on Pearl Street. A proximity beacon had already commanded the garage doors to open.

After the hovercraft stopped, centered in its spot in the first garage bay, four passenger doors swung up and out, and everyone exited the craft. The cargo door opened silently, and everyone pitched in to get the boys' luggage into the house.

As the boys entered the house, they had their first whiff of home in ten days, and it smelled wonderful. Sam brought all the luggage straight to the laundry room and started on the first load. Once he had the washer going, he went to the living room and plopped on the couch.

After getting a glass of water, Joe looked over at his dad relaxing on the couch. "Hey dad, since the woods are all clear, I was thinking of getting Teddy and Austin and some of the rest of the guys to go explore some more in the VFW Woods."

"Hmmm. Well, I don't see why not. The Army said the woods are clean. Their word is as good as gold in my book."

Mary was quick to join in. "Sam Scott, you WILL go with them."

"Aww Ma, we'll be okay. Dad can stay home," Austin argued.

"No sir, young man. No sir. He goes, or you stay on this side of the Fox River," Mary declared.

"Mary, it's okay. It really is," Sam said gently. "You can't protect them all the time. Look, if it makes you feel any better, we can have Scoobie go with them."

Scoobie was their house AI robot. They had programmed it to understand and speak 20 languages. It also had multiple sensors that could sense danger and alert those within earshot and also call for help if needed.

Mary looked at her three men and yielded. "Ok, but at the first sign of alarm from Scoobie, you listen to it and do whatever it says to keep safe."

Just then, the girls came bursting through the front door. They had been across the street at their friend Desiree Robinson's house. Desiree's mom, Tabrika, had volunteered to babysit the girls while Sam and Mary went out to Rockford.

Mary jumped up from the couch and caught all three girls' hugs, as they all fell together back onto the couch.

Mary picked up her comm and called her best friend.

Tabrika was quick to pick up. "Hi, girl. How'd it go?"

"Fine. Sam and I got to the airport terminal early, so we had most of a steak lunch before the boys' plane arrived. Did the girls behave?"

"You even have to ask? Of course, they did. Say, Martin asked me to ask you two out for dinner next Saturday. Talk it over and check your schedule and get back to me."

"Wow, that would be great. Nothing comes to mind schedule-wise but let me check with Sam and get back to you. Love ya, friend!"

"Love ya back! Say hi to the boys."

"Ok, will do!" Mary hung up just as Joe and Austin ran out the door to Ted's house.

But after just a few minutes, Joe burst back in and yelled, "Mom, we got Ted, and we're gonna go get the rest of the guys. Can you get Scoobie?"

"You guys want to go to the woods now?" Mary asked.

"Sure, why not?" Joe said. "It's only 2:30. Plenty of time left before dinner."

Sam called out, "Scoobie!"

"Sam!" Mary yelled.

"Don't worry, hon. I told you it's all safe over there. Relax, they'll be fine."

Scoobie woke up from sleep mode and emerged from the charging station in the foyer. It glided silently over and gave a greeting. Sam opened an eye wide for the retina scan and then spoke after the green light flashed.

"Scoobie, go with Joe and Austin. Do not let them out of your sight."

The robot responded with a "yes, sir" and turned towards Joe and waited for him to move. Joe ran out the door, with Austin and Ted close behind. Mary stepped out and watched as the boys and Scoobie went from house to house, gathering all the other boys. Joe, the ringleader of their little band, led everyone east down Pearl Street.

Mark came up next to Joe. "Hey, where're we going?"

"The VFW Woods! We're on a mission of discovery!" Joe announced.

Ted chimed in, "Cool, what did you find out about the sign!?"

Joe told the gang about the sign he and Ted had come across a few weeks earlier. Next, he told them all about his and Austin's most excellent adventure at their grandpa's farm and how they had dug up a treasure trove of old stuff about a game called baseball.

"Wow, you found all that in one trip? Some trip!" Ted exclaimed.

As they came to the Rt. 120 bridge ruins, Joe turned and got all the guys in tight to go over the game plan.

The gang of neighborhood friends Joe had put together included well over 20 young boys. The basis of that large group was a core group that he'd known all his young life. This core group was comprised of his younger brother Austin, of course, and their neighbor, Ted Lee Banks, plus Mark Samuelson, Billy Cross, the triplets: Jim, John, and Jeff Gander, Dan Simpson, Norm Gould, Steve Dearing, Jim Hart, Ken Orbison, Roy Hobson, Doug Jeffries, and Bill Adams. After listening to Joe's plan, they all filed into a single file line behind him.

Joe carefully stepped down into, traversed, and then climbed up out of the old bomb crater. Everyone followed suit, except Scoobie. As a newer robot model, Scoobie could glide at an elevation of up to 12 feet off the ground. It easily glided over the crater, without so much as a dip. Once they were all gathered over on the east side, Joe led them on the same path he had taken before with Ted. After making their way through the same underbrush he had fought through a few weeks earlier, they arrived at their destination, the ruins of the old VFW hall.

Joe led them inside and showed them what he had found, including the old VFW Post 4600 sign. He then led them all out the east door and toward the remains of the old fence where he had found the "No Pepper" sign.

Austin spoke up, "So what are we looking for now, Joe?"

"Anything, any relic. Let's spread out. Yell if you find anything and be careful! My dad says the Army gave the all-clear, but there could be snakes in here."

"Snakes!?" Ted yelled. "I hate snakes."

Billy Cross gave Ted a nudge forward. "There's no snakes in here, Ted. C'mon, let's go."

Joe had Austin and Scoobie go with him. Some of the guys had already found an opening and were on the other side of the old fence. Joe walked down the line of fence and vines that led away to the east. Coming to a small bomb crater that had long ago filled in with weeds and brush, he stepped over and through the opening and noticed the ruins of a small cinder block structure with some shreds of aluminum strips. Joe cleared away what he could, so he could step inside the small structure. Then he spotted something.

"Hey guys, I found something!" Joe yelled.

Everybody else came running over at the sound of Joe's voice, dodging trees, brush, and small bushes.

Ted got there first. "What'd ya find?"

"It's some sort of metal thing with U-shaped openings sticking out. And right over down here is a metal bench, or what's left of it. It's pretty messed up. Look at all those holes! Probably from bullets."

Multiple "wows" were heard. Joe was able to dislodge the artifact from the fence easily and took it with him. Next, he doubled back down the same fence line (or what was left of it). He made his way slowly down, while the other boys scattered again, trying to find their own relics. Some fairly large trees blocked his path, so he had to veer left several feet before continuing on.

As he continued to walk along, he took another step and felt something different under his feet, just below some sand and leaves. He got down on his knees and scraped away the debris. His efforts paid off, and he uncovered a dull, white rubber-something on the ground. Joe saw a square but could tell he had not cleared everything away. After a few more sweeps of debris, it became crystal clear in his mind. The geometry of what Joe was looking at was instantly recalled from one of the DVDs he had watched at Grandpa Moses's house.

"Oh my gosh! I found a home plate!!! Everybody! Quick! Everybody come over here! I found a home plate!!!!"

Everyone came running over, but only Austin looked excited. The rest had blank looks on their faces.

They almost all spoke at once, "What's a home plate?"

Austin answered them, "Baseball guys! We just found a diamond!!!"

"A diamond? It looks like a piece of rubber to me!" Roy Hobson yelled.

"No, Austin's not talking about a jewel. He's talking about a baseball diamond. This is an old ball field! A baseball field!" Joe yelled back.

Bill joined in the questioning, "What the heck is a baseball diamond or ball field or whatever?"

Joe was quick to answer. "It's a sport that died before the war a hundred years ago. It's been dead for a long, long time. Before the war, it was called 'America's pastime.'"

"That's impossible. Everybody knows America's pastime is soccer!" Jim Hart argued.

Mark Samuelson was quick with a rebuttal, "No way, Jim! Lacrosse all the way."

Some chimed in to agree with Mark, while others vocalized support for Jim's assertion about soccer. Soon, a friendly shouting match erupted.

Joe turned his head towards the gang and yelled back, "You're wrong, guys. I'm tellin' ya. You're all wrong. Baseball was once the biggest, most popular game in all of America, a long, long time ago."

Austin was quick to back up his older brother. "It's true, guys! It's true, I tell ya!"

The other boys instantly quieted.

Mark Samuelson broke the silence, "So now what?"

"Let's keep looking," Joe said. "I'm sure there's more to find here. There's got to be more."

But after another ninety minutes of hunting for relics, they found nothing but shell casings. And, despite their find, they returned home with more questions than answers.

Coming into the house, Joe plopped himself on the couch, exhausted from the day's adventure. But as soon as he got comfy, Mary yelled, "Dinner time!"

CHAPTER SEVEN

Learning the Curve

Grandpa Moses always enjoyed the long drive from Dyersville to McHenry. There was not a cloud in the sky as he and his best buddy, Wesley Wainwright, took off early in the morning in the old Mack truck. The day before, he had hired some local farm hands to load up all the baseball items into the trailer.

Wesley was 20 years younger than Moses and had a CDL. Those were rare in that age of driverless vehicles. He, like Moses, liked all things old and especially liked vintage big rigs, particularly ones that were still roadworthy that he could drive.

While Moses's collection contained mostly ancient farm tractors and, of course, the 1959 pickup, he also had an old 1963 Peterbilt and this old 1969 Mack truck.

Motoring east on U.S. Route 20, they were slightly behind schedule as they passed out of the Hill Country region of Galena, Illinois. Earlier, Moses had insisted on stopping for a brief tour of U.S. President Grant's home in Galena. Moses was a history buff, especially of America's two civil wars. He was fascinated by the life of Ulysses Simpson Grant and his part in the First

American Civil War, as well as his later service as the 18th President of the United States.

The "short visit" had lasted two hours and was the sole reason they were running behind. Wesley was determined to make up for lost time and had put the hammer down after those two hours had passed. Once into the flatlands of northern Illinois farm country, the road straightened out, and he could cruise at 70mph to Rockford and make up for some lost time.

Traffic was unusually light, with the occasional driverless cargo drone flying overhead or driverless auto gliding past them on the road at 85mph.

Wesley was a tall, wiry guy with a bald head. He had met Moses at a tractor show 20 years earlier, and they had struck up a quick friendship. Though quite a few years younger than Moses, Wesley considered him an older brother. They had frequently forayed for parts for their antique tractor collections and had been quite successful, from time to time, finding old John Deere, Case, Massey Ferguson, and Ford tractors and parts. Every once in a while, they'd stumble onto some old parts for Moses's 1959 pickup.

Wesley was quite a fan of lacrosse, having played on a traveling, semi-pro team in his thirties. Then, when marriage and three kids came along, it was time to leave his traveling days behind him. The family put down deep roots in Dyersville. But he still played lacrosse once a week in a church league, since he thoroughly enjoyed the camaraderie of just getting together and playing the game. When Moses called him up, excited about the find out at the back of the barn, Wesley was thrilled and wanted to know more about the dead game.

"So, getting back to this old game called baseball, what do the boys figure on doing with it?" Wesley asked.

"Well, Joe's of a mind to learn the game enough to teach his buddies and then play an actual baseball game to see if they like it," Moses answered.

"Judging by the size of the haul in that trailer behind us, it seems like they'll have no shortage of equipment or knowledge to do just that," Wesley remarked. "How long do you figure it'll take before they can actually play?"

"Well, I suppose that depends on school, homework, chores, and the like. I suppose maybe before winter sets in," Moses mused. "If not, then spring for sure. Mary's got the four oldest grandkids involved in a lot of activities through the fall and winter."

"Well, based on what little I've seen of Joe and what you've told me about him, he seems like a very inquisitive young boy. I'm sure he'll learn all about the game and be teaching it to his buddies before you know it."

"Yep, I'm sure he will," Moses agreed.

"Why don't you call Mary and let her know the NAV has us getting into McHenry about 2:30 this afternoon."

"Is that allowing for a lunch stop?" asked Moses.

"Uh, no," Wesley replied.

"I'll tell her 3:30 max then. You hungry yet? I'm hungry. Just saw an ad pop up on the NAV screen for a chicken place coming up. Let's stop there."

"Alright. Chicken sounds good. I'm buying," Wesley stated.

"The heck you are! You're in my truck, and I dragged you into this junket to McHenry."

"Moses, you know darn well anytime our schedules coincide, and I have time to hang with you and drive this old truck, I'm so there."

"That may very well be, but …"

Wesley cut him off, "No, sir! No, sir! My treat! End of discussion!"

Just as soon as the words left his mouth, the NAV computer announced the chicken joint was one mile ahead on the right, and if they would like to stop, they should begin decelerating now.

⚾ ⚾ ⚾

Mary and Sam had been preparing for Moses's arrival all morning. The large pole barn out back behind their home had been neglected the last six months, with many items thrown in there haphazardly. The entire family had been recruited by Mary to tidy the place up and make room for this treasure trove that was fast approaching from the west.

Joe rose early to get a head start on the rest of the family, which thoroughly impressed Sam. Austin joined in at the same time the girls did, a few hours later. It was hard work, but they had just gotten everything put away when they heard the telltale sound of the air horn from Grandpa Moses's Mack truck.

It wasn't every day that an 18-wheeler — vintage 1969 — rolled into McHenry, much less down the street where they lived. Although Sam had seen the big rig on the trips out west to Dyersville, he'd never actually seen it in motion. It was a sight to behold.

Having been replaced by driverless cargo drones, the old 18-wheelers had mostly disappeared from the rebuilt nation's roads, with the exception of occasional appearances in local parades. Anytime these old, monstrous big rigs were seen in motion, people stopped to watch and listen.

Word had gotten all around their neighborhood that an ancient big rig was rolling into town today. When Moses sounded the air horn, throngs of people came out of their homes to come and gape at the sight. Compounding the hullabaloo was the police escort that was mandatory when large, manually driven vehicles rolled into town.

Wesley had already braked and downshifted into low gear as they made the right turn onto Pearl Street from State Rt. 31. He immediately caught sight of people standing at the curb (and a lot more rushing toward it), trying to get a peek at this big rig from another era before the war. Before he could get his arm all the way up, Moses beat him to the cord and pulled hard. The air horn duly responded with a loud blast that made people jump back and then laugh.

Joe stood there with his family and friends and smiled widely when he heard Grandpa blow the air horn.

The police escort slowed to a stop, with the Mack truck just behind them. Joe could see his grandpa clearly smiling from ear to ear in the passenger seat, as Wesley applied the air brakes and brought the behemoth to a full stop. Grandpa could not resist and gave a second, even longer, blast of the horn, to the delight of the crowd.

Joe ran up and was the first to greet Wesley as he exited from the cab of the Mack and made landfall. Grandpa emerged next and was helped down by some neighbors. His feet had hardly touched the ground when Joe threw his arms around him and refused to let go. Mary shed a tear and joined in.

"It's great to see you, Dad, really great," Mary said, embracing her dad.

"It's good to see you too, sweetie."

Sam stepped over. "Dad, great to have you back in McHenry."

"Good to be back, son, good to be back. What's for supper tonight?"

"Grilled shrimp, of course," Sam chuckled.

"Grilled shrimp it is. I had a fine chicken lunch, somewhere between Galena and Rockford. Can't believe it, but I've worked up an appetite again."

Mary laughed. The shrimp thing had been a running joke between her dad and Sam, for as long as they had been married. When Mary and Sam were first dating, Sam would frequently say, "Where's the shrimp?" whenever they showed up at a family party. Only, tonight, there really would be shrimp — and steak — on the grill.

Moses got everyone's attention and motioned for them to quiet down. "Listen everyone, we need some space to back this rig into the side driveway and up to the barn door. We could also use a hand emptying the trailer. Got quite a load back there."

Folks from further down the road headed back home, but a decent enough number of immediate neighbors hung around, as Wesley deftly re-entered the cab of the big rig, pulled around to the side driveway, and backed her down all the way to the barn door. With 15 neighbors, plus family, chipping in, they had the trailer emptied in no time at all. Joe had already worked out a plan of where he wanted each numbered carton put inside the old barn.

Once they were done, the family members all extended a hand of thanks to the neighbors that had helped. Mary had already quietly told Sam she'd ordered more shrimp and steaks, and that he should tell all the neighbors to plan on staying for a party. They all accepted but asked to be excused for a short time to go home and clean up.

Joe figured there would be about an hour's pause before the festivities began. It was enough time for him to head to the carton nearest to the barn door, carton number 42. After unsealing it, he found an entire box full of baseball gloves and baseballs. He tried a few gloves on until he found one that felt good on his hand.

He took a ball and pounded it once into the palm of the glove. The smell of leather, already strong once he had unsealed the carton, now came on even stronger with each pounding of the ball into the ball glove's pocket.

Joe let up and sort of plopped the ball into the mitt a few times and grinned. Then he tossed the ball slightly into the air, just a little higher than his head. He stuck the glove out swiftly, but the ball bounced off the tip of it and careened away toward the wall and onto the ground. He picked the ball up from the ground and repeated the toss into the air. This time, he caught it.

He smiled and giggled, then he tossed the ball a little higher. He caught that one, too. Joe smiled even wider and laughed a little more. The next one he tossed even higher, but this one went a little wild. He took a step, but he quickly realized it would not be enough and made a quick sprint to catch the ball.

Just then, Austin and Teddy walked up and stood at the entrance to the barn.

Joe looked over and yelled out, "Hey, guys, grab a mitt."

"A mitt?" Ted asked.

Joe pointed. "A baseball mitt, over in the open box. Try a couple on until you find one that feels good on your hand."

Ted and Austin walked over to the unsealed carton 42. They peered in and each picked a mitt up, trying a few on until they both found gloves that fit their hands well.

"This one feels great. Fits like a glove!" Austin joked.

"Yeah, this one fits me like a glove too!" Ted added.

"Funny, guys, real funny. Stand over there on the other side of the barn. I'm gonna toss the ball to you first, Ted. Try to catch it. Throw it back to me, then I'll toss it to you, Austin."

Joe took the ball in his throwing hand and gently underhanded it to Ted.

Ted reached out his mitt and caught the ball.

"Uh-huh, a natural!" Joe yelled out.

"What's that mean?" Ted asked.

"It's from a very ancient movie. The guy was born to play baseball," Joe explained, as he made an overhanded toss to Austin, who caught the ball without incident.

"Yeah, this does sort of feel natural to me. Feels real good," Austin said.

Austin reared back and threw the ball back to his older brother. The ball let out a smack as it landed squarely in Joe's mitt.

"I'm gonna throw one a little harder, Ted. Be ready," Joe warned.

Ted caught the ball and returned the toss with equal velocity. Joe caught it. It was then he noticed the sound of the ball hitting the pocket of the glove when caught in the right way. Joe found the sound was delightful, mesmerizing even.

All three were smiling and even giggling a little. Without even saying it, they all felt they were rediscovering something magical, something very, very good.

They paused the play when Joe suggested they go outside to allow longer and higher throws. Once outside, they resumed throwing and took turns tossing the ball high, low, on the ground, soft, hard, long, short. They were having a blast and couldn't get enough of it, even when they missed a catch or made a poor throw.

Sam and Mary had spotted them and had stepped out onto the patio to watch. Mary smiled. Sam made a comment that he wanted to join them right then and there, but Mary had stopped him, saying, "No, not just yet, hon. Hold on."

After about 15 minutes, Joe stopped after catching a high one. He looked at the ball and nodded several times. Then he looked over at Ted. "Hey, wanna learn the curve?"

"The curve?" Ted asked, looking confused.

"Yeah, it's called a curveball."

"I wanna learn it too, Joe!" Austin yelled.

"Sure!"

Joe walked up to Ted and Austin and showed them the grip of the ball he had learned while watching one of the instructional DVDs on the art of throwing a baseball. Grandpa had insisted on watching a few of the DVDs before the boys flew home.

After Ted got a feel for the right grip and placement of his fingers on the seam of the ball, Joe had him pitch to him from around 50 feet away, while Austin stood by and watched. Ted's first pitch bounced into the ground five feet in front of Joe, then bounced up and nearly hit him in the forehead.

But Joe got the mitt up in time and deflected the ball away as he laughed, "Whoa, Ted!"

After getting the ball back from Joe, Ted paused and fixed his fingers on the ball as he had before. He reared back and threw the ball again, at the target of Joe's mitt. This time, he tried to add a little more speed. The ball sailed in a little wild and bounced into the grass. Joe leaped to his right to catch or stop the ball. Too late. It skittered past him and rolled into the bushes. He retrieved the ball and tossed it back to Teddy, who repeated his moves and tried again. The ball came in, headed toward Joe's mitt, before it broke down and to his right. Joe reached over and down and caught the pitch. They both smiled.

A fourth attempt went wild to Joe's left.

"Maybe learning the curve is gonna take a lot more practice," Ted sighed.

"Yeah, I think so," Joe agreed. "But we'll keep doing it and figure it out."

"Hey, boys, let me in on this action," Sam yelled out, as he ran over to the boys. Mary had tried to stop him a second time, but Sam would have none of it.

"Sure, Dad, go inside the barn and look in the open carton to find a mitt that fits."

Sam walked over to the barn and up to the opened box and foraged through a few mitts. None of them fit. He opened box 41 and immediately saw a yellowed, thick, nine-inch by twelve-inch envelope. He unsealed it and grabbed the thick stack of papers and pulled them out. The top page had the words "Nokona Glove Factory, Nocona, Texas." As he briefly rifled through the papers, he could tell right away the packet contained detailed patterns and instructions for making something. Unsure of what, he put the papers back in the envelope and the envelope back into the box. Gazing down, he saw the mitts. These were clearly bigger mitts for adults. He tried a few on and, after finding one that fit well, headed back out to the boys.

Sam and the boys formed a square and started tossing the ball counterclockwise. When the first ball came Sam's way, he reached out to catch it, but it careened down toward his foot and squarely struck his big toe. He bit his tongue and hopped around a few seconds before shaking it off. The boys looked concerned, but Sam quickly recovered and threw the ball to Joe, who threw it to Ted, who threw it to Austin, who threw it — a little softer this time — back to his dad.

"Don't worry about me, Austin," Sam said. "Throw the next one as hard as you did the first one. I've got it now."

When Austin got the ball again from Ted, he complied with his dad's wishes and threw the ball to him a lot harder. This time, the ball smacked squarely in the deep pocket of the mitt and made that same mesmerizing sound the boys had heard in the barn. When Sam heard it this time, he paused, "Hey, that sounds nice, real nice."

They continued tossing the ball back and forth. With each throw, Sam got a little more comfortable and was amazed at how good it felt to engage in this strange thing called "catch."

"So, Joe, what do you figure on doing with all the stuff in the shed?"

Joe stopped, looked at his dad, and smiled widely. "Well, I guess read everything about the game, watch more of those old movies, and study and practice it a lot. Hopefully, my friends will too. Then, we'll play a game and see if we like it."

CHAPTER EIGHT

The Immersion

It was chilly outside when an excited Sam arrived at work, earlier than usual, and headed straight for Eduardo's office. He had called Sam during the party over the weekend, asking him to come by his office first thing Monday morning, that he had some news about the "No Pepper" sign.

"Good morning, Eduardo!" Sam greeted him. "How are you?"

"Excellent! Had a great weekend with the family. Eduardo Jr.'s lacrosse team won the championship!" Eduardo beamed.

"Hey, congratulations! I remember you telling me your son was doing quite well in lacrosse."

"Thanks! Yes, yes, he is. He just loves the sport. My other son, Louis, not so much."

"How come?" Sam asked.

"He just doesn't like it all that much. Soccer, he dislikes even more. Too much running, he says," Eduardo answered, rolling his eyes.

"Ha! That's for sure. I never got into soccer myself, either. Well, I'm sure he'll find a sport that appeals to him. So, you called, what's up?"

"It's about the sign your son found, 'No Pepper.' I found more information about it. Where your son found that sign was more than likely a baseball field before the war. I'm thinking the field was for a local youth league back then. Professional baseball players would often play pepper, but the youth leagues didn't want the kids to play it because of the risk of injury. So, the youth leagues would post those signs on the fences of their ball fields. Pepper was pretty much dead, until it became popular again, in the 2030s, with the professional baseball players. Of course, you know how kids love to imitate the pros. So, it spread to the youth leagues, but a lot of kids were getting injuries to their faces, losing teeth and such."

"Huh, interesting," Sam said. "What led you to conclude the old fence was part of an old baseball field?"

"Well, I took a field trip over there myself with the Army Corp last week. They were doing survey work in the area. I did some exploring and found the remains of the fence where your son found that sign," Eduardo explained. "In my mind, and based on the material we have archived now, that is an old baseball field. Of course, they blew much of it to bits in the battle. What remains is overgrown with vegetation. But, in my opinion, it was definitely a baseball field before the war."

"Wow, that's something. I remember now Joe telling me they'd gone back over there and found something called a 'home plate' still stuck in the ground."

"Huh. Interesting. Well, I got another thing for you as well. Just last week, a gentleman who lives over on Elm Street dropped off a stack of old local newspapers from before the war. They were tucked away in the attic of a house he had just bought. I came across one copy that had a story about a youth baseball league anniversary. I'm not 100% positive, but I believe they took the photograph at the baseball field your son found."

"No kidding? Hey, I'd like to see a copy of that when you're done with it."

"Sure, I'll let you know. Hey, say hi to Mary for me. You know we're overdue to get together with you guys. Let's do it soon."

"Sure, maybe this weekend," Sam suggested. "Let me check with Mary and get back to you. Thanks, buddy, have a great day."

"You too, my friend," Eduardo said, settling in at his desk to start his workday. "You too."

As Sam walked to his own office, his thoughts focused on what he'd just heard, and he pondered what he should do with the information. Obviously, he would tell Joe, but what else? These events of the last several weeks seemed … bigger than that.

A puzzle formed in his mind, that had all the pieces in motion. Then he realized these events seemed like they happened for a reason — like they were orchestrated, even.

As he connected the dots, he felt amazed. The "No Pepper" sign. The trunk in the attic at his father-in-law's house. Then the note in the trunk that was almost missed. A treasure trove of baseball stuff in the ground and in pristine condition. It seemed all too real. Now this latest update from Eduardo.

Then he thought, *Maybe I should call Tyree.*

With that, Sam picked up the comm and dialed Tyree Williams of the Army Corp.

"Operations, Master Sergeant Tyree Williams speaking, how may I help you?"

"Tyree, Sam Scott here."

"Hi, Sam. How've you been?"

"Doing well, and yourself?

"Excellent. Mary and the kids doing okay?"

"Sure are. How's Monique and your kids?"

"All good here, too. All good. What's up?"

"Glad you asked. Look, let me come over to your office," Sam implored. "I need 15-20 minutes of your time."

"C'mon over. I actually have a lull going on right now."

"Great, I'll be over in five."

Joe was excited. It was now mid-November. He'd gotten the entire gang back together for the first time in several weeks. In fact, they had not all been together in one place since they had ventured into the VFW Woods and found the home plate, back in late September.

Austin, Ted, and all the neighborhood boys were gathered at Joe's house to watch the baseball DVDs. They were all talking over one another, excited to see what was in store. So, Joe pointed to his friend Mark and signaled for the famous whistle, an ear-piercing attention-getter.

With the deed done and the room quieted down, Joe spoke. "Ok, listen up, guys. I've told you about all the baseball stuff we got from my grandpa's farm. Now we're gonna watch some DVDs that are all about baseball. We got two movies, plus some DVDs with lessons on baseball. My mom's making popcorn, so settle in. They filmed one movie in my grandpa's town, way before he was born. The other movie, I'm not sure where they filmed it, but it's a cool movie, anyway. We can take a break before we watch the DVDs with the baseball lessons. When we watch those, we have to pay extra attention!"

"Why? What's the big deal?" Steve asked.

"Well, the way I figure it, if we want to learn about this game, we need to, we need to ..." Joe struggled for the right word.

"Immerse—" John offered.

"Immerse? That's a big word," Bill interrupted.

John continued, "I like doing the crossword puzzles in the newspaper. My mom helps me with the bigger words. Yes, 'immerse.' Think of this as binge-watching. We're going to study this baseball stuff and get a real good feel for it. Think immersion, dude. Like when you're submerged over your head in water."

"Yeah, that's it, John. That's a perfect description. Leave it to you, Mr. Know-It-All. It's one thing to throw the ball around and catch it and all, but to actually play a game of baseball is a lot harder than that. So, we need to do our homework and get this right or not do it at all," Joe insisted.

Just then, a sudden commotion erupted, as Anne rushed in, yelling, "It's snowing! It's snowing!"

Winter had arrived in McHenry.

CHAPTER NINE

Spring Training

It had been a cold, snowy, but short, winter. By mid-March, the temperatures had already moderated into the upper 50s. The unseasonably warm low 60s arrived in the last half of the month. Perennials were already a few inches out of the ground, and the tree leaves were emerging early, too.

Spring, for the first time in anyone's memory, had come early to McHenry.

During the winter, the boys had spent hours upon hours immersing themselves in all things baseball, via the media horde from the Dyersville treasure. Mary had insisted that Joe include his twin sisters in some of the instructional video sessions. He had reluctantly complied.

Snow had piled high and then quickly melted in late February. The boys had lived, breathed, and learned baseball. They learned baseball phrases, baseball rules, and baseball techniques. All, of course, after their school homework. Whenever they could, they'd gather in the barn and toss the ball around, until the cold drove them back into their homes.

Sam relished his many games of "catch" in the barn with his

two boys or the twins. It warmed his heart when one of them approached him on a Saturday and asked, "Dad, wanna play a game of catch?"

A four-day thaw, at the beginning of February, had given the boys a small window of time to go outside the barn and play catch and try their hands at a game of pepper. They had an absolute blast, and no one got hurt. Well, at least not seriously hurt. Billy Cross had a ball bounce up and hit him in the chin and had quite a sting and a minor bruise to show for it — plus two stitches.

The boys had all learned a valuable lesson from Billy Cross's minor injury. Paying attention and respecting the ball when it was in motion was very important. It was a lesson they were sure to remember, as they delved deeper into the game.

It was one thing to watch movies and read books; it was quite another to do what they were learning. For some of the boys, especially Joe and Ted, it all seemed to come naturally. One thing that none of the boys expected was this growing sense of anticipation for warmer weather and dry ground, so they could do baseball, rather than watch it and read about it.

By mid-March, the boys had determined it was dry enough to engage in practice drills, taking turns at the various positions on the field and, of course, getting their fair share of at-bats at the plate. It was all paying off. The boys were having the time of their lives learning the intricacies of the game at each position, as well as the hitting aspects of baseball.

Joe and his dad scouted out some suitable places to try the game out when the weather warmed up. They settled on the sprawling, 20-acre DeVita Park, the area's largest soccer and lacrosse field complex, just north of their home.

It was within walking distance of the boys' neighborhood. Sam had checked with the respective league presidents of the local soccer and lacrosse clubs, and they had picked out a particular part of the park that was not in use by either sports club in March.

The day finally came when Joe, Austin, Ted, and the rest of the gang were to meet at DeVita Park for their first-ever baseball practice, and hopefully, a game. Sam offered to help, along with some of the rest of the dads. Joe was beside himself with excitement and had flown out of bed to get ready.

Mary made a fabulous breakfast, while Sam was busy gathering up the gear. The boys were wolfing down their food, when the twins announced they were coming to participate in this "baseball stuff" in person.

Joe attempted to object but caught a look in his mom's eye that said he'd better not try to shut out his sisters from that glorious, early spring day.

After breakfast, Sam and a large contingent of family and neighbors met out in front of the Scott home and made the short trek to DeVita Park. Sam had gotten a call the night before from both league presidents for the youth soccer and youth lacrosse groups, letting him know that none of the fields would be in use that day. A perfect day for a real baseball game!

When they arrived at the field, Joe took charge, directing kids and grownups where to put bases, equipment bags, lawn chairs, and other gear. It took a good thirty minutes to lay everything out. When they were done, Joe got all the gang together and picked Ted to coach one team, while he coached the other.

All the guys and gals spread out over the outfield and infield. Joe grabbed a ball and bat and walked over to the home plate. He tossed the ball into the air and swung the bat. The sound of the ball hitting wood made a familiar crisp, cracking sound that had become a sweet sound to his ears. The first hit was a ground ball to third base. Teddy and Billy were standing there, close to one another. Ted waited for the ball to come to him. He fielded the ball cleanly and threw the ball to first base, where

Mark Samuelson was standing. Mark caught the ball and tossed it back to Joe.

Joe already had another ball in hand before Mark tossed the ball back to him. Joe repeated the motion and hit a ground ball to the shortstop position. Dan Simpson and Steve Dearing were standing there together. Steve raced to his left and scooped up the ball and tossed it to Mark.

Joe hit the next ball to second base, where Jim and John Gander were stationed. The ball came right at Jim, but his older brother, John, stepped in front of him and caught the ball after one bounce and threw it over to Mark. Jim gave his brother a push and a look.

Joe hit the next ball hard into the air, out toward Jeff Gander and Ken Orbison in left field. The ball sailed past both of them. They took off running, but Ken got a jump on Jeff and ran as fast as he could. With the ball descending rapidly, Ken reached up and caught it, just before Jeff caught up to him.

Joe hit the next ball to left center. His twin sisters, Nellie and Anne, were there, and Nellie reached up, without having to move her feet at all, and caught the ball. She smiled and tossed the ball to Dan Simpson.

After 30 minutes had gone by, Joe remembered one video where guys playing pickup games of baseball would toss a bat into the air for a guy to catch, in order to decide who picked the first player. So, he grabbed a bat and tossed it over to Teddy. Ted, as if reading Joe's mind, reached out and caught it with one hand. Joe then placed his hand on the bat, just on top of Ted's hand, then he and Ted alternated putting their hands one on top of the other until there was no more bat left to climb. The last hand on the top of the bat got to choose the first player. Joe was the winner.

"Figures you'd win the first toss!" Ted grumbled.

"Yeah, well, I don't usually win contests, so I'm not feeling bad at all," Joe laughed.

"Ok, so what's next?" Ted asked.

"We'll alternate choosing players until everyone is on a team," Joe explained.

"Ok, let's go!" Ted yelled.

"Ok, I choose Billy," Joe announced.

"Mark," Ted stated, making his first pick.

Back and forth they went, until each had their team for the game.

On Joe's team were Austin, Billy Cross, Steve Dearing, Ken Orbison, Jim Gander, Norm Gould, Doug Jeffries, and Joe's sisters, Anne and Nellie.

Ted's team had his brothers, Jerry and Tom Banks, Mark Samuelson, Dan Simpson, John Gander, Roy Hobson, Jeff Gander, Eduardo Chavez Jr., and Jim Hart.

The parents had all come to watch. They'd brought lawn chairs and had them arranged all along the third-base side of the field.

Once Joe and Ted had corralled their respective players for their first attempt at playing a game of baseball, they let each player know where they were going to play on the field. Joe and Ted had worked it out ahead of time to have a printed line drawing of a baseball field, and they both got to work penciling in names at the various positions, as well as determining who batted in what order.

Joe's lineup card consisted of:

1. Austin Scott - Shortstop
2. Billy Cross - Second Base
3. Steve Dearing - Third Base
4. Ken Orbison - First Base
5. Jim Gander - Center Field

6. Norm Gould - Catcher
7. Doug Jeffries - Pitcher
8. Joe Scott - Left Field
9. Anne Scott - Right Field

At Mary's insistence, Anne and Nellie would take turns playing right field.

Ted's lineup card had:
1. Jerry Banks - Second Base
2. Tom Banks - Shortstop
3. Mark Samuelson - First Base
4. Ted Banks - Pitcher
5. Dan Simpson - Catcher
6. John Gander - Left Field
7. Jeff Gander - Centerfield
8. Roy Hobson - Right Field
9. Jim Hart - Third Base

Sub's going in were Bill Adams and Eduardo Chavez Jr.

Sam had studied up on the rules, whenever time permitted, over the winter. He felt comfortable enough with them, at this point, that he had volunteered as the umpire for the first game and donned the safety gear from the treasure trove of equipment.

Joe called everyone together at home plate and said a prayer. Once said, Ted's team fanned out to their respective positions, while Joe's team headed over to the first base side and took up positions to watch their first batter, Austin Scott, come to bat.

The weather was perfect. A balmy and unseasonably warm 74 degrees, along with sunny skies and a light wind from the southwest. Sam looked at his watch and made a mental note, *"1:10 PM, Saturday, April 4, 2167."*

Ted Lee Banks went to the pitching rubber staked down in the grass. Dan Simpson got into position behind home plate.

Ted looked around at the rest of the guys tossing the ball around, and he saw their smiles and determination to play the game well. He smiled, too.

Ted looked at Dan and effortlessly caught the ball Dan threw to him for his warm-up pitches. Taking his mitt off, Ted rubbed the baseball with both hands and took his place with his right foot on the pitching rubber. He put his mitt up to his face and breathed in deeply. The smell of the leather was something magical. He put the mitt back on and put the baseball into the pocket. He set up for the windup and threw his first warm-up pitch for a strike. Dan fired the baseball back to Ted. His next warm-up toss was also a strike. Back and forth they went, for seven more pitches.

"I'm ready!" Ted yelled.

With that, Sam Scott put his mask on and yelled out, "Okay, let's play!"

Austin Scott stepped up to the plate.

Ted set up for the first pitch. He paused for a moment, then reared back and threw a fastball. Austin saw it coming and began to stride into the ball while his bat came around.

He missed.

"Strike one!" shouted Sam.

"Yes!" yelled Ted.

"Crap," Austin muttered.

Dan tossed the ball back, and Austin got ready for the next pitch. Ted again paused in the windup (it seemed natural to him), reared back, and let loose another fastball. Again, seeing it coming in, Austin bore down, as he stepped into the pitch and swung the bat in one smooth motion. The ball contacted the "sweet spot" of the barrel and rocketed upward and outward. The trajectory carried it between John and Jeff Gander in left and center field. They saw when the ball was hit but hesitated for a split second before they both took off running to catch up with the baseball before it landed. A gentle wind was all that was needed to push the ball a little more toward the left. John Gander was the first to come close to the ball, as its descent was nearing the ground. He reached up with his mitt, while in a full run, but the ball had a little more travel in it and overshot his outstretched mitt by mere inches.

At contact, Austin had taken off running toward first base. He could not help but watch the ball as it traveled high and far. He smiled, in part because of the awesome sound of the baseball when it had contacted the wood bat, but also from sheer delight at how high and far the ball was traveling! As Austin rounded first base, 60 feet away from home plate, he saw John Gander's failed, but valiant, attempt to catch the ball.

In the meantime, Jeff Gander had correctly judged the baseball was nearer to his brother but that his brother would not catch up to it, despite his speed. So, Jeff had altered his path and angled out to a spot just beyond where he felt the ball was going to land. It was a keen move, and he arrived just after the ball had landed and bounced. Jeff reached out and caught the ball on the first bounce and fired it into second base, where Jerry Banks was already in position. Austin flew into second base, just ahead of the throw, and slid across the grass and into the base.

"Safe!" barked Sam. As the only umpire, he had run out toward the pitcher's area to be in an excellent position to make a call at second base.

"Yes!" Austin shouted.

Mary Scott, while watching all this unfold, had yelled for Austin to run. When he wound up at second base, she jumped up and down, cheering. Some neighbors turned to look at Mary and laughed. Sam looked over too and smirked. But her enthusiasm was infectious, and with a runner on second base to start the game, the other spectators began to get caught up in the rush.

Joe yelled out for the next batter, Billy Cross.

Billy stepped up to the plate. Ted repeated his pitching motion, reared back, and threw a curveball. Billy strode into the pitch but held up his swing when he saw the ball curving out of the strike zone. Dan reached over to his right and barely caught the ball.

"Ball," stated Sam, very matter-of-factly.

Dan tossed the ball back.

Ted repeated his routine and threw a fastball.

Again, Billy strode into the pitch, but this time he let loose a swing. He missed.

"Strike one!"

Two pitches later came the call: "Strike three, you're out!"

Billy trudged back to the sidelines, realizing that hitting that small, white baseball was much harder than he thought.

Joe walked over and patted Billy on the back. "Don't worry, Billy, you'll get 'em next time!"

Steve Dearing had also patted Billy on the back, as he walked up to take his turn to bat.

Steve stepped toward the home plate and looked at his good buddy, Ted. "Teddy, I'm gonna take the first good pitch you throw and send it over Roy's head out in right field."

Ted laughed, "Bring it, buddy!"

Ted set up for the pitch, then wound up, reared back, and threw a slower pitch right out over the plate.

Steve saw the ball coming and noticed that it seemed slower than the last pitch he saw, when Billy Cross had swung and missed for the strikeout. Steve hesitated for a brief fraction of a second and then started his swing. He contacted the ball but, instead of hitting it into the air, it became a ground ball to second baseman Jerry Banks. Steve took off running hard toward first base. Jerry waited for the ball to roll into his mitt before turning and throwing the ball to first baseman Mark Samuelson, who caught the ball just a moment before Steve stepped on the base.

"Out!" yelled Sam. "Two outs!"

Ted turned around and yelled out to Roy in right field, "Hey, Roy, did you catch that ball?"

"Nope, I never even moved," came his reply.

"Next time, Ted, next time," Steve yelled back, as he walked back to his team, sitting in the grass.

As the game continued, Mary Scott's old high school friend, Mike Drucker, arrived and put down a lawn chair very near her. As a writer for the McHenry Herald newspaper, he had won the Pulitzer Prize the year before for his series of articles on the efforts to eradicate the flu epidemic of the previous year.

Mike Drucker's nephew, Dan Simpson, was catching behind the plate. Mike had received word from his sister, Sarah, that Dan was going to be playing an ancient game called baseball. As a feature editor for the McHenry Herald, Mike was intrigued by the idea of doing a story about these McHenry boys playing a pre-war game that had long since been extinct. With his boss's permission, he had come out to see what this game called "baseball" was all about. Although he was a huge lacrosse fan and a season ticket holder for the Rockford Rockets national lacrosse team, Mike was unprepared for what was unfolding before his eyes.

Mary turned to her old friend. "Well, Mike, what do you think so far?"

Mike paused for a moment. "This is different. I'm so used to seeing all the players in lacrosse and soccer pretty much in motion throughout a game. This game is something entirely different."

Mary smiled. "It is very different, I know, but there's a certain finesse about it. I'm still taking it all in. The kids have studied so hard, and practiced even harder, just to get to the point where they felt comfortable playing this first practice game and ..." Mary paused in mid-sentence with wonderment at the thought that had just come into her head, "… and to think this is the first time in over a hundred years that anyone has ever played a game of baseball! Wow, let that sink in."

"A hundred years?" Mike asked.

"Sam's been working with a co-worker at the federal building to research the recovered records on the sport. So far, there's no record of a baseball game having been played since a 5,000-pound bomb was dropped on a baseball stadium in Charlotte, North Carolina, at the outset of the war. The bomb killed all the players and spectators in attendance."

"Creepers! Why the heck did they do that? When was that?" Mike asked, with a horrified look on his face.

"April 11, 2061," Mary replied.

Mike paused as the date registered in his head. "April 11 … why does that ring a bell?"

"The next day, April 12, 2061, was 200 years to the day from when the First American Civil War started."

"Damn!"

"Mike!!!"

"Oh, I beg your pardon, Mary. How many died in the stadium attack?"

"One thousand, seven hundred and seventy-six souls, including all players and members of the press."

"Huh, the press too," Mike replied. "There's some irony in those numbers, for sure."

"That's what I thought when Sam told me. I guess the stadium could hold something like 35,000 people, but the sport was on its last legs already."

"Thirty-five thousand?! Thank goodness it was nearly empty when that attack went off. What killed the sport?"

"They're still trying to uncover that from the records they're restoring. But it seems money played a factor, and a three-year strike by the professional ballplayers. Then there was the huge jump in popularity of soccer and lacrosse at the amateur and professional levels. Seems like it all made a perfect storm and killed the game."

Mike thought for a second, then replied, "Well, here we are, over a hundred years later, and both soccer and lacrosse are still competing to be America's pastime, ahead of basketball and football."

Mary laughed, "That's funny you used that phrase. Sam also found out that's what they used to call baseball, back 175 years ago. America's pastime."

"No kidding?"

"No kidding!"

With that, both of them noticed a lot of clapping and yelling from the other neighbors that had assembled to watch the kids play. Mike and Mary turned their heads back toward the boys on the field.

Joe was having an animated discussion with his umpire dad about a call he had just made regarding a play at the plate.

Spring training was in full swing.

CHAPTER TEN

The Boys Just Wanna Play!

Monday morning, Joe was still a little sore from the game two days earlier, but he could not wipe the smile off of his face. He and the boys had an absolute blast playing an actual baseball game! For sure, there had been more than a fair number of errors and strikeouts, but hey, as he had told his buddies after the game, "What did you expect for our first time playing an extinct game?!"

Indeed, while it had been the first game of baseball played in over 100 years, something had happened. As the parents and grandparents watched, many of them, on their own volition, sent messages to family and friends to stop by and take a look. Many had, along with what seemed like every kid within a ten-block radius.

After the game, the kids who saw what this baseball game stuff was all about mobbed Joe. They had peppered him with a myriad of questions, and amidst the din and noise of it all, Joe told them all to show up at his house after school on Monday for any questions they had about baseball. As excited as he was, Joe was tired, and his left arm was a little sore, after being hit by a pitch from Ted.

Ted was, indeed, a natural at the sport — but he was only human and imperfect at that. With runners on first and second in the fifth inning, and the count one and two, Ted had drilled his buddy with an inside fastball that "got away from him," as he recalled after the game. The ball sailed in and hit Joe in the upper arm. It stung, for sure, but Joe shook it off while trotting to first and waved his mom and dad off when they attempted to check on him.

On Monday afternoon, as young Joe turned the corner of his street, he looked twice at the mob of kids standing around at his house, waiting for him to show up. He stopped in his tracks and took it all in. He was about halfway down Pearl Street, when Randy Washington spotted him and yelled out his name. All the kids there turned and took off running towards Joe.

"Hold on, guys, hold on! Let me get to my porch and put my stuff down."

With that, the crowd made a way for Joe to finish the last steps to his house and up the stairs to the porch. After putting his stuff down, he turned to the guys and gals assembled in the yard.

"Ok, I'll try to answer every question ya' have, but only one question at a time. Hold your hand up, just like in school, and if I point at you, it's your turn to ask a question. Deal?"

"Deal!" was the boisterous response from the crowd.

As he answered questions and went over Saturday's game in his mind, he could not help but think something big was, indeed, in the making.

Mary ran in from the backyard when she heard the phone ring. She was expecting a call from her dad at 3:30, and sure enough, the clock next to the phone showed it was exactly 3:30.

"Hello, Dad."

"Now, how did you know it was me?"

"Dad, you always call on the dot to whatever time you message me you're going to call. You never miss it!"

"Is that right? Well, maybe next time I'll call two minutes late, just to throw you off!" Moses joked.

"What, stop a good thing?!" Mary protested.

"Well, alright, since you put it that way. Say, I wanted to call and see how things went on Saturday. I wanted to be there so bad, but things are busy here."

"Oh, Dad, it was a sight to behold."

"How's that?"

"It was love at first sight for me. It was the finesse of the game that grabbed my attention."

"Ya' don't say! How did Joe do?" asked Moses.

"He was two for four."

"Two for four? What does that mean?"

"He batted four times, and he got a hit two times," Mary explained.

"That's right, that's right. I remember that now from one of the DVDs or tapes. Wow, good for him! How about the girls? How'd they do?"

"Funny you should ask. They loved it too. Seems we may have some budding ball players in the twins."

"Is that right?"

"Yep! Nellie and Anne each got a hit."

"Well, that settles it. I'm going to clear my calendar and pay a visit to watch a game," Moses announced.

"That sounds great, Dad. When are you coming out here?"

"I need to tie some loose ends up first, and then I'll get back to you this evening or tomorrow morning. Love you, sweetie."

"Love you too, Dad."

Moses hung up and stomped the floor with his right heel so hard, it got Josephine's attention in the next room.

"Old man, what's the matter?!"

"Oh, Josephine, I'm so mad at myself for not being there for the kids' first try at playing a baseball game. Why did I let myself get so wrapped up in this other stuff? In the end, it's all trivial junk, anyway."

"Well, don't just stand there and sulk. I heard what you said about clearing your calendar. Get to it and clear it out, so you can get back to McHenry soon. Before you know it, those kids will be all grown, and you'll be in Glory."

The words hit Moses hard and got his attention. "Well, I suppose you're right, Josephine. I suppose you're right."

Joe sat patiently, as friends, acquaintances, and strangers peppered him with question after question. Eventually, he lost track of how many. He started taking notes of the questions he could not answer right then and there.

He told everyone he would double-check the answers and to show up at the same time the next day, so they could continue their discussion.

One thing that was clear, though. Even though a lot of the kids didn't understand the sport much at all, interest in the game was catching on fast. *The boys just wanna play,* " he thought to himself, then spoke it out loud after everyone but Ted had left.

"The boys just wanna play. What did we do, Ted?"

"What do you mean?" Ted asked.

Joe paused for a long moment, while he stared down at his mitt, still in his left hand. He slowly raised it and put his face into the pocket of the glove, closed his eyes, and breathed deeply. Opening his eyes, he turned to his buddy and said, "I mean, like, did we just do something so totally awesome that it could, like, change the nation?"

"Uh, wow, that just gave me goosebumps!" Ted exclaimed, staring at Joe with wide eyes.

"Not as big as what you get when your friend hits you with a baseball, I hope!" Joe fired back, as they both broke into laughter.

"You wanna come inside for a lemonade?" Joe asked, after they had recovered.

"Sure!"

When the boys entered the front room, Mary Scott was already in the kitchen making some lemonade. She was enjoying her unexpected day off, which her boss had given her for a job well done on a year-long project that had ended the week before.

After having spent some time doing yard work, she was quietly sitting in her easy chair in the front room, taking a quick break. She overheard the conversation between her son and Ted, and the funny thing was, when her son made the comment that gave Ted goosebumps, she had gotten goosebumps too.

She made a mental note to call her old friend, Mike Drucker. Maybe a story about baseball would interest him. He had already seemed interested at the practice game on Saturday. With his reputation and connections, who knew, maybe the national media would pick it up.

Mary served the boys lemonade and some small talk with them for the next 20 minutes. Afterward, she headed back into the kitchen, picked up the house phone, and called Mike Drucker.

"Hello, Mike Drucker, McHenry Herald."

"Hi Mike, it's Mary."

"Hi Mary, how's Sam and the kids? Say, how's Joe doing after getting hit with that baseball?"

"They're all fine, including my budding young baseball player. He's got a sore spot, he said, but he's a tough kid. Hey, thanks for taking my call. I wanted to ask you if you could meet me and Sam for lunch tomorrow. I'd love to talk baseball with you and see if you'd maybe consider doing a story about it and the boys. Lunch will be our treat."

"Would I?! Darn right. You must have been reading my mind or something. I've been thinking about the game. When and where for lunch?"

"Oh, how about 12:15 at Happy Jacks?"

"Ah, yes, the legendary Happy Jacks! See you then, and leave your money at home. This has the makings of a national story! I'm buying!"

CHAPTER ELEVEN

Press Pass

In recent weeks, Eduardo Chavez's team had come across a lot of baseball material during their ongoing data restoration project, so Sam took the liberty of inviting Eduardo to join them for the Tuesday lunch junket at Happy Jacks. Mary had sent a quick message to Mike, and as expected, he was fine with the lunch party growing to a party of five.

McHenry's Happy Jacks had been a legend for as long as anyone could remember. The original restaurant had been housed in the remodeled frame of an old ranch house, built in the 1950s. Converted to a restaurant in the 1980s, it passed through 3 different owners, until 2061, when it was destroyed by a tornado in the first year of the war.

Some 50 years after the war, the last owner's great-great-grandson came across a scrapbook from the restaurant's heyday and was inspired to rebuild and reopen the place. Given the state of the American economy, family and friends thought he was nuts, but he plodded ahead, undeterred, during the latter stages of "horse and buggy mode."

In retrospect, it was that sort of American, can-do spirit that played a large part in the transition phase of recovery from the Second Civil War.

The rebuilt Happy Jacks looked nothing like the old one shown in the ancient photos on the walls. But, at five times the size of the original, it remained an icon in town, serving generous portions of subs, burgers, hot dogs, salads, fries, and of course, ice cream, shakes, and malts.

Mike had arrived early and was waiting for Mary, Sam, young Joe, and Eduardo. They made quite a noisy entrance (as was the custom for the Scott family).

Sam extended a hand out to Mike, and they shook hands.

"Hi, Mike, good to see you again. Of course, you know Mary. I'd like to introduce you to my oldest son, Joe, and my co-worker at the federal building, Eduardo Chavez."

"Thanks, Sam. As always, Mary, good to see you. Glad to meet you, Joe. Eduardo, a pleasure to meet you as well."

Eduardo extended his hand. "Mr. Drucker, I must say it's an honor to meet a Pulitzer Prize-winning reporter."

"Come on now, none of this 'mister' talk. Please, call me Mike."

"Very well, Mr. Mike!" Mary laughed, teasing her old friend.

Mike hugged Mary, and they all began to take their seats. But Mike motioned to the counter and said, "Listen, let's all get in line and place our orders, and then we can sit and have some small talk before we get down to business."

Minutes later, back at their seats, they enjoyed a casual conversation over a classic American meal of hot dogs, burgers, fries, and soft drinks.

After ten minutes of eating and small talk, it seemed like the right time to dive into the principal topic, that extinct game, called baseball, that Joe was trying to bring back.

"So, Joe, tell me about this old game you played the other day," Mike began. "I stopped by and saw a part of it. Very different, very different indeed, but in a good way."

"Well, Mike—" Joe started, before being interrupted by his dad.

"Son, mind your manners."

"That's okay, Sam," said Mike. "I did insist on no "misters.""

"Just the same, I try to instill manners and decorum. He's still young and needs to address you as Mr. Drucker," Sam said firmly.

With that settled, Joe corrected himself, addressed Mike as Mr. Drucker, and started over again describing his early forays into the VFW Woods, as well as the magical weekend out in Dyersville, with his Grandpa Moses, where they had found the huge treasure trove of baseball equipment.

Joe continued, "My friends and I studied the game real hard over the winter. Did a lot of playing catch in the barn, and outside, on warmer days. Played a lot of pepper in the barn, too, because we couldn't hit much until a few weeks ago. With the weather getting warmer, we all got serious about batting practice and all, so as not to stink up the place when we finally played our first practice game."

"I see. So then, what was your first impression after having played a full game?" Mike asked.

"Well, some parts are easy to explain, and some parts are a little hard. But every one of my buddies thought it was magical. We can't wait to play the next game."

"Is that right? Say, Eduardo, Mary says you have some good information on baseball. What can you tell me?"

"Well, Mike, as you may have heard, my department at the federal building is in charge of transferring old books, documents, periodicals, magazines, and newspapers into digital format. It's taking years, as more and more material is provided to us to scan—"

Mike interrupted and seemed a little irritated, "Hold on a second, Eduardo, hold on one second. Why has it taken so long to get to this type of material? I mean, the country technically recovered from the war quite a few years back."

"Mike, understand that everything, and I mean everything that was digital, was destroyed worldwide. After the Second Civil War ended here, as I'm sure you know, we were in the dark ages, literally and figuratively. The other nations were not much better off than us, so they couldn't help us at all, except for the Israelis, but even their help came later.

"It was every man for himself, just to survive each day, living mostly off the land. After a while, smarter heads prevailed and realized we needed to work together if we were ever going to rise from the ashes as a people again, never mind a nation. Thankfully, what was left of the federal government and the armed forces started to get help out across to the rest of the nation, by horse and buggy, literally. Even though some military vehicles were hardened against an EMP attack, the entire gasoline refinement and delivery infrastructure was wiped out completely. They had vehicles that could run, but no fuel delivery system for them. They had gasoline reserves they could 'can' for vehicles, but that broke down when the famine hit. Someone hatched a plan to try and utilize vintage steam locomotives. They had some success with that, but working locomotives were too few and far between to make any serious difference.

"But what about the electric fleet? There was a sizable number … oh wait …" Mike halted, as he knew what the answer was going to be.

"Fried by the EMP," Eduardo replied. "It took many, many months of searching to find a paper schematic for the electric gas pumps. Thank God for the mechanical pumps! Point being, with all the knowledge we had in digital format wiped out, we had to triage the technical data we found in paper format and decide what should be recovered first, and that was after we figured out how to build computers again!"

Mike paused for a moment. "Huh, kind of like the chicken and egg riddle."

Eduardo nodded. "On steroids, to the tenth power."

"Yes, I recall now that's where the Israelis stepped in with the whole computer thing. That was a key saving grace back then," Mike said.

Eduardo continued, "Precisely. Once they came to the rescue with that knowledge, the ball started rolling again to where we could start to recover our data, or should I say, re-enter our data. At first, we were keying in data by hand, data entry-style, but that was very time consuming.

"Once we found the schematics for scanners, that's when we went with high-speed scanning, once we figured out how to build those again. That sped up the knowledge restoration process, but it still took a very long time because of all the stops and restarts — for a myriad of reasons.

"I forget the exact order, but infrastructure and food processing and distribution were the first order of the day. Then, if I recall correctly, that was followed by healthcare and pharmaceuticals. The rest, I'd have to dig up my notes. But I know that dead last was sports, which brings us to my current work at the federal building and our present conversation.

"We recently received another shipment from the Library of Congress. This new shipment had many, many books on sports, including this old game called baseball that Joe has been exploring.

"Also, our friend Sam here had approached me to check out what I could find out about an old sign that Joe had found in the VFW Woods. It was a sign with two words on it: 'No Pepper.'"

Mike interrupted, "No Pepper? Joe, does that tie into the pepper you mentioned earlier that you and your friends played in the barn over the winter?"

"Yes sir, Mr. Drucker."

Eduardo then explained pepper and its integral relationship to baseball as a pre-game warm-up to fine tune hand-eye coordination. Then, for the next fifteen minutes, he explained what his team had uncovered about baseball from the Library of Congress shipment the team was scanning. When he was finished, Mike rubbed his chin. The others sat quietly for a moment, still eating, but staring at Mike to gauge his reaction.

After Mike himself took a huge bite out of his hamburger and washed it down with a swig of iced tea, he broke the silence. "Hmmm. Okay, I think we have the makings of a great story here. There's a lot of neat elements and angles here that really intrigue me.

"You've got history, an extinct game, buried treasure, as it were, and the kids taking a quick liking to this long-forgotten game. I'm certain I can convince my boss to let me write a feature article, especially since there is more than just sports involved here."

At that, Joe smiled. "Really, Mr. Drucker? A front-page story?"

Sam followed his son's comment with a gentle admonishment. "Hold on there, son, Mike said nothing about a front-page story."

"True, Sam, true, but you just never know how a story can unexpectedly take off. Still, no promises, young man. But, then again, I've been in the newspaper business long enough to have seen stories take on a life of their own. One never really knows for sure how the reading public is going to respond to a story."

"Fair enough," Mary responded.

"Listen, would it be alright with you both if I stop by the house and speak some more to your boys? I'd like to dive in more about these old media files found at your dad's farm. I may even want to make a trip out to interview him too."

Mary chimed in. "That'd be just fine. Let me or Sam get back to you with some good time slots when Joe will be available."

"Great, that's great." With that, Mike stood up and thanked Eduardo and the Scotts for their time and excused himself for his next appointment.

Eduardo turned to Sam and thanked him for the invite, then left to get back to the office, as well.

Mary and Joe lingered for a bit with Sam and talked about the conversation that had just concluded with Mary's longtime friend.

"Well, Joe, what did you think about that?" she asked.

"Aww, Ma, that was so cool! I can't wait till Mr. Drucker comes over and I can show him some of the old baseball media."

"That will be very fun," Sam agreed. "But right now, we have to get back to work. Turning to Mary, he said, "I'll take Joe home. I know you have a one o'clock meeting."

"Thanks, hon."

⚾ ⚾ ⚾

Khalil Jackson had been the managing editor for the paper for 15 years now and was still enjoying every minute. With a Pulitzer Prize on the paper's record, courtesy of his star reporter, Mike Drucker, Khalil was enjoying that year in particular. Things were good on the home front and the work-front, and that day was no exception. As Khalil sat thinking about the last few years, Mike burst through the door in his usual, exuberant style and broke the early afternoon calm.

"Boss! Have I got a story! It has so many cool elements to it, you're not gonna believe it!"

"Whoa, slow down there, tiger. Okay, have a seat and talk to me in a calmer manner."

"Sure, sure," Mike responded, as he took a seat.

"Ok, whatcha got?" Khalil inquired.

"You ever hear of an old, extinct game called baseball?" Mike asked.

Khalil pondered the question, "No, not rea … hey, wait a second … you know, I may have heard something about that just the other day, now that I think about it. I briefly overheard my son talking about some old game he'd heard about that some kids had played a day or so ago. I'm almost certain he said the word 'baseball.' So, what is it?"

Mike told Khalil about the just-concluded lunch with his old friend Mary, her son Joe, husband Sam, and the federal worker, Eduardo. In particular, about young Joe Scott's involvement in uncovering an old game called baseball, and of his grandfather's critical role in this discovery, out at his old farm in Dyersville, Iowa. Mike could hardly contain his excitement over all the elements of the story, particularly its ties to pre-Second Civil War America.

Khalil sat patiently and took it all in. When Mike was finished, they both sat quietly for a moment, then Khalil finally said, "I want you to keep a tight lid on this story. What are your next steps?"

"Well, I'm going to make an appointment to go over to the Scott residence and interview young Joe at length and also see what some of these old media files are about. I'll ask Rachel if she is free to come along and get some good pics."

"Don't forget some good shots of the treasure brought back from Iowa."

"Yep, yep, got it."

"What about this Grandpa Moses?" Khalil asked. "He seems like an interesting fella."

"Well, I'd like to head out to Dyersville, and interview the grandpa, as well," Mike responded.

"Fine, fine, yes, do it, and I'll look forward to your draft in what, a week's time?"

"Give me two, boss. I'm not sure about Joe's schedule yet, and I'm finishing up my current project."

"Ok, two it is. Remember, keep a tight lid on this one."

"Sure, you bet. Thanks, and have a great rest of your day, boss."

"You too, Mike. Stay in touch."

Mike left Khalil's office and called Mary to check Joe's schedule, so the interview could get onto the calendar. The next evening at 6 PM worked for all parties concerned. While he was at it, Mike asked if he could get Mary's dad's number. Mary happily provided it, and Mike was quick to call Moses. To his delight, he found that Moses was coming to McHenry the next day to surprise his daughter and family.

"Perfect," Mike thought. *"I can interview both Joe and the grandpa at the same time."*

But Mike still knew he would have to make a trip out to Dyersville in order to get some pictures for the story. He and Moses agreed that next week, Wednesday, would work just fine for that.

Later that evening, as Mike started drifting off to sleep, he couldn't get baseball off of his mind. A vision popped into his head of many familiar faces from the press, all staring intently out of a booth high above the ground.

He couldn't make out what they were all looking at. Every one of them had a look of great anticipation, much like he remembered all rookie reporters having after being issued their very first press pass to a big game. He smiled as sleep came on and the vision faded.

The alarm rang at 5:30 AM and roused Mike from a deep sleep. He lay there for a few minutes, thinking about the day ahead.

After rising and getting ready for the day, he called Moses to check if the scheduled interview with him and Joe was still on.

Moses assured him it was. So, later that evening, Mike drove over to the Scott residence.

After some coffee and small talk, Moses suggested they all go outside onto the front porch. After the three of them settled in, Mike began the interview. "So, Joe, tell me again how this all began."

For the next several minutes, young Joe retold the story about the first and second visits to the VFW Woods, the rusted, old "No Pepper" relic, and all that had transpired previous to yesterday's lunch. In between Joe's recountings, Moses added important details regarding the trunk in the attic, which led to the unearthing of the vaults, which revealed the baseball treasures within, and his subsequent delivery of them to McHenry.

Mike asked many questions about the first game Joe, his siblings, and his friends had played the week prior. Joe patiently answered all of them. All the while, Mike's co-worker, Rachel, was busy snapping photos of Joe and Grandpa Moses.

Mike paused and asked one last question of Joe. "So, what is it about this old game of baseball that has you and your buddies so mesmerized?"

Joe paused for a moment to think about the question and how to answer. "You know, when we were out on the field playing the game, there was this magical thing about us all being out there in the different field positions but understanding each one and how they all work together.

"One minute, the ballgame can be centered on fielding the ball in the infield, and in the next minute, the focus is way out in the outfield. Then there's the hitting part. When you're up to bat, it's just you against the pitcher. Do you swing the bat? Or don't you? Then there's the runner. In every other sport we play, the person with possession of the ball is the one scoring a point. In baseball, you might never have hit the ball during an at-bat, but you can still score the winning point. How cool is that? Plus, Mr. Drucker, it's just a cool game. If we brought it back all the way, I think a lot of people would love it!"

"What do you mean when you say, 'brought it back all the way?'" Rachel asked, while looking at Mike.

"Great question, Rachel," Moses responded. "Joe, let me answer that."

"As I studied the old media files and pored over the old, printed material with my grandsons, it became apparent that baseball was once America's pastime. In a time long since forgotten — long before any of us were born — it was a pastime where Americans would peacefully relate to one another in a positive way for a few hours. Regardless of beliefs or economic status, they'd come together for a few hours, out of sheer love of the game, enjoy a cold beer or cold pop, along with hot dogs and peanuts and cracker jacks, and soak it all in.

"They could alternate between watching and chatting with family, friends, and even complete strangers, some of whom may even have been rooting for the other team.

"There they all were: one. When the game was over and the seats emptied, everyone who had come in peace, left in peace, young and old alike."

"That's right, Grandpa, young and old alike," Joe solemnly agreed.

Mike paused for a moment. "Hmmm, great power in that. So, do you see any benefit of this dead game being played by others again, after all this time has passed?"

Joe smiled wryly and answered, "Mr. Drucker, as of 1:10 PM on Saturday, April 4, 2167, the game of baseball is no longer dead! It's being resurrected! With your help, through this story you're working on, I hope the game is played, watched, and enjoyed again by people all over the country, young and old alike, forever."

At that, Moses, Joe, and Mike all got goosebumps. Mike had the thought come to him that this story was going to attain a life of its own.

"Well, Joe, I will say this for sure. You best polish up your shoes and get a haircut, because if this story breaks the way I think it's going to go, you are going to be one busy lad doing interviews."

Later that evening, Mike gathered his notes and started typing. The feature article on baseball just flowed out of him. At 1 AM, he was done and retired for the night. As sleep came quickly, the vision he had earlier came back into his head. He remembered being startled by it again, but sleep quickly overwhelmed the images.

CHAPTER TWELVE

Extra! Extra!

Just two days later, Mike gave Sam Scott a heads up that the feature story about Joe and his rediscovery of baseball would be in that day's extra afternoon edition of the Herald.

Sam loved the fact that the Herald had decided, five years earlier, to print a newspaper again, instead of just having the news published electronically. There was something about reading a printed newspaper and smelling the fresh ink.

After the war, with all electronics inoperable, newspaper employees around the country scoured museums and antique shops looking for working printing presses, typesetting equipment, and typewriters. The nation, at the time, was desperate for information, and the newspapers were determined to get the news out to the surviving citizens.

Many years later, after reconstruction had reached a pivotal point, the news could again be published electronically, but the preceding years of printed newspapers had left an indelible and positive mark on the recovering nation. However, after that developmental tipping point, many news outlets, despite the sentimentality of it all, opted to discontinue the printed newspaper. The Herald had initially resisted the trend, but had eventually gone along with it, as one of the last holdouts.

But decades later, and only after much demand, the Herald began printing newspapers again. Occasionally, they would print an extra edition in the afternoon, as the news warranted, because it always generated generous sales.

The unusual nature and angle of Mike's story about young Joe Scott, his Grandpa Moses, his family and friends, and Joe's rediscovery of a pre-war game had caught the keen eye and interest of Mike's boss Khalil. Khalil had originally thought to put the story on the front of the "Weekender" Sunday pullout section. But, after reading Mike's draft write-up, he had a gut feeling. So, it was on Khalil's order that the Herald published an extra edition that particular Friday afternoon.

The smell of fresh ink on the printed pages of a newspaper had always appealed to Sam's senses, but this edition was especially exhilarating. In fact, at the start of his lunch break, he had raced down to the corner stand and purchased a dozen copies to give out to family and friends later that evening. As he returned to work and settled back down at his desk, he reread the front-page headline, for what felt like the thousandth time: "Extinct Game Finds New Life." *"Wow,"* he thought. *"I still can't believe it. My son's on the front page!"*

Sam, still beaming with pride and excitement, put his comm on "Do Not Disturb" and began to carefully read. As he did, he got goosebumps. Not just because the story's main character was his son, or because the story was so uplifting and filled with a dream-like sense of something good and noble, but because it was also a bridge to the nation's past, a tumultuous past at that.

When he was done, Sam felt the overwhelming sense that this story was about to change their lives forever.

〇 〇 〇

Mike's instincts had been spot on. His feature story on young Joe Scott and his rediscovery of the long-lost game of baseball had taken the nation by storm. After all the live media and print interviews with Joe and his family, including Grandpa Moses, Mike was feeling a little tired. He was looking forward to a quieter Monday, when his comm rang.

"Hello, Mike Drucker here, how can I help you?"

"Mr. Drucker, this is General Livingston of the Army Corps of Engineers. How are you today?"

"Well, good, and you, General?"

"Fine, just fine. Hey, listen, I read your story and thought it was fantastic. Nice job getting it into prose that grabbed our attention. Never heard of baseball before, but from what I read in your story, it sounds like it was a really great game to play and to watch. That leads to the reason for my call. I have something for you that's baseball related. Can you come by my office at the federal building this afternoon at 1 PM?"

"Well, sure."

"Great, see you then."

After hanging up, Mike, excited and unsure of what to expect, found that he could no longer focus on the day's tasks. Needing something to do to hurry the slow-moving clock along, he resorted to giving his workspace a thorough spring cleaning, which Khalil had been hounding him to do for weeks. But his mind raced the whole time, wondering what the general could possibly have to show him. He finally gave up on getting any work done at all when, in his distracted state, he caught himself about to shred his current reimbursement receipts. Fortunately, though, it was almost time for the anticipated meeting. Leaving his desk in disarray, he practically raced over to the federal building to see what the general had in store for him.

After checking into security and getting his visitor's badge, he headed up to the 77th floor, the U.S. Army Corps of Engineers Midwest Central Command Headquarters.

When the elevator door opened, he was met by a uniformed, and armed, U.S. Army soldier. He greeted Mike politely and immediately escorted him to the general's office, whereupon General Livingston invited him in and greeted him.

"Mr. Drucker, I'm really glad you could take some time out of your busy day to come over here and see what I have to show you."

"The pleasure's all mine, General. And please, call me Mike. Now, what do you have for me, sir? I'm dying to know!" Mike replied excitedly.

The general paused for a moment and stared into Mike's eyes. "Well, of course you know how New York, Chicago, Atlanta, and Charlotte have been uninhabitable our entire lives, combined."

"Yes, yes, of course."

"Well, I've just gotten word of a scientific breakthrough that can change all of that. Scientists from Oak Ridge National Laboratory in Tennessee and the Science Academy of Nuclear Physics in Tel-Aviv, Israel, along with folks at Dow and DuPont Chemical, have developed some sort of device, in combination with a chemical aerosol. They say that we can use it over radioactive sites to neutralize all levels of radiation. They're doing an experimental application in three days on the southside of Chicago."

"Wow. That sounds fantastic! But why the southside?" Mike asked.

"No particular reason, really. They just looked at a map and picked an area. The reason I called you, though, is that the particular area they selected apparently has the ruins of an old, large baseball stadium used before the war."

"Really? Who found that out?"

"Eduardo Chavez," the general answered.

"Eduardo, wow. That's interesting. How'd he get involved in this?"

"Eduardo and I do lunch every so often. We were talking one day over lunch about our younger days. Seems, earlier in his career, Eduardo was a cartographer. He had a side hobby of collecting old pre-war maps of the nuked areas. When I found out about that, I thought it might be helpful to have him join our targeting meetings for the experiment, as an observer. Once we settled on the target area, I asked him what buildings of any note had existed there before the nukes hit. Mike, I have to tell ya', he rattled off a bunch of places I'd never heard of. The last thing he mentioned, though, was an old sports stadium tied to this extinct game called baseball you wrote about."

"Wow," Mike breathed. "What an incredible find! So, can I write about this, or is it top secret?"

"Top secret? Not at all. Write about it? Well, I think you could write a better story if you came along for the experiment," the general said, smiling.

"Seriously?! I'm flabbergasted! Are you sure?"

"Absolutely! Say, how would you and young Joe like to fly along for the ride, courtesy of the United States Army and Air Force?"

"Would I? You better believe it! Thank you so much! Of course, I can't speak for Joe, but I'll reach out to his parents today. When do you need to know?"

"Forty-eight hours work?" the general suggested.

"Yes, that should be time enough."

"Ok. I presume you'll fly no matter what the Scott family decides?"

"Yes, yes, of course. Where will we meet?"

"Meet me here at my office at 0700 hours this Thursday. We'll take a chopper ride over to King Air Force Base and board the plane there for the flight to Chicago."

"Awesome, General. See you then."

After leaving the meeting with General Livingston, Mike contacted Sam Scott to inquire if Joe could tag along on this special science mission. After a few safety questions in a conference call with Mary, they both enthusiastically gave the okay. He also mentioned that Grandpa Moses was in town and would love to come, if there was room.

Mike checked in with General Livingston the next morning to see if there was room for one more. With a "go" from the General, the flight now featured Joe, Grandpa Moses, and Mike.

⚾ ⚾ ⚾

The alarm sounded dull at first, but then grew louder as Joe awakened from a deep sleep. He cracked his eyes open to see the time: 5:45 AM. He shut his eyes, hoping for 15 more minutes of sleep, but Grandpa burst into the room, threw open the shades, and yelled, "Rise and shine, young man! We have a big day today."

Grandpa Moses had insisted the alarm be set early, so they could both get ready and out the door in time for a hot breakfast at the Scott family's favorite local breakfast stop: the Lincoln Cafe, on Riverside Drive.

Once dressed and out the door, it was just a one-minute walk to the cafe.

The Lincoln Cafe had been a restaurant for as long as anyone could remember. Before the war, it was known as the Little Chef. It sustained heavy damage during the artillery barrage on the first day of the Battle of McHenry and had lain in ruins for the better part of five decades, before being rebuilt and renamed after America's 16th president of the United States, Abraham Lincoln.

Opting to dine outside, Grandpa Moses and Joe both ordered a hearty meal of pancakes, eggs, hash browns, and toast.

Grandpa got his customary black coffee, while Joe settled for chocolate milk and orange juice.

"So, what are you thinking right now about all of this?" Moses asked.

"Not sure," Joe answered, chewing thoughtfully. "It's been awfully crazy with all the reporters and interviews and stuff."

"Well, never you mind about all that. You keep your head on straight and don't let this popularity go to your head, you understand me?"

"Sure, Grandpa. What about you? You had reporters and stuff out at the farm."

"Some, but certainly not as much as you. Tell you the truth, it's been kind of fun toying with them all and talkin' you up and all about this baseball discovery," Moses chuckled. "Say, what about today? What do you think about this experiment? It sure sounds promising."

"I know, right? I mean, I've only ever read about Chicago in my history book at school. Flying over it today is gonna be weird. You think we'll see anything we can make out from before the war?"

"Well, son, my hopes are not high on that. Satellite photos show mostly heaps of rubble and melted steel. You know, a while back, I saw pre-war aerial photos of some old skyscrapers in the downtown area. If memory serves me correctly, they called them the Willis Tower, the Hancock Building, the Aon Center, and the Trump Tower. Now, the pictures show piles of rubble over a hundred and fifty feet tall at each site. The rest of downtown looks similar.

"One strange thing, though, were two old churches. They called one Holy Name Cathedral. I think they said it was Catholic. They called the other Moody Bible Church. That one was apparently Protestant. They're both standing, though damaged. I prefer to think of that as a divine message."

"Wow, will we be flying over them?" Joe asked.

"Don't think so. We're headed to an area that was south of the downtown area. The downtown area was called 'the Loop.' South of that area they called 'the Southside.'"

"Why'd they call it 'the Loop?'"

"There were elevated trains in those days, and a loop of elevated train tracks surrounded downtown," Moses explained. "People would take the trains to work and back and work inside that area.

"Wow, that sounds neat. I love trains!"

"Well, the trains of that era were a lot slower than the ones we have now."

"Well, I'm glad we're living in this time then," Joe announced. "Sure, seems like the people back then must have been miserable and had a hard time doing anything right."

The maturity of his oldest grandson's comments surprised Moses. "Joe, you have no idea. I'm sure it wasn't all bad, but by the time the war broke out, things had gotten pretty bad."

⚾ ⚾ ⚾

At exactly 7:00 AM, General Livingston welcomed Mike, Joe, and Grandpa Moses into his office. A highly decorated veteran, General Livingston had received his fourth gold star a year earlier and was just recently offered a position at the White House in the Kennedy administration, as an advisor to the Joint Chiefs of Staff. He was due there in two weeks and had not even packed yet.

After getting the final approval for the day's experiment, he wondered anxiously what the outcome would be. He knew success would be transformative, not only for the country, but potentially for the world. Thus, he was eager to tag along. He loved flying and took to the air as often as he could.

The ride out to King Air Force Base, next to the commercial Rockford International Airport, was quick aboard the jet-powered helo. Upon setting down, the general and his guests were quickly whisked away to a hangar for a quick briefing on the flight to the ruins of Chicago, and the old Southside, in particular.

"Good morning, everyone," the general began. "I'd like to introduce you to our friends, starting with Dr. Yosef Mizrah of the Tel-Aviv Science Academy of Nuclear Physics. Dr. Mizrah is a special civilian attaché to the Israeli Defense Force liaison office at the Pentagon in Washington D.C. He's joined here today by Dr. Rashied Davis from Dow Chemical, Dr. Evette M'busa of DuPont de Nemours, and Dr. Stanley Knight of the National Science Foundation, based out at Oak Ridge National Laboratories in the great state of Tennessee."

Handshakes and pleasantries ensued for a moment, before the general continued.

"Also joining us today is Pulitzer Prize-winning reporter, Mike Drucker, of the McHenry Herald, Joe Scott, of whom I presume some of you have now read about in Mike's stories about the old game of baseball, and Joe's grandfather, Brian Woodbridge—"

Moses butted in, "You can call me Moses. Been called that most of my life. Not looking to change now and get all proper using my birth name."

The general seemed slightly annoyed at being interrupted, but quickly smiled and extended grace to the old man. "Moses, beg your pardon. That's a great nickname."

Dr. Mizrah spoke up, "General, what's the flight plan for today?"

"I was getting to that. After takeoff, we'll head out on an east-southeast heading, over Interstate 90. Near the ruins of O'Hare airport, we'll make a right turn more toward the southeast. The application of the aerosol will begin on the outskirts of the south side of the city, via a fleet of heavy drones. We'll continue the application, pretty much on a southeasterly heading, all the way to the lakefront. Once the aerosol is deployed, we'll activate the device aboard the mother-ship we're about to board here in a minute."

Dr. M'busa spoke next, "What means are we using to test the radiation levels before and after?"

"We just checked the levels yesterday, via drones. The general reading remains fairly high at 1,000 rads," the general responded.

"Good Lord, after all this time?" Dr. Davies chimed in.

The general paused, then spoke, "That's down from Day Zero, when it was 3,000 rads."

Moses jerked his head towards the general. "Day Zero. I've not heard that phrase in a long, long time."

Moses suddenly had a pained look on his face. Joe knew what that meant and tugged his grandpa's sleeve. Moses turned and looked at Joe, smiled, and then seemed to come back to the present.

There was silence from the group for a long moment. Everyone, in their own way, silently recalled the history of the nuke exchange that killed 80 million Americans in a single day, now referred to as "Day Zero" in the history books.

Dr. M'busa broke the silence, "Will we get instant readings after we begin the application?"

"Yes, we have robotic soldiers all along the test area. The surface winds are calm, at five miles per hour. Perfect for today's test."

"Well, let's get this bird in the air, General. I'm eager to see what happens today," Dr. Davies said.

The general nodded. "Well, alright then, let's go."

With that, the general and his entourage of scientists, civilians, and members of the flight crew all walked the 100 yards to the mobile jetway of the aircraft and climbed aboard.

The Boeing 807-M was the largest vertical takeoff and landing airplane in the world. Developed 20 years earlier, as the very first post-war-designed aircraft for the company, the 807-M had a length of 265 feet, was 75 feet tall, and had a wingspan of 240 feet. The commercial version could hold 500 passengers.

This military variant had modular interior components that could quickly be swapped out to change it from all-troop carrier mode to all-cargo mode, or variants of both, as well as modules designed for scientific work, among other specialized uses. Four General Electric GE 140-VM VTOL Hydrogen-Powered Turbofans powered both the commercial and military variants.

This particular 807-M was outfitted with a single passenger module that accommodated 50 passengers in business class-style seating. It also had a science module that held the military and scientific support staff for the experiment, accompanying equipment, and communications modules. Last, and at the rear of the aircraft, was the module containing the Wide Beam Neutron Device, developed in cooperation with the Israelis.

With everyone aboard, the flight attendant gave the mandatory safety talk. Once complete, the Air Force pilot welcomed everyone aboard and told them to enjoy the flight.

The tower at King AFB gave the go for pushback and staging on pad 59-A.

The Boeing 807-M was pushed away, about 400 feet from the terminal, via robotic tug. Once on pad 59-A, the captain fired up the giant engines. A distinct whine built, as the engines lumbered to life.

Joe had a window seat in 10A and watched in awe as the engines powered up and rotated upwards into the vertical position. Grandpa had just finished telling Joe about the marvels of these GE engines, when the pilot gave the five-second countdown to liftoff.

At full thrust, the engines had a roar that was an unmistakable conveyance of raw power. When the countdown reached zero, Joe and everyone else aboard could feel the aircraft begin to hover off the tarmac and then climb skyward rapidly.

At 500 feet and still at full thrust, the pilot hit the rotation button, and the engines rotated back down toward the horizontal thrust position. Joe could feel the aircraft pick up ground speed as the terminal drifted out of view to the rear. Their airspeed continued, higher and more and more forward, as the engines were now roughly at a 45-degree angle. The power in the engines was staggering to experience firsthand. Joe recalled his short flight out to Dubuque, the previous summer, on the smaller A-720 with its older-style, long takeoff roll. This experience was a thrill and a half.

At 2,000 feet and climbing, the engines were now locked into their full horizontal position and thrusting the 807-M at 250 miles per hour. The pilot made a banking left turn, and Joe could clearly make out Interstate 90 down below, as they started flying toward the east, toward the ruins of Chicago.

At 10,000 feet, the pilot leveled off and set a course to the east-southeast. The flying time to the ruins of O'Hare Airport would be 20 minutes or less. In the meantime, the pilot frequently checked the RAD meter on the plane's instrument panel. It showed a steady green as the big jet flew over decreasingly populated areas.

At roughly ten minutes into the flight, the 807-M approached the Fox River over Elgin. With a population of 25,000 people on the west side of the river, the RAD meter slowly climbed as the jet flew over the river and continued east.

Within a minute of passing over the river, the RAD meter quickly entered the yellow zone. At this level, they considered limited, short-term exposure relatively safe for humans, but long-term exposure was still not permitted.

Over the ruins of Schaumburg and the junction of I-90 and I-290, the RAD meter jumped into the red zone. At these levels, it was unsafe for humans to spend any amount of time on the ground.

The plane's guidance computer, aware of the high radiation levels on the ground, sounded an alarm and automatically climbed the aircraft to a safer altitude of 15,000 feet. The climb brought the RAD meter to the borderline of green and yellow.

In the science bay, the collection of civilian and military personnel had been busy going through their checklists and preparing to order the drones to begin the aerosol application.

General Livingston had stood quietly, amid the noise of engines and the cacophony of scientific jargon, for the last several minutes, but decided he'd had enough.

"Alright, can someone, in plain English, explain to me how this all works?"

Dr. Knight turned, looked, and smiled at the general. "Of course, General. In a few minutes, we will begin the aerosol application over the target area. The fleet of 200 heavy drones is already hovering in their designated application zones.

"Once we send the commit order, the drones will begin deployment from an altitude of 500 feet. The chemical agent has a special gooey consistency that makes it stick to anything it lands on. Once the chemical is fully deployed in the target area, we will point the Wide Beam Neutron Device down toward the ground and begin the second phase of the experiment.

"The Wide Beam Neutron Device interacts with the chemical at a subatomic level that, in turn, interacts with any radioactive elements in the vicinity, interrupting the element's rate of decay and essentially fast-forwarding it to safe background radiation levels."

"What exactly is in this chemical we're about to spray, Dr. M'busa?" the general quickly added.

"There's a lot of science to explain that, and of course, top secret information—"

The general interrupted, "Yes, I'm well aware of that doctor. Okay everyone, let's get this show on the road."

Robotic Soldier 1910051959 was stationed in an area on the south side of the ruined city. On the military maps, they labeled it "Armour Square." Not much was known about what the area used to be like, prior to its destruction.

Impervious to radiation, the Robotic Soldiers were perfectly suited for the experiment being conducted overhead.

Aboard the science module, it had already been predetermined, before liftoff, that Dr. Mizrah would give the go/no go for the beginning of phase one of the experiment, the release of the aerosol. At ten minutes past the hour, satisfied that all readings were good, he gave the "go" signal. General Livingston then gave the order for the drones to deploy the aerosol.

After having been dispersed aloft, over a wide area, the aerosol quickly raced toward the ground. The chemical was three times as heavy as air. Once on the ground, the tacky substance stuck to everything it landed on.

The squadron of pre-deployed Robotic Soldiers, equipped with RAD meters and cameras, began to live stream information to the science module in the Boeing high above. At their stations already for 10 hours before the flight, the RAD meters on the robots had held steady all that time at 1,000 rads, plus or minus 50, which was lethal, within minutes, to all human beings and animals.

Up in the science bay, Dr. M'Busa was assigned the task of giving the go/no go for the firing of the beam device. After hearing all the feedback from the science team and determining that the aerosol deployment was complete, she made a final assessment and gave the "go" signal.

General Livingston then gave the order to fire the beam.

The Wide Beam Neutron Device was cloaked in secrecy. They had mounted it within its own specialized module, the entrance to which was secured by two very large MPs with weapons at the ready.

When the general gave the order to turn on the beam, it took only a few seconds for Robotic Soldier 1910051959's RAD meter to change and show a rapid decrease in the radiation levels. Within 60 seconds, the RAD meter showed 750 rads. In another minute, 437 rads. Then, at the end of the third minute, the level had collapsed to a background level, safe for humans. At this point, the Robotic Soldier was pre-programmed to begin a grid pattern scan of the area to measure the rads, all the while sending live video feed up to the aircraft overhead.

An hour later, the Robotic Soldier came across a pile of concrete rubble and melted steel.

Among the rubble, there was one section of a high wall that had stayed pretty much intact, even after the thermonuclear blasts over a hundred years earlier, albeit a bit charred. The robot's computer instructed the camera to zero in on the wall, as it had detected human language written there. The presence of human language caused it to send an alert upstream to the Boeing 807-M's science module's video screen wall. When the video images began rapidly flashing, with a bright red border, on one of the smaller screens, all eyes were drawn to it.

General Livingston ordered that the feed be switched to the main, giant screen. There was already exhilaration among the personnel in the science module at the high rate at which the rad levels had essentially collapsed to near zero. Curious eyes gazed at the words on the video wall, as one of the military guys tried to make out what was written.

"Comiskey Par … ? What's that? It looks like the second word is partially blown away."

Joe, who had been distracted by a question from Mike

Drucker, snapped his head to the screen when he heard the words. He replayed the words again and again in his head, until his memory recalled one of the old videos he had watched with Grandpa. He stood there stunned for a second at what he was seeing on the screen and then blurted out, "Those are the remains of Comiskey Park! Home of the old Chicago White Sox Major League Baseball team!"

Everyone turned and looked at Joe. Mike put his hand on Joe's shoulder, laughed, and shouted, "Extra! Extra!"

CHAPTER THIRTEEN

Littlest of Leagues

Joe was up to bat and facing Ted again. Since learning the game of baseball, Ted was becoming an increasingly tough pitcher to hit. Still, Joe figured he was batting about .300 against his buddy, which meant that for every ten at-bats, he was getting on base three times.

Earlier that morning, Ted had shown a little pride and predicted that the next time Joe faced him, he would strike him out. Joe had laughed it off and said, "I doubt it, buddy!"

The two continued to joke around, while Joe sent a message to the gang that a game was on later that morning, at 10:30. After Joe sent the message, Ted looked Joe in the eyes and said, "I'll make you a bet that I strike you out. If I do, you owe me a chocolate malt. If I don't, I owe you a vanilla malt!"

"You're on!" Joe yelled.

With no official baseball fields anywhere, the gang had settled on making one in an empty corner lot, a block over from the Scott residence. League officials had kicked the boys out of DeVita Park more than once, when the soccer and lacrosse leagues needed every available space. Joe and his friends finally learned the times and dates of games and practices, so they knew when they could play a pickup game of baseball at DeVita Park. Saturday mornings like this were out, and thus the need to find an alternative place to continue to explore this old game. The empty lot was perfect.

They all arrived together, there at the corner lot, at 10:30 sharp. But they were surprised to see an unexpected guest, Earl Donnerson, setting up a lawn chair down the third-base line, past the infield.

Earl Donnerson had made his fortune in the dairy industry and had a heart of gold. It was a widely accepted fact that he was also the most giving and benevolent man in town, probably in all of McHenry County.

Joe walked over and greeted him. "Hello, Mr. Donnerson. What are you doing here?"

"Well hello, Joe. I was sitting on my front porch and saw you and your friends walk past with your gear. Thought I'd come and watch, if that's okay."

"Sure, that's cool! Enjoy the game." With that, Joe walked back over to his friends, who were patiently waiting for him.

They got busy right away setting up bases from the Dyersville treasure and used a discarded plastic snow fence, that Joe's dad had got, to set up an outfield fence.

Joe had cut the grass the night before, expecting that his friends would want to play a game that Saturday morning. So, with a clear blue sky, puffy white clouds, and a gentle wind blowing, the game began.

By the bottom of the second inning, the score was 3-2, with Joe's team in the hole against Ted's. The first two guys up to bat from Joe's team reached base on a bunt single and an error. The next two batters struck out. The fifth batter walked. So, with the bases loaded and two outs, it was Joe's turn to bat.

Joe stepped over to the plate, grabbed a little dirt, and rubbed it into his hands. He looked around and made a mental note of where the outfielders and infielders had positioned themselves for his at-bat, then he made eye contact with his teammates standing on all three bases. Teddy's words and their friendly wager earlier that morning played over and over in his head. Joe hesitated before stepping toward the plate and decided it was best to shut down the inner chatter of that memory. It would be better, he thought, to psych himself up to get a hit off of his good friend, no matter what.

Joe stepped into the batter's box. It had been crudely outlined with some white sand. Joe gazed up into Ted's eyes and said, "Bring it, bro."

Ted stared back at Joe and fired off a shout, "Get ready for a strikeout!"

Ted was determined to win the wager. He brought the mitt up to his face and nestled the baseball within. He discreetly put his fingers onto the seams of the ball, in the fastball con-figuration, as he waved off the catcher's sign for a curveball. Pausing for a moment, he looked at the runner on third, then he turned and zeroed his concentration on the catcher's mitt. Rearing back, he threw the ball as hard as he could toward the mitt. Joe, expecting the pitch to be a fastball, was ready, saw the ball coming in hot, and swung his bat. The bat tipped the ball, and it bounced over beyond the third base foul line, where Mr. Donnerson and some others had gathered to watch, out of curiosity. Foul ball, strike one!

After having the ball tossed back to him by Mr. Donnerson, Ted positioned himself for the next pitch. The sign came again for a curveball. Ted waved it off and then acknowledged the sign for an off-speed pitch.

Joe remained in the box and was already ready for the next pitch as he saw Ted's arm rear back and let the ball fly. Joe was convinced, in his head, this would be a fastball as well and timed his swing accordingly. But he quickly realized his swing was way out in front of the pitch. In a millisecond, he debated whether to check his swing or slow his swing a bit to let the ball catchup to the bat. He opted to slow his swing, but it was too late. Strike two!

Ted was smiling wide and looked at his friend and said not a word. Joe looked back and smiled. "Bring it, bro!"

Ted stepped off the pitching rubber to grab some dirt of his own and rub it in his hands. He then wiped his hands on his pant leg and settled back into the mound, placing his right foot on the rubber and staring down his catcher. When the catcher flashed the sign for a fastball, Ted nodded in approval, and the catcher set up with his mitt on the outside of the plate. Ted knew what that meant.

Joe saw the catcher put his mitt toward the outside of the plate but had a hunch it was a ruse. He somehow had a feeling that Ted was going to try to blow a fastball right down the middle of the plate.

Ted remained stoic after getting the fastball sign and setting up for the pitch. Pausing again to stare the runners down and keep them honest, he turned toward the plate and stared hard at the middle of the catcher's chest to focus on his target, ignoring the position of the mitt. He reared back and let the baseball fly. He could physically feel himself throwing the ball harder than the first pitch, and as he released it, it seemed as if time slowed down.

Joe saw the ball coming and had again timed his swing for a fastball. The ball's trajectory was headed exactly where Joe was expecting. With his bat in motion, Joe could feel himself swinging the bat a little harder than he had for the first pitch. It seemed as if time slowed down for him, as well.

The ball was traveling at 55 mph, with a rotation of 30 revolutions per second. At the point of release, given Ted's height of 5 feet 11 inches, the ball started its rapid trip to the plate at slightly below 6 1/2 feet off of the ground. The ball was coming in rapidly and descending.

Joe's bat weighed 32 ounces. At mid-swing, the bat was traveling just under 60 mph when it made solid contact with the ball.

Joe distinctly heard the telltale crack sound that always indicated a baseball bat hitting a baseball at speed, "square up," as he had learned. He had quickly grown to love that sound, in the short time he had spent learning about the game.

The effect of a 55-mph baseball hitting the opposing force of a wood bat, which was headed at the ball at just under 60 mph, was something that grabbed Earl Donnerson's attention. Having read about the newly resurrected game of baseball in the paper a few weeks back, he, by his own admission, was intrigued.

Joe watched in utter amazement as the ball immediately rocketed skyward off of his bat. As it arced high into the sky toward left-center field, both the left and center fielders took about two steps and then froze, realizing the ball was leaving their newly made sandlot field and flying into the tree-lined lot next door.

A tall row of maple trees, 30 feet high, lined the perimeter of the back of the lot. Joe, Ted, and everyone from both teams, along with Mr. Donnerson, were in awe and watched the flight of the ball as it disappeared over the tops of the trees.

Joe let out a yell and started his home run trot around the bases. His teammates met him at home plate and mobbed him. Joe turned and looked at Ted. "What was that you were telling me this morning, buddy? Oh, I remember. I'll take vanilla, please!"

Ted just laughed it off and yelled back, "Nice hit, Joe! Nice hit! I should have thrown a curveball!"

Old man Donnerson clapped and cheered wildly for the kid he had read about in the papers. He was instantly hooked.

He had half run to home plate to join the kids mobbing Joe.

"Young man, I'd like to talk with you after the game."

Joe looked up at Mr. Donnerson and replied, "Sure thing, Mr. Donnerson."

The game continued, and soon it was the top of the ninth, with the score tied at six. Ted was up to bat, with the bases loaded and two outs.

Joe looked at Ted and half smiled when Ted yelled out, "Bring it!"

Ted settled in at the plate and took a deep breath.

Joe stared down at the sign and got the fastball signal from his catcher. Joe shook it off and gave the nod to the next sign, an off-speed curveball. He brought the mitt up to his face, put his fingers on the seams for a curveball, and made the delivery.

The ball left his hands at six feet off the ground, at a velocity of 42 miles per hour. Rotating at 28 revolutions per second, the raised, rotating seams of the ball grabbed air, causing the ball to break sharply down and away from Ted.

Ted was an excellent hitter and had correctly guessed that Joe would throw his wicked curveball as his first pitch. Ted had stepped a little closer to the plate and a few inches forward, more toward the mound than his usual stance. Seeing the breaking ball clearly, Ted hesitated, just a millisecond, to time his swing accordingly.

Ted's swing had the bat traveling at 61 miles per hour when it contacted the curveball low and on the outer edge of the strike zone. Ted also heard the distinct crack sound of a well-hit baseball.

The ball rocketed off the barrel of the bat, sharply down the left-field line, like a rocket. It was a line drive that kept elevating for three-quarters of the flight before it fell toward the earth. The left fielder ran as hard as he could, but he could not catch up to the ball before it just barely cleared the fence, inches fair.

Teddy let out a loud, "Yes!" and started his trot around the bases. His teammates, of course, mobbed him as well when he crossed the plate.

Mr. Donnerson cheered again.

With three up and three down in the bottom of the ninth, Joe's team lost 10-6. It was their first loss in five games of baseball.

Both teams lined up and shook hands while also chanting, "Nice game," to each player they met in the line.

Afterward, Mr. Donnerson met up with Joe and thanked him for the entertaining two hours he had sitting and watching the game. He shared how he had been following the newspaper stories of Joe and this rediscovered game of baseball and that he had taken a quick liking to the game, personally.

"Young man, I've been following this story since it first appeared and like the way you handled yourself out there today. I have a proposition for you."

"What would that be, sir?"

"Well, I received word today about the VFW Woods and the old ball field. Since the Army Corp gave the all-clear for the land there, a lieutenant I was speaking with was wondering if anyone had any interest in clearing the trees and making it a ball field again. The man I spoke to had also read about your exploits in the paper. The lieutenant and I were just having a casual conversation when he blurted the thought out."

"That would be great!" Joe exclaimed. "But who would clear the land?"

"Don't you worry about that. I know people."

"That would be awesome! I have a lot of friends that want to play baseball that are already playing in soccer or lacrosse leagues. I've been wondering if we might start a league of our own for baseball."

Mr. Donnerson took that comment in and paused for a moment. "That would be the littlest of leagues to start in these parts in quite a long time. You all know how big soccer and lacrosse leagues are in town.

"You know, when I was watching you and your friends play, it was as if I could sense God Himself smiling down on you. As far as we have come in my 80 years of life, I could never get past the sense that something was missing from our culture.

"Mark my words, Joe, mark my words, you bringing this game back is going to be another very important chapter in the recovery of our country. Yes sir, young man, mark my words. You will get your league and then some, because I am personally taking an interest to make sure that it happens."

Joe turned and looked at his friends who had been quietly listening, then turned back towards Mr. Donnerson "Wow, I don't know what to say except thank you! I can't wait to see what happens!"

CHAPTER FOURTEEN

A Fine Diamond

Grandpa Moses awoke at his usual time of 5 AM on Saturday. After spending his customary time reading his Bible and praying, he went downstairs at 6 AM, after the first aromas of bacon and brewed coffee reached his nose. It was great to be in McHenry for a visit with the family.

Mary was like a well-oiled machine in the kitchen. Sam cooked a mean breakfast as well, but today Mary was in the mood to cook a nice breakfast. Sam didn't mind cooking dinner instead and was planning a nice one later that evening. Moses marveled at the talented team the two of them made.

After arriving the evening before, Moses had an extended phone conversation with Mr. Donnerson before bed, all of which was organized by Mary. Moses was looking forward to taking Joe over to see Mr. Donnerson to discuss making a real baseball field for the kids to play on. For now, though, the focus was on a hot breakfast.

The kids had all slept in that morning, after a busy week, so Moses and Mary had some rare daddy-daughter time, while everyone else was still upstairs. But before too long, there came a sudden rush of sound and laughter as all the kids and Sam came bounding downstairs at once. After Mary got tons of hugs from everyone, they all mobbed Grandpa to give out some more love.

Joe sat down next to Moses and looked up at his grandpa, "Good morning, Grandpa!"

"Good morning, young man. Say, we have a big day ahead of us, don't we?"

"We sure do!"

"So, how many of your friends do you have interested in baseball now?"

"Well, with the gang, and counting friends from school, maybe 60. Say, what do you think Mr. Donnerson is going to do for us?"

"Well, after speaking with him at length last night on the phone, I think today is going to be a wonderful day for you and this coming-back-to-life sport of baseball, thanks to you."

"Hey, you helped a lot too, you know. If it hadn't been for you and your farm, who knows if anyone would have found all the baseball stuff buried in the ground there."

"Well, there was that letter in the attic from our ancestor," Moses reminded him.

"Yeah, but someone else could have just seen it all as nothing but junk and tossed the whole thing back into the corner of the attic — or worse, into the burn pile — and the letter would never have been found. Fate, I guess."

"Fate? Where did you hear that word?"

"At school," Joe answered.

"Son, I much prefer the word faith, which is the belief in something unseen."

With that, the other conversations at the breakfast table stopped. All eyes were on Grandpa Moses, recognized as the family historian and spiritual adviser.

"I still remember a conversation I had with my dad when

I was 11 years old. It was just before he died of influenza. He told me how, before the war, it was as if half of America had developed a hatred for the other half, for one reason or another. The idea of Americans accepting one another's viewpoints on issues had vanished. You either were in one camp or another, and each camp viewed the other as an enemy who could not be trusted. Based on that information, it is pretty obvious that a spiritual desert existed way back when.

"Within that context, it's no surprise we started a shooting war that led to the eventual deaths of 90 percent of the U.S. population. When it was all over, and for some time afterward, there was this long period of grief, remorse, and introspection among the survivors. It must have been mighty humbling for the surviving elected leaders, struggling to bind up the nation's wounds, especially after they were actually shooting at one another months earlier.

Joe looked quizzically at Grandpa. "Then what happened?"

"Well, son, a lot. For the first several years after the war, the once again United States of America limped along with a decimated population, no functioning electrical grid, and almost no communications grid, except for Ham radio operators using vintage tube equipment powered by vintage generators. There was no food or medical distribution system to speak of. No computer systems, no fuel refineries, and nearly no functioning autos, trucks, trains, or planes. Compounding all that was disease, famine, a breakdown in law and order, and the lack of a strong central government to assist the states in their respective recovery efforts."

"That sounds awful," Joe stated.

"It was beyond awful," Moses continued. "The pockets of survivors in small towns had to fend for themselves but fared much better than their bigger city brethren. The biggest loss of life was in the larger metropolitan areas. Even the cities that had not been nuked were a nightmare when it came to survival. At least in most of the countryside there was wild game, fish, arable land for primitive farming, and most importantly, life-giving freshwater from wells. Lakes and rivers also provided valuable water, but it was, of course, an immediate threat to anyone that drank it untreated. The larger metropolitan areas that had lakes and rivers nearby fared somewhat better than the other metropolitan areas that did not.

"People had to learn to work together again, in order to survive. But it was not until Inauguration Day, in January of 2081, that things truly began to change. Newly elected President Vedder challenged the survivors to put aside any remaining malice and to continue coming together, in order to bind up the nation's wounds. She challenged us, spiritually, to revisit and embrace the faith of our forefathers, in regards to brotherly love, grace, union, and just being decent, kind, and understanding citizens again. A people that would be quick to listen and slow to speak. That would lend a hand whenever and wherever the opportunity arose. What happened after her speech was described as if there was a gentle healing rain that washed over the broken heart of an entire nation."

"The new birth of freedom," Joe recalled from his history lesson.

"Yes! Yes, that's right, son. And from that moment forward, a renewal took place in the hearts and minds of Americans that has continued to this very day.

"Fate? No, not fate. Rather, providence itself is at work here. The good Lord is bringing back America, but purged of all that had corrupted her from before the war. The war served as a refiner's fire. We would all do well to remember that until our dying breath."

There was a silence in the room for a moment. It was broken only after Joe rose and embraced his grandpa tightly. "I love you, Grandpa, so much."

"I love you too, all of you," Moses replied.

Sam stood up and looked at his oldest son. "Listen, through my friend in the Army Corp, Master Sergeant Tyree Williams, they have assigned you an escort today, a Sergeant Mattingly. So, Joe, you and your brother Austin better mind your manners today with Mr. Donnerson and the sergeant — and also keep an eye on your grandpa."

"Thanks, Dad, don't worry. We'll all be fine."

Grandpa stood up next. "Boys, I'll see you out front in 10 minutes." With that, he kissed Mary on the forehead and thanked her for breakfast, then hugged Austin, Anne, Nellie, and Lynn.

Ten minutes later, Joe, Austin, and Grandpa Moses met out front and headed over to the Rt. 120 bridge at the Fox River. Once there, they met up with Mr. Donnerson and Sergeant Mattingly from the Army Corps of Engineers. Mike Drucker was also there, along with a staff photographer for the Herald. After general greetings, they all made the trek over the bridge and into the VFW Woods.

At six feet, four inches tall, Sergeant Mattingly was a big, burly guy with a dark complexion, jarhead crew cut, and a no-nonsense look about him. But, when he spoke, it was clear that the sergeant was a friendly man, despite his imposing presence.

"So, Joe, I'm glad I could meet you in person. I read the story about you and your grandpa. What are you guys hoping to do with this old game?" Mattingly asked.

Joe thought about the question for just a second. "Well, it's like this, sir. If we can help bring back an old game that was once called America's pastime, I think the country will have taken another step forward along the line of recovery."

Grandpa Moses and Mr. Donnerson both stopped and looked at each other. Sgt. Mattingly turned and looked at Joe. "Young man, that was quite a mature answer."

Joe smiled at the sergeant and then looked at his grandpa.

"I've got a good teacher right next to me." Grandpa smiled and tapped the top of Joe's head.

The group continued on deep into the woods, past the clearing, and into the remains of the old VFW hall. New to his post in McHenry, Sergeant Mattingly had only heard about this place and was in some awe to be standing inside of the ruins.

Over one hundred years earlier, that building, and battlefield had been a place of horror and valor. But were it not for the destroyed buildings they had passed along the way to the VFW hall ruins, the forest, wildflowers, and other vegetation could have conspired to hide its past infamy.

Walking towards the interior south wall of the hall, the sergeant stepped on a large piece of metal that had, at one point, been up in the ceiling as perhaps a part of the roof or heating ductwork. Curious, he lifted it to see what lay underneath. He saw a framed object, somewhat heavy, and he could tell that the front of it was glass.

It rested atop some shattered plywood, which had kept it elevated off of the floor and away from the inevitable pooling of water. The framed object was caked in dust and grime. The sergeant wiped away the dirt and grime until he could make out the shape of a man and his horse.

After wiping away more dirt, he noticed the man was kneeling, with his hands folded in prayer, beside his horse. The man was dressed oddly. Then, it hit him. This was the artist's rendering of America's most famous Revolutionary War hero and first president of the United States, General George Washington!

"Guys! Come on over, you've got to see this!" he shouted.

They all rushed over to the sergeant, who was holding an intact, framed print, with the glass miraculously unbroken.

"What is that?" Joe asked.

Sgt. Mattingly was quick to answer. "That, my friends, is a famous print depicting General George Washington kneeling beside his horse at Valley Forge, Pennsylvania, during the American Revolutionary War, in the winter of 1777."

Mattingly stared for a moment and continued, "Wow! *The Prayer at Valley Forge*. We learned about this at West Point. The original of this print is hanging in the Oval Office in the White House. I don't get it. How did this print survive, still intact, all these years?"

Joe looked at his grandpa, then at the sergeant, and without skipping a beat, answered him. "Providence, Sergeant, it must be providence."

Sgt. Mattingly set the print down and leaned it up carefully against a pile of rubble nearby, while making a mental note to come back to get the print on the way back. They climbed over the rubble at the east door and passed the small clearing. Within a few minutes, they were standing in the area where Joe and his buddies had found the old home plate.

Mr. Donnerson listened as Joe recalled the earlier trip and explained where they had found the home plate. Joe also pointed out the remains of the fencing for the old ball field, as well as the trees that had grown up where the old outfield and most of the infield had been. All the while, Mr. Donnerson, walking on ahead of the group, was writing tons of notes. He reached the far edge of the remains of the field and yelled out to ask Joe what this fence was for, way out from where they had found home plate.

"That was called the outfield fence, Mr. Donnerson. If you hit a ball hard enough and over the fence—"

"A home run, like you did the other day when you hit one," Mr. Donnerson finished.

"That's right!" Joe said proudly.

Mr. Donnerson walked back to the group. He wrote down a few more notes and then looked at the sergeant and asked, "What is the status of this place?"

"Well, it's still technically a military zone, but as you already know, the no-go restrictions were lifted a short time ago. Not sure what the status is beyond that. But I can find out and get back to you."

Moses looked at Mr. Donnerson. "So, what are you thinking?"

"Well, I'm thinking that one way or the other, we're going to fix this place up and give these kids a real live baseball field to play on. I can't think of a better place to start than here. I think our lost men and women in arms would fully approve of our plan to make this a place of peace and fun again, while respecting their memory."

Joe and Austin smiled.

Mr. Donnerson continued, "We have a lot to figure out though, before someone throws a pitch at this place again, a lot to figure out."

"Well, count me in," offered Moses. "I'll do whatever I can to help you. I know quite a few heavy equipment operators, out near Rockford, that would be interested in a project like this."

Sgt. Mattingly paused, then added, "I'm certain the Army Corps of Engineers would have an interest in this as well. Scuttlebutt is they've been looking for a new PR project, and this one would fit the bill nicely. It'll need to be run up the chain of command, of course."

The group nodded to one another, with determined looks. With that, Sgt. Mattingly headed back toward the VFW hall to pick up the old print of General Washington, while the rest of the group followed along.

They filled the return trip with all kinds of talk and suggestions, as well as a question-and-answer session, with lots of questions about baseball asked by Mr. Donnerson and Sgt. Mattingly. Joe did most of the answering and, now and then, deferred to Grandpa Moses when he was unsure.

Mike Drucker had taken copious amounts of notes, and his favorite staff photographer at the Herald had taken many photographs of the day's adventure. They would come in handy as the story continued to unfold.

The next few weeks were a whirlwind of activity. Mike's follow-up story in the McHenry Herald went national, and a producer from Good Morning USA called to arrange an on-air interview with Joe, Moses, and Mike Drucker. Moses refused to go on air unless Mr. Donnerson was included, so he was added, as well. Their interview was held the following week, on Friday. The story was published the next day.

The story had caught the attention of the McHenry community and the surrounding area by storm. It seemed as if anyone with a tractor or a chain saw wanted to come out and be a part of this volunteer corps of citizens clearing up the baseball field-turned-battlefield-turned-woods.

Moses's phone rang almost nonstop after the story broke. Longtime friends he hadn't heard from in years called in to offer free use of heavy equipment and the labor to go with it.

When he asked if they had read up on baseball, over three quarters had read the articles, but they still had very little understanding of the game. They were, however, eager to see a live game and learn. A universal theme was that they all wanted to help and see where this all led to.

A week later, Mr. Donnerson, Moses, and 100 volunteers were assembled at the remains of the old VFW hall. Before going over the plan for the day's work, Moses announced he would say a prayer of protection for those assembled. When he was done, Mr. Donnerson's hand-picked foreman, Sam Washburn, addressed the crew.

"Everyone, on behalf of Mr. Donnerson, Grandpa Moses, and his grandson, Joe Scott, we thank you for taking time out today for the start of this project. I understand that, by now, most, if not all of you, are familiar with the baseball stories written by our local hometown boy, Pulitzer Prize-winning reporter, Mike Drucker.

"I've read his series of articles on the exploits of Joe, his brother, Austin, his friend, Ted, and the rest of their buddies, as well as the Scott family's beloved Grandpa Moses. We are assembled here today as volunteers who now join with them and their desire and efforts to resurrect an old game called baseball. A game that was once called America's pastime, a long, long time ago, before the war.

"From the death of baseball, just before the war, to the war itself and its aftermath, America struggled to just survive, much less thrive. Those days, thankfully, are now far behind us. The news is increasingly better for all of us, as the nation has gotten back on its feet in some huge ways in the last several years. With the pace continuing to speed up, the future looks bright once more.

"Now, I believe that any nation that loses some or all of its culture loses a part of its identity. In the whole grand scheme of things, I expect our nation would continue to progress without delving into the past and digging up some old game — literally and figuratively.

"But, after reading about baseball and what it once meant to our country a long time ago, surely we can't hurt ourselves by re-weaving this game back into the fabric of our nation. So, we're gathered here to begin this project to do just that.

"The Army Corps has generously donated a team of 20 soldiers, all skilled in heavy equipment operation and tree removal. We've got plenty of heavy equipment here today.

"For today's work, we have four teams assigned to tree removal. Each team has a team leader who will, separately, go over the safety protocols we'll need everyone to follow. You all have your marching orders for afterward. With that, let's get to work."

The gathering of 100 quickly split up into four teams of 25. The pre-planning had been vital to ensure, first and foremost, safety, but also smooth and efficient tree downing, sectioning, loading, and hauling of the timber to the local mill on the west side of town, in the old gravel pits. Once an area was cleared, root removal was performed. It was determined beforehand that stump grinding would not be sufficient, so heavy equipment was used to dig up the bigger roots for disposal.

By day's end, the area was cleared of timber.

Before heading home, the volunteers gathered together to gaze out over their hard day's labor. Joe, Austin, and Moses stood arm in arm and stared in wonder at what was once a forest.

Mr. Donnerson, though not usually one for speeches, broke the silence. "Well, everyone, you've all done a mighty fine job today. I know it still looks rough, but if you close your eyes and imagine, what we have before us now is the makings of a fine diamond. Yes sirree, a fine diamond indeed."

CHAPTER FIFTEEN

Good Morning USA!

At the sound of his customary 5 AM alarm, Grandpa Moses awoke and began his morning routine. This Friday morning, though, he also had to awaken Joe and Austin. Mary, Sam, and the girls would join them later at the new ball field site, but for now, the boys were Grandpa's to shepherd through their earlier-than-usual morning. First, however, he read from the book of Ecclesiastes.

As he read, the words in chapter three, verse 11 particularly struck him:

"He has made everything beautiful in its time. He has also set eternity in the human heart, yet no one can fathom what God has done from beginning to end."

When he finished, he placed one hand on top of each of the boys' heads and prayed silently. When he had finished, the boys knew better than to ask what he had prayed. Previous attempts were always met with the same answer: "God loves prayers said in secret, so I'm not sayin', because it's a secret!"

Twenty minutes later, they were all in the kitchen where Grandpa had cooked up a hearty breakfast of bacon, eggs, and hash browns, with toast, juice, and chocolate milk.

"So, what's supposed to happen today on the show?" Joe asked.

"Well, the information given to me was that first, Mrs. Tubman will interview us about how this all started. Next, she'll ask you, your brother, and your gang of buddies to put on a little demonstration of baseball, after a commercial break. When the camera comes back on, that'll be the cue to play ball. Have you figured out a lineup and where everyone is going to play?"

"Yes sir, got it right here in my shirt pocket." Joe patted his chest.

"Who's pitching?" asked Grandpa, with a knowing smile.

"Funny, Grandpa, very funny. Austin is!"

"What?" Austin shouted out. "Since when?"

"Since last night. I thought about it, and I figured we don't have a lot of time on the air, so when they say go, you'll be pitching to me to start the game. That way, we'll both be on the air at the same time, right from the start. Mom thought that was a cool idea. Besides, you're my kid brother and I really want you to pitch."

"Well then, okay. I guess I'll lead things off by striking you out!" Austin wryly offered.

"Dream on, little brother!"

Grandpa saw where this was going and cut them both off. "Alright boys, let's finish up our meal here and then get upstairs and finish getting ready."

⚾ ⚾ ⚾

Good Morning USA, the nation's top-rated morning show for five years running, had hit the road and landed in McHenry. The fact that they were there in McHenry, to do their show live, had sent the entire area into a frenzy. They had even received permission from the Army Corps and city officials to do the show live from the grounds of the old VFW hall.

While the baseball field was still being constructed, the dirt was level enough for Joe, Austin, Ted, and the gang to do a baseball demo, live on air, all at the special request of Good Morning USA host Laura Tubman. Laura had taken an early interest in the baseball stories written by Mike.

Laura was a direct descendant of Harriet Tubman, an influential heroine of the First American Civil War. Harriett was Laura's seventh great-grandmother, who became famous for escaping slavery in Maryland, in 1849, and then leading hundreds of slaves to freedom, via the famous abolitionist-organized Underground Railroad that had made Harriet's escape possible in the first place.

At 28, Laura had become the youngest national morning show anchor in American broadcast history. Her reign, for the last ten years, at the top of the ratings heap as the anchor of Good Morning U.S.A. had landed her many awards and accolades in and out of the broadcasting industry.

Known for being highly intelligent and a tough interviewer, she pulled no punches with politicians, regardless of party affiliation. She had long ago declared on live TV that she had been and would always be an Independent, politically speaking, that is.

For today's show, however, she was ready for a light-hearted, feel-good piece.

The morning was bright and clear as Laura arrived on location at the ruins of the old VFW post. In the background, there were many pieces of heavy equipment and an enormous pile of logs still awaiting transport to the mill west of town.

There was a cacophony of noise from two sources: her fellow employees getting ready to go live in 30 minutes and a large crowd of locals excited to be a part of history.

Laura had done her homework about this lost game but still

had lots of questions. She was excited that they had the grounds in good enough shape that they could broadcast a live demo of the game to the nationwide audience.

Before she had left home, Laura's husband and her two oldest boys told her they would watch the show and that the producer needed to be a little generous with the baseball demo time, to give the viewers a chance to study the game, if ever so briefly. Laura assured them she had received firm promises the live demo broadcast would air for a full ten minutes.

The show's producer, Arnie Harris, had been the producer of the Good Morning U.S.A. show since its inception 15 years earlier. Day's prior, Arnie had a long discussion with Laura about the baseball demo that Laura had pushed hard for.

Laura's initial ask was for a full 20-minute live demo segment. Arnie argued that five minutes should be good enough. In the end, though, it was Laura's persuasiveness that caused Arnie to compromise and land on 10 minutes. Early in the morning, at his hotel room, he'd prayed to God it would be some of the best 10 minutes of demonstration they had aired in a long, long time.

A week earlier, the show's advance crew had already mapped out everything — where the stage and audience would be, the background, and the spot where they wanted the boys to demo the baseball game. With three different cameras set up for the demo, Arnie was confident everything was in place. He had a gut feeling today's show had the makings of something special, if everyone played their parts right. Adding to the confidence, it was a perfect weather day.

⚾ ⚾ ⚾

Grandpa Moses, Joe, Austin, Ted, and all their young buddies arrived just before the limousine that pulled up and discharged Laura Tubman. They were awestruck that she was there in

McHenry. A few minutes later, Sam, Mary, and the girls showed up to take their places in the reserved seats down the baseline, along with Mr. Donnerson.

A countdown clock showed 15 minutes to airtime.

The Scott family all came over for a moment to huddle with Grandpa, Mike Drucker, Mr. Donnerson, and the boys, to encourage them and exchange small talk. Mary tousled the hair of her two sons and gave them each a big hug. Sam leaned over and did likewise and said one word to them both.

"Shine."

Mary hugged her dad and whispered into his ear. Grandpa looked his daughter in the eyes and said, "You too, munchkin, you too."

Ten minutes to airtime.

Joe gathered up Austin, Ted, and all the rest of the gang that would take part in the demonstration game.

"Ok, everyone knows their part, right?" Joe asked.

Everyone nodded.

"Ok, don't screw it up. Take some deep breaths and remember to have fun out there, just like we did yesterday in the game at the park. Hands in, everyone."

Everyone stuck their right hand into the center for a hand sandwich and, on the count of three, yelled, "Play ball!"

Five minutes to airtime.

The crowd quieted down when the audience prompter held up the five-minute cue card. People took their seats and snapped some more pictures as the clock ticked down to zero.

The stage director yelled out, "Five — Four — Three — Two — One!" He snapped his hand down, and the show's opening song played, followed by the announcer's tagline.

"Live from McHenry, Illinois, it's time to say Good Morning U.S.A. with your host, Laura Tubman, and our news and weather team, Alex Michaels and Lauren Livingston!"

Laura was front and center and ready for the last note of the jingle.

"Good Morning U-S-A! Wow, what a fabulous crowd! How is everyone doing here in the great city of McHenry, Illinois?"

The crowd roared with approval.

"We're so excited about today's show. I don't know about you guys, Alex and Lauren, but I had a hard time sleeping last night."

"For sure, Laura, for sure. How often do we get to do a live demonstration of an extinct game?!" Alex joked.

The audience laughed.

"Well, remember, Alex, we're here today because the game is no longer extinct — we think," Lauren answered.

She joined the audience in laughter, before she continued, "That's right, that's right. We're so excited that joining us here today are some special guests. With us today is Joe Scott, his younger brother Austin, the Scott family's beloved Grandpa Moses, and Pulitzer Prize-winning reporter, Mike Drucker, from the McHenry Herald newspaper. All of them played a part in the re-discovery of this long-lost game called baseball. But first, here are today's headlines from Alex Michaels and the national weather forecast from Lauren Livingston."

The show proceeded with the news and weather segments and then broke for a quick commercial break. During the break, Laura shared a few quick pointers with Joe and the rest of the guests assembled on stage. The stage director motioned, did another five-second countdown and then, at zero, pointed straight at Laura.

"Ok, we're back live from McHenry, and seated here with us are our special guests. From left to right, reporter Mike Drucker, Grandpa Moses, Austin Scott, and Joe Scott. So, Joe, how on earth did all this start?"

For the next several minutes, there was back and forth between Laura and the "special guests." Laura then called up

Earl Donnerson and asked him questions about the volunteer effort to clear the land, which had been so crucial for the day's demonstration game.

Mary Scott had been a little fidgety in her seat, leading up to the first question Laura asked of Joe. But she was encouraged by her son's poise and his answer to the first question. As the interview went on, her initial nervousness gave way to quiet and simple joy. Grandpa was his usual storyteller self, and Mike Drucker did a great job of weaving things together. It was as if they had all rehearsed this. Austin was a little quiet, but got a laugh when he said he was going to strike his brother out in the baseball demonstration segment after the break.

After a full ten minutes of back and forth with the guests, it was time for another commercial break. During this second break, the boys hustled over to the makeshift ball field and got a few warm-up tosses in. Laura, the rest of the crew, and the stagehands all pivoted over to the field as well.

Austin was warmed up and feeling good, especially after the way he had pitched the day before.

The stage director shouted out the five-second count down again. At zero, he again pointed to Laura.

"Good morning, U.S.A.! Here we are again, live from McHenry, Illinois. As promised, here is our live demonstration game. I'll hand over the mic to Grandpa Moses, who, along with Mike Drucker, will provide commentary during this full ten-minute demonstration of the game called baseball."

Mike took his cue. "Thank you, Laura. It's a pleasure for Grandpa Moses and myself to add a bit of explanation and commentary. To start things off, Austin Scott will pitch to his brother, Joe …"

Out on the mound, Austin listened to Mike's intro but soon tuned him out and took a deep breath. He was determined to strike his brother out on national TV. Originally, Ted was going to pitch, but Joe had recognized the golden moment that was right before him to have his younger brother pitch. They were very close, and Joe had told him, "Your pitching has come into its own."

Austin cleared his mind, stared at his brother, and then looked for the sign. There it was: fastball.

"Wow," he thought to himself, *"this is pitch number one on national TV, the first one in over one hundred years."* The thought brought out a slight hint of a smile, which Joe saw and smiled back.

Austin went into the windup, reared back, and offered up a fastball for his first pitch.

Joe was determined not to embarrass himself on a live, national TV broadcast by striking out at the hands of his younger brother. He knew him well and figured his first pitch would be a fastball. He was right, and the ball came in hot. Joe timed his swing perfectly but missed the ball.

Mike Drucker yelled out, "And there it is, folks, pitch number one on a national telecast, the first in over one hundred years. Great opening pitch by your grandson, Moses."

"Yes it was!" Moses replied. "A brother-to-brother challenge, Mike. The younger comes out on top against the older, at least for that pitch."

Austin let out a quiet, "Yes!", under his breath. He waited for the next sign, which was a curveball.

Joe was slightly annoyed at himself, but not enough to let it get into his head. Two strikes left.

Austin brought the mitt up to his chin. His right hand grabbed the ball, and, instinctively, his fingers found the seams and configured for a curveball. He reared back and let it fly.

Joe had guessed another fastball was coming. By the time he picked up the rotation of a curveball, it was too late. His bat swung and missed by a full foot, as the ball broke sharply, down and away, out of the strike zone.

Drucker was again quick to comment, "Whoa, that was a big swing, but the ball dropped down and away so much that Joe Scott had no chance to hit that ball."

Austin let out another quiet, "Yes!", and for a split second, fantasized about the next pitch being a "Swing and a miss, strike three!" He was again given a curveball sign, but shook it off. Next was a changeup. He shook that one off, too. Catcher Norm Gould was slightly annoyed and offered the fastball sign. Austin nodded, went into the windup, and let it fly.

Joe was convinced that, after being wrong on the last pitch, his brother was now throwing a fastball, for sure. He picked up the rotation and, in his mind, yelled, *Fastball!* He had guessed right. Oh, had he ever guessed right.

Mike Drucker's call was loud, "And Joe Scott hits a long fly ball deep into left-center field. It's going past both fielders and keeps rolling. Billy Cross grabs it, bobbles the ball, and fires it into second base. Joe is headed for second base. Here comes the throw, and Joe Scott is in with a stand-up double!"

Mary felt bad for Austin but elated for Joe. She, along with everyone else, cheered wildly.

Mike Drucker then introduced the next batter. "Now batting, Ted Lee Banks."

Ted had almost not made it to the game. The day before, he was feeling lousy, but after a good night's sleep, he felt better when he woke up and let Joe know to put him in the line-up for the demo.

Ted stepped into the batter's box and was also determined not to be embarrassed on national TV. He locked eyes with Austin's glove and reminded himself of his sidearm delivery.

Austin was highly annoyed his big brother had hit his pitch for a double. He was determined to not make the same mistake again. A curveball would be his first offering to Teddy.

Teddy had settled on Austin again. Still staring at Austin's glove to see if he could see the grip of the ball on the delivery.

Austin had been working on his delivery after watching one of the old instructional DVDs on the art of pitching. One thing he had learned was that he tended to "tip his pitches," which is to say the batter was picking up his grip on the ball in the mitt and determining if it was going to be a fastball, slider, or curveball. He had tried the new delivery the other day, during a game, and it seemed to have worked. He was sure Joe had made a lucky guess. Austin gripped for a curveball, reared back, and let it fly.

Ted had missed the last game Austin pitched and quickly realized his friend had changed his delivery. He couldn't make out the grip and held on to his original idea that a fastball was coming. By the time he saw the break in the ball, mid-flight, it was too late. He had started his swing and could not adjust in time.

"STRIKE ONE!!!" yelled the umpire.

Austin let out a whoop.

Mike Drucker was now in a groove. "The first pitch to Banks is a called strike. Grandpa Moses, that looked like a curveball."

"Yes sir, it was. Austin's been working hard to improve his delivery and not let the batter know what pitch is coming. We worked a lot on that yesterday to prepare for today's show."

"Fair enough. Let's see what comes next, as Banks steps back into the batter's box to get ready. Austin Scott stares intently at the catcher, waiting for the sign. He shakes off the first and gives a nod of approval for the second. Here is the wind-up and the pitch. Banks swings and misses for strike two!"

Joe had been jumping around out on second base, trying to distract Austin. Their friend, Bill, was playing shortstop and kept feigning moves toward second base, in the event Austin made a pickoff attempt. Joe figured that the time was right to try to steal third base. He'd already decided that, as soon as his brother made the next pitch, he was going to do it.

Moses continued the commentary. "Boy, that was a great pitch that broke down and in. No way Banks was going to be able to adjust to that pitch."

"The count is no balls and two strikes," Mike informed the audience. "Moses, what's Banks thinking now?"

"I would have to believe another curveball is coming."

Austin set and then looked back twice at his older brother on second base, to keep him honest. He was so intent on striking out Ted, he didn't notice the extra half-step Joe had taken in his leadoff at second base. Austin zoned in on the catcher's mitt and let a fastball fly.

Ted had guessed a fastball was coming and was right.

At the release, Joe took off for third base like lightning.

Ted, in a millisecond, could tell the ball was breaking away more than the last pitch and would, more than likely, sail out of the strike zone. He had also seen Joe take off in his steal attempt of third base.

Behind the plate, Norm Gould saw the curve breaking. He shifted toward his right to be in a position to stop a potential wild pitch and also be ready to fire a throw to third base to try to throw out Joe in his steal attempt.

Jim Gander, over at third base, had seen Joe take off and raced in to get into position to get a throw from Norm.

Ted held up his swing and heard the umpire yell, "Ball!" Out of the corner of his eye, he saw Norm catch the ball, jump up, and throw hard to Jim. Joe slid into third, just under Jim's tag. The third base umpire yelled, "Safe!" Joe pumped his fist and stood up, with an enormous smile on his face.

⚾ ⚾ ⚾

Back in Boston, the Good Morning USA control room was wired to receive instant feedback from a multitude of sources regarding any segment of the show. At number one in the morning ratings, Operations Director Harmon Musial and the rest of the crew of Good Morning U.S.A. were always in tune with the feedback ratings and trends for the popular hit morning show.

That day's show was going to be a little different, and Harmon's curiosity had been piqued, after he had read the series on baseball by Mike Drucker. The story had caused quite a sensation, even out in Boston.

Bostonians everywhere were looking forward to the morning's segment on baseball. They were eager to tune in to get a firsthand glimpse of this demonstration of baseball.

When the baseball segment started, Harmon kept looking back at the live feed monitors and the feedback portal. The feedback meter rose as the segment began, and continued to rise. Harmon swung his attention between the live feed monitor and the feedback meter. He grew increasingly astonished at the rapid ascent of the feedback meter into record territory. He was witnessing a phenomenon with the response from America, from coast to coast, on this baseball segment.

Then, Harmon heard the phones begin to ring in the switchboard room next door. It was as if every alarm bell in the city rang at once. Through the glass, he could see all 25 operators on their phones, taking notes, hanging up, and getting another call immediately. One operator held up a hastily written sign, which said, in big, black, bold marker: "Press Baseball Crazy!"

Back in McHenry, they finished the baseball demo. The boys in the field had come in and were all crowded around Laura to answer questions. Then Joe popped a surprise.

"Miss Tubman, I know your show normally airs from the

studios in Boston. I have a surprise for you and the crew back in Boston."

"A surprise? I love surprises! Especially on national TV. What is it?" Laura asked.

Joe was handed a large manila envelope from his mom. He handed the envelope to Laura. Laura opened it up and glanced at a photo. Puzzled, she asked, "Thank you, Joe, but what is this a picture of?"

Joe gave a quick glance over to his grandpa, who was in on the surprise. Then he looked straight into the TV camera and, without skipping a beat, answered, "That, America, is a 150-year-old photograph of one of the most famous baseball fields that ever existed. It was in Boston and was destroyed in the Great Boston Firestorm during the Second Civil War. It was called Fenway Park."

⚾ ⚾ ⚾

Back in Boston, Harmon stood frozen, looking at the live feed monitor. The cameraman back in McHenry had zoomed in on the photograph of the old Boston ballpark, from before the war, from before the maelstrom.

Harmon got goosebumps, as tears formed in his eyes. Others in the control room just stood in silence and stared at the monitor. The feedback meter had smashed the all-time record by a factor of 10. Baseball was a hit again!

CHAPTER SIXTEEN

From The Top

President Frederick Kennedy started his day like all others, with a quiet time of reflection and reading his Bible, followed by his daily call with his priest, Father David Mulcahey, for prayer and encouragement for the day's challenges.

President Kennedy was a true patriot, devoted husband to his wife of 20 years, Anne, and a doting father to his five kids: Dwight, Martin, Sarah, Elizabeth, and Susan.

He was the first Black Irishman to be elected as president of the United States. His ancestry was also noteworthy, having both President John Fitzgerald Kennedy and President Ronald Reagan in his genealogical tree.

The president was riding a tremendous wave of popularity in the polls, mainly because of surging economic activity that was "raising all boats."

After the early morning national security briefing, the president had returned to the family residence of the White House. There he sat quietly with his oldest son, Dwight, watching the baseball demonstration segment of the show that was being live broadcast from McHenry, Illinois.

The president had heard bits and pieces about baseball from his son, and he had read Mike Drucker's stories about the newly rediscovered game. At his son Dwight's insistence, the president had agreed to take a rare but brief morning time-out to watch the baseball demonstration segment with him. The affairs of state had been clipping along at a hectic pace and had, naturally, been a far higher priority than this lost game re-discovered. They were joined by the president's chief of staff, Carl Rosenthal.

Having visited the Eisenhower Federal Building in McHenry a few years earlier, the president was familiar with the lay of the land in and around the city. He recalled flying over McHenry the previous year, in Air Force One, before landing at King Air Force Base in Rockford, Illinois.

As the president sat and watched the demonstration baseball game, he felt an increasing sense of curiosity and wonder as the demo played out. By the time the segment was over, he looked over at Dwight and made a comment that what he had just watched looked like fun. He then asked Carl to reach out to Mike Drucker and the Scott family to see if they would be up for a visit to the White House.

"Yes sir, Mr. President. However, you're booked pretty solid this week and next—"

The president, typically polite, interrupted Carl, "Yes, I recall. How about a one-hour working lunch out at that hot dog joint next week?"

"I think that can be arranged, Mr. President."

"Thank you. I'm looking forward to meeting this young boy. Also, get me any information we have on this game. I'd like to read up on it some more. You know, come to think of it, I seem to recall, when I was very young, my great-granddad mentioning something about an old game he would go see in Boston. I wonder if he meant baseball? Also, curious if you can find out what part this game played in pre-war America."

"Mr. President, I will see what I can dig up. I have an old friend at the federal building in McHenry. He was mentioned in Mike Drucker's series on the game."

"Thank you, Carl. Well, we're both a tad late for our next meeting."

"Yes, sir, I'll join up with you in a minute. Let me get the inquiries going on this."

As the president and Carl left the family residence of the White House, Carl stepped aside and turned to his aide to give instructions regarding the president's requests. The aide nodded in the affirmative and headed off in one direction, while Carl pulled out his phone.

Eduardo Chavez was in a good mood. Things were going very well with the latest batch of printed material for the Data Restore Project. He was coming off a great weekend with his family, celebrating three birthdays and a high school graduation. When the phone rang and he answered it, he heard a familiar voice.

"Carl Rosenthal? Is that you?!"

"Indeed, it is my friend. And how is Eduardo Chavez on this fine day?"

"Shalom, my friend! Shalom! Man, it's great to hear your voice. When's the last time you and I connected?"

"Well, let's see," Carl pondered. "If I recall correctly, it was around Christmas, two years ago."

"Wow. Shame on us for not connecting sooner. What can I do for you?"

"Listen, I have a special request from the president—"
Eduardo interrupted, "THE President?!"
"Yep, the president would like a briefing paper on baseball—"

Eduardo interrupted again, "Baseball? Man, I'm hearing that word a lot these days."

"The president saw the baseball demonstration on Good Morning USA this morning and wants to meet Joe Scott and Mike Drucker. He wants to read up on the game beforehand, so that he's prepared when he meets them."

"Well, you're in luck, my friend. We've come across a mother lode of material on the old game. I can have something for you in a few days. Good enough?"

"Perfect, Eduardo, perfect. Listen, I owe you one. When do you want to come to D.C. for a VIP tour with the family?"

"You know, that sounds like a lot of fun. Let me talk it over tonight over family dinner and get back to you soon."

"Sounds great, Eduardo. Thanks a bunch, and I will give the president the good news."

"Ok, thanks, Carl. I'll be in touch soon."

It was noon in McHenry when the phone rang at the Scott residence. Moses picked up. Sam and Mary had both gone to work at the federal building, after the morning's excitement.

"Hello, you have reached the Scott residence," Moses announced.

"Hello, my name is Sarah McDougal. I'm calling from the White House, on behalf of the president of the United States. Is Joe Scott there?"

"Is this a joke?"

"No sir, I can assure you it is real."

"Wow! Well, Joe is not here at this very moment," Moses replied.

"Are you his father?"

"No ma'am, Brian Woodbridge, his grandfather. You can

call me Grandpa Moses."

"So, you're the Grandpa Moses I saw on TV this morning!"

"One and the same man."

"That was a fun segment. I really liked the demonstration baseball game."

"Glad you liked it. The boys put a lot of thought and effort into making sure the demonstration game went well."

"Well, it went well enough to capture the interest of the president of the United States. He's extending an invitation to come to the White House and tell him about this old game your grandson has rediscovered."

"Are you kidding me?"

"Not at all, Mr. Woodbridge. I'm quite serious."

"Wow, that sounds fantastic. How can we reach you later? I need to call my daughter and son-in-law."

After they exchanged information and Moses hung up, he called Mary at her office. Grandpa could tell by the tone of her voice that she was shocked. Mary bridged in Sam, who was equally shocked. They asked where Joe was at that moment, and Moses told them he was playing catch with Austin and Ted, over at the park.

⚾ ⚾ ⚾

"Ouch! That one really stung my hand, Joe!" Austin yelled out.

Ted laughed.

"C'mon, little brother, I didn't throw it that hard," Joe replied.

"The heck you didn't. This ball glove may be over a hundred years old, but it's hardly used and has plenty of padding in the pocket."

Ted laughed again. "Hey, guys, what did you think about this morning? Just think, we were on national TV. My mom and dad have been getting calls all day from family and friends from all over."

"I know, right? I just got a text right now from my mom to call her. Something about a call my grandpa just got from someone important," Joe replied.

"Like who?" Ted asked.

"Like, I don't know. Hang on while I find out." Joe brought his comm up toward his face and called his mom. He listened intently as she explained the call she just had with Grandpa. Austin and Ted watched curiously and started getting excited when they saw Joe's eyes get bigger than they had ever seen before. Joe hung up, and his mouth was wide open.

Ted yelled, "Well … what's up?!"

Joe looked down at the ground and then looked up, as his mouth formed a mile-wide smile. "Wow! Guys, it looks like I'm going to the White House!"

Austin fell to the ground in a mock faint.

Ted burst out screaming.

$$\text{⚾ ⚾ ⚾}$$

The practice of using the presidential plane to pick up average Americans and bring them to Washington D.C., via Reagan National, had started 25 years earlier, under the Rosenfeldt administration, to further strengthen the post-war bonds between the government and the people. When the plane was not carrying the president, the aircraft's call sign for those special civilian missions was changed to "Patriot One." The flights had become an enormous success. So much so that the overwhelming support of the populace had silenced initial critics.

And so, the giant Boeing 877 landed at King Air Force Base, next to Rockford International Airport, where the Scott family entourage was waiting for that day-long outing to the nation's capital to see the president of the United States.

Upon the 877's touchdown, the military motorcade that had earlier traveled to McHenry to pick up the day's special guests, along with General Livingston, drove up to the giant aircraft. General Livingston, his staff, the Scott family (including Grandpa Moses), and Mike Drucker walked up the stairs to the aircraft and were shown their seats.

After the obligatory safety briefing, the four mammoth General Electric GE 140-VM VTOL Hydrogen-Powered Turbofans powered up. Within two minutes, the giant airplane had lifted off to an altitude of 1,000 feet. It hovered for a few moments before the engines began assuming horizontal flight configuration, when it quickly sped up and headed for Washington, D.C.

The flight from King Air Force Base in Rockford to Reagan National on the banks of the Potomac River was uneventful and featured an unclouded day for the entire trip.

Flying at an altitude of 44,000 feet, Patriot One was in the lower range of the stratosphere, way above the haze. Thus, the sky above was a deep ocean blue. Joe's view from the window seat was spectacular. He loved to fly, and it showed in his mile-wide smile.

Upon touchdown at Reagan National, next to the nation's Capital District, the Secret Service drove up in the presidential motorcade and headed to the front of the aircraft. The Scott family deplaned first and were guided to the presidential limousine. A Secret Service agent opened the door, and there he was: the president of the United States. President Kennedy invited the Scott family into the limo. Joe was speechless.

⚾ ⚾ ⚾

The ride to Skobel's Hot Dogs in Alexandria, Virginia, was relatively short. The White House Advance Team had already secured the facility 24 hours earlier and had been on site since, while still allowing regular customers to come in and dine. Two hours before arrival, security tightened, as the United States Secret Service began screening all customers.

The motorcade pulled up, right on time, at 12:30 PM. All the Secret Service agents in the motorcade quickly exited their vehicles and established their security presence, pre-coordinated with the Virginia State Police and the City of Alexandria Police Department.

The president and son, Dwight, exited first, followed by the Scott family, and then Mike Drucker. Chief of Staff Rosenthal and some aides, as well as, of course, the obligatory press corps and Secret Service agents, joined them as they all walked into Skobel's Hot Dogs.

Elias Skobel had opened his hot dog joint ten years earlier, and it had become an instant hit, not only among the civilian population, but also with members of the military stationed across the Potomac at the Pentagon.

When Elias was just ten years old, his grandad had written down a recipe for something called a "Chicago-style hot dog" that his grandad had cooked from time to time. Family lore had Elias's great-great-grandad born and raised in Chicago before the war came along. He had owned a small hot dog stand called, appropriately enough, Skobel's Hot Dogs.

Elias had been beyond excited when the Secret Service showed up with the White House Advance Team to check out his place and plan out the security details. When he was asked if he would host the president for a working lunch, he, of course, said yes. While he had not voted for the president, he was taught at a young age that, when the election is over, you stand behind the president and let bygones be bygones. It was all for the general good of the nation.

Elias and his staff were ready when the cue came, and the president of the United States walked into his hot dog joint.

It immediately impressed Elias when the president walked briskly up to the counter and said thanks for hosting him and his working lunch today. He extended a hand of greeting to Elias, to which, of course, Elias obliged. The president then added a personal touch by asking Elias's employees their names and, one by one, exchanging pleasantries and handshakes with them, as well.

"Well, alright then, lunch is on me today," the president announced.

Sam quickly interjected, "Mr. President, please extend me the honor of going back to work next week and telling my coworkers that I bought a hot dog lunch for the president of the United States."

The president paused, then laughed out loud as he saw the look on Sam Scott's face. "Well, alright, Mr. Scott, but I insist on buying ice cream for dessert, right here, after our chat. Deal?"

Of course, he wasn't about to say no to the president of the United States, so Sam stuck out his hand. "Deal!"

After everyone had placed their orders and sat down, Chief of Staff Rosenthal re-introduced all the parties present. Immediately afterward, the president, a devout Catholic, invited those present to bow their heads as he said table grace. With grace said, table chatter resumed, and the president turned to Joe.

"Young man, I want to thank you and your family for taking the time out of your busy schedules to come and have lunch with me today. Mike Drucker, I love reading your stuff. I thank you as well. Your series on baseball was very enjoyable. To Mr. and Mrs. Scott, Austin, Anne, Nellie, and Josephine, thank you as well. Last, but not least, a thank you to Grandpa Moses."

After all of those present uttered their thanks in return for the invitation, the president said, "So, Joe, why don't we start from the beginning, and you tell me how this all came about?"

Joe spoke first, and then Grandpa. Joe started from the very beginning. When Moses retold the story of the burial vaults on his property and all the baseball stuff that had been discovered within them, meticulously preserved, the president interjected.

"Like a giant time capsule. I find that part fascinating. To think a citizen, at the time, had the forethought to do something like this. Trying to preserve a part of our cultural heritage in the event of a worst-case scenario. It gives me goosebumps."

The president looked around at everyone and continued. "Do you realize that the sum total of the Smithsonian artifacts recovered after the war amounted to less than five percent? We lost practically everything in Air and Space. Thankfully, someone grabbed a piece of the tail of the Wright Brothers' Flyer before the flames got to it. We lost the Air and Space Annex at Dulles, and all of Dulles itself. Why, just about everything the Smithsonian had in a nearly 950,000 square foot warehouse in Landover, Maryland, burned to ashes. The National Archives lost fifty percent of its collection. Thankfully, not the Founding Documents."

Grandpa Moses's moment had arrived. Not even Joe knew what was about to happen.

"Mr. President, I have a gift for the people of the United States. I was rummaging around in my attic a few days ago and was looking inside the trunk I spoke of a few moments ago. Something caught my eye in a bottom corner on the inside of that trunk. The thought came to me that the trunk may have had a false bottom to it. Sure enough, a few minutes later, I had it opened up. Inside was a single page of paper in a manilla envelope. Here it is."

Grandpa carefully took the aged envelope out of his satchel and opened it up to take out the solitary sheet of paper he had already read several times himself. With a slight smile on his face, he presented the sheet to the president. The president had a confused look on his face, but he took the sheet from Moses, looked at it, and his eyes got wide as he read the heading and the brief paragraph.

Clearly excited, he turned and looked at his son, then at the others in the room, then he read the letter out loud. "The heading at the top says, 'The keys to the past are contained herein.' Below that, a single paragraph that reads, 'To the bearer, below are the exact GPS coordinates for 100 burial vaults across the midwestern region of the United States, wherein you will find a rich treasure trove of preserved cultural heritage of the people of the United States. These artifacts are the property of We the People and are to be transferred into the custody of the Smithsonian Institute and the National Archives.'"

The president looked stunned, as did everyone else in the room. He looked over at a Secret Service agent and instructed him to take possession of the document and not let it leave the president's side.

"Grandpa, you said nothing!" Joe yelled.

"I know, I know. I wanted to keep it a secret for today."

Conversation with the president then picked up where it had left off. The president got excited when Joe started talking about the ball fields being developed back in McHenry, on the hallowed grounds of the VFW segment of the Fox Valley Battlefield site, no less. The president, well-educated in U.S. history, was very aware that the Fox Valley Battlefield site was the Second Civil War's version of the First Civil War's Battle of Gettysburg.

"Wow, that sounds exciting, Joe. Do you have any idea when the first official game will be played there?" the president asked.

"Well, the work is moving along pretty quickly, but I guess they're having trouble finding sod."

The president looked over at Chief of Staff Rosenthal. "Carl, take a look at that and see if we can help these folks out with a little help from the feds. Also, make a note for me to call Rodney Maris."

"Yes sir," Carl said, as he added the requests to his notes.

"Well, Joe, I have a proposition. If you'll have me out to your first game on the new field, I would be delighted and honored to attend in person."

"Wow, Mr. President, that would be awesome! What position do you want to play?"

Everyone in the room burst out laughing.

"Well, Joe," the president smiled. "I was thinking I would watch the game, as opposed to playing in it."

No sooner had the president finished his words, when Dwight tugged his father's sleeve and whispered into his ear, "Dad, can I go with and play baseball?"

The president looked deep into his son's eyes and winked. "Joe, would you have room that day for Dwight to play?"

"Would I?! Really? Wow, that would be awesome. Are you sure that's okay?"

The president smiled and laughed, then looked at Joe. "Young man, this approval comes from the top!"

CHAPTER SEVENTEEN
Is This a Dream?

The news cycle for the last 48 hours had been dizzying for the Scott family, Grandpa Moses, Mike Drucker, and Mr. Donnerson. Video images of President Kennedy's "working lunch" at the hot dog joint had gone viral.

The Scott family phone had been ringing off the hook since their arrival back in McHenry. The same was happening for Mike Drucker and Mr. Donnerson. All the major U.S. news crews had been visiting all over McHenry and were now camped out in front of the Scott family home. They had also been busy doing live news feeds from the ball field, which was rapidly taking shape, on the grounds of the old VFW hall. All under the watchful eye of Mr. Donnerson's army of volunteers, and with a little help from the Army Corps of Engineers.

Mr. Donnerson was enjoying his black coffee that morning, while supervising the crews who were busy at work with fencing, scoreboards, concession stands, lights, and bleachers. He was so focused that he did not hear the hum of the tandem flatbed trailer pulling in with an oversized load. The driver exited and asked a volunteer who was in charge. After he was pointed to Mr. Donnerson, the driver quickly walked over to him.

"Would you be Mr. Donnerson?" the driver asked.

"I would be."

"Mr. Donnerson, my name is Rodney Maris. I own the largest sod farm down in Peoria. I got a call yesterday from the president of the United States. We're old friends from our Navy days. Well, anyway, he ordered this truckload of sod to be delivered here, pronto."

Mr. Donnerson stood there speechless for a moment. "Wow, I guess it helps to have friends in high places. All the sod farms around here have been hit with some sort of blight or fungus. Your timing is perfect! I can't thank you enough!"

⚾ ⚾ ⚾

Reggie Spalding had taken great delight in making serious headway on his family tree. After years of struggling to locate genealogical records that were older than the war years, he was delighted when the National Data Recovery Project announced that a vast number of genealogical records had just recently been restored, with the help of the Mormon Church in Utah. As a fan of history, Reggie was thrilled by all the records he was uncovering concerning his family lineage.

He had also become quickly enthralled by the baseball talk all over town, after viewing the live demo game on Good Morning U.S.A. Adding fuel to his curiosity was the huge news story of the president's meeting with Joe Scott and his intentions to visit McHenry to watch a game.

Reggie had found an additional set of records just the night before and was closely examining them when he came across the name Albert Spalding. As he studied the information on his ancestor, he got very excited reading about the Spalding sporting goods company and empire founded by Albert, which had begun in 1876. Of particular interest to Reggie was his ancestor's company's association with the newly rediscovered game of baseball.

When he had finished reading all the newfound material, he pushed his chair back from his keyboard and lit his evening smoke in his favorite pipe. Reggie smiled as his thoughts went into overdrive.

⚾ ⚾ ⚾

The president had been briefed that morning on the security situation around the globe and was in a cheerful mood because of it. The news was good and encouraging all the way around. His next meeting was with General Livingston. The general had just been re-assigned to Washington a few weeks earlier, after a five-year stint in McHenry at the Eisenhower Federal Building.

He had accumulated many accolades during his assignment there, the crowning achievement of which was the immense success of the Chicago experiment with the Wide Beam Neutron Device.

Upon being ushered into the Oval Office for a private meeting with President Kennedy, the general stood at attention and saluted the commander-in-chief.

"At ease, General, at ease. Please, have a seat."

"Thank you, Mr. President," the general said, as he relaxed and took a seat on the sofa, next to the president.

"General, I've thoroughly read your report on the Wide Beam Neutron test in Chicago. I'm very impressed with your report. Very detailed and concise. You've taken very complex, technical stuff and put it into layman's terms. My compliments. You and your team have done tremendous work, not only on behalf of the nation, but on behalf of the world. I'll be conducting a press conference in a day or so to announce the results to the nation and the world. I would like you to be there in person, along with the key leadership of the team, and especially the Israeli ambassador."

"Yes sir. Thank you, Mr. President. It would be an honor to attend."

"The honor will be mine to introduce you and your team to the nation. The achievement here is breathtaking. I believe this is Nobel Peace Prize type stuff we're talking about."

The general looked a little stunned at the president's comment and insisted, "It was a team effort. I want to be very, very clear about that."

"No worries, General, no worries. If it comes down to that, I'll personally make sure I nominate all the proper individuals for the team. Listen, on another matter entirely, what can you add to this whole baseball story thing that seems to be taking on a life of its own? You were out in McHenry for some of this. What do you know?"

"Mr. President, I have two sets of twins at home. Twin, 8-year-old girls that are huge into soccer, and a set of twin, 10-year-old boys that are equally avid fans of lacrosse. I can say, with certainty, that all four of them are closely following this baseball story and have been asking a lot of questions about it.

"My boys were able to play a game with Joe Scott and his friends the other day, and they came home super excited. One of them wants to quit lacrosse right away and join the new youth baseball league that an elderly benefactor is organizing. Separately, the ball field complex at the old VFW site is essentially done. I'm told that the sod delivery was a huge missing piece of the project. They asked me to convey sincere gratitude for your personal efforts to secure that shipment."

"That's fantastic," the president said. "Yeah, Rodney Maris and I go way back. Best buds in the Navy from our beginnings at Annapolis. We both served on the U.S.S. Yorktown. Good old CVN-93. We served on her for two tours of duty in the Pacific Fleet. Seems like all he ever talked about back then, during his second tour, was getting home to Peoria and taking over the family sod farm business. We still keep in touch all these years. He's a good man and has been a good friend. Well, anyway, I can't wait to see the field. You know, I also heard about the ruins of a ballpark found during the Chicago experiment. What can you tell me about that?"

"Well, from what I've gathered, in conversations with Eduardo Chavez and Joe Scott, is that, before the war, a professional baseball league had been around for well over a hundred years. There were ballparks in many major cities, including two in Chicago. The ruins of the ballpark we found on the south side of Chicago had a cornerstone with the year 1991 on it."

"Anything recoverable from the ruins?" the president asked.

"I seriously doubt it. Everything there is pretty charred."

"I see. Well, Carl will contact you with details on the press briefing in a day or two. Thank you for your time today, General. It's been great meeting you in person."

"Likewise, Mr. President. It's an honor to serve the country, and I'm looking forward to the press conference."

⚾ ⚾ ⚾

Mr. Donnerson, Joe, Austin, Grandpa Moses, and the gang, as well as a large group of family and friends and a large contingent of the press, including Mike Drucker, stood silently, looking at the first finally completed ball field.

Joe and Austin had seen videos and plenty of pictures of ballfields. Some, they had wound up sharing with Mr. Donnerson and the landscape architect in charge of designing this brand-new one.

However, nothing could prepare them for the sight before their eyes that early morning.

To see the field in person, completed, was awe-inspiring. Lush green grass. Orange-ish dirt infield. White chalk foul lines. The scoreboard in left field, behind an outfield fence with a crushed limestone warning track. The tops of which were capped off with yellow, plastic safety tubing. Each foul line perfectly aligned, extending out to their respective left field and right field foul poles, which were painted safety yellow and reached 50 feet into the sky.

They had secured outfield distance placards in left field, center field, and right field, listing the distance from home plate to each placard at 210 ft, 240 ft, and 210 ft, respectively.

There were bleachers up and down both foul lines and all along the outside of the outfield fence. A brick dugout with a metal roof. Also, a high backstop that wrapped around and continued out toward first and third bases.

The press and announcer's booth were there too, high behind the backstop. The sprinkler system was on, and in the early morning light, the sun was glistening off the water droplets, clinging to the tips of the newly sodded grass.

Joe looked at the infield again and took particular note of the pitching rubber, the brand-new bases, and the white home plate, all from the Dyersville hoard.

He recalled the old home plate he had found earlier, amidst the ruins, and remembered how weathered and forlorn that one was after sitting there, unused, for over a century. The new home plate was so white, so untouched, and so beckoning.

No one spoke for several minutes, until Joe broke the silence. "Wow, would you look at this! Is this a dream?"

Mr. Donnerson turned and looked at Joe, "Young man, that is indeed a dream come true. A genuine baseball field. The first one built in well over a hundred years! And to think you started all this when you came across an old, rusty metal sign."

Mary Scott arrived at her desk at the federal building at 7:30 AM and had just sat down when the phone rang.

She picked it up and, before she could utter a salutation, a booming voice came over. "Hello, is this Mary Scott?"

"Yes, it is. How can I help you today?"

"This is Harry Scully, president of the American News Network. We broadcast Good Morning USA."

"Oh, wow. Yes, how can I help you?

"I just received a call from the president of the United States a few moments ago. He's asked our network to broadcast the upcoming game he will be attending with his son, Dwight. I think the idea is fantastic, and we're going to play it up big.

"I'm sending an advance team today to scope things out and make the arrangements. I would like to invite you and your husband to be in the broadcast booth during the pre-game ceremony and help add some color commentary about your son's exploits and success in bringing this game back to the American people."

"Um, wow, that would be incredible. Can I get back to you later today with an answer?"

"Certainly, later today would be fine."

"Ok, thank you so much." Mary hung up and mumbled to herself, "Is this a dream?" She picked up the phone and called Sam, thinking, *This is going to be a fun conversation.*

Sam had just finished a meeting when he saw Mary was on the private line.

"Hey, beautiful, what's up?"

As he listened to his wife, his eyes got bigger and bigger as she relayed to him the conversation she had just had with the president of the ANN, Harry Scully.

"Of course, I'd love to be in the booth! Oh my gosh, that's awesome! Joe and the kids are going to freak! Are you sure this is going to be a national telecast?"

"Hon, when the president of the American News Network says so, I'm kind of thinking so!" Mary laughed.

Sam paused, then laughed. "Is this a dream or what?! I love it!"

"Well, hon, that would seem to be the phrase of the day, because that's what I just said, moments before calling you."

President Kennedy's news conference had gone very well, according to his aides and the instant polling that was available in real-time. They had given General Livingston and members of the Chicago Experiment team a chance for a Q&A after the president's speech.

There was visible excitement in the eyes of the reporters as they realized the magnitude and full scope of the experiment's success and its implications for the continued regrowth of the United States and its economy.

The president had stated that an estimated up to five million new jobs could be created if the four radiated metropolitan areas could be de-radiated, rebuilt, and re-inhabited. The five million number, he mused, was probably on the low side, since the combined area of all four affected metro areas was over 1,200 square miles.

As he walked back to the West Wing of the White House, the president asked if everything was on track for the next week's big day in McHenry. Chief of Staff Carl Rosenthal assured him it was and, if any snags came up, he would let the president know.

"Carl, if this event next week goes off the way I think it will, we're going to need someone to make a whole lot of baseball equipment. A whole lot."

"Mr. President, I'm certain, if it comes to that, someone will step up to do just that."

"You know, I spoke to Dwight this morning. He's beyond excited for next week. He looked at me and said, 'Is this a dream?'" the president said, as he smiled and laughed.

CHAPTER EIGHTEEN

Opening Day Part 1: The Pregame

The dawn's early light awakened Joe after a fitful night of sleep. After rubbing his eyes and peeking out the window, his thoughts turned to the big day ahead. He shook his head in disbelief. Then he thought of his grandpa. He just knew that Grandpa Moses was probably up already and out on the front porch drinking coffee and reading his Bible or praying. Joe meandered over to the washroom first and then downstairs into the kitchen. After pouring himself a glass of chocolate milk, he headed out to the porch, and sure enough, there was old faithful in the middle of his morning routine.

Grandpa Moses was in silent prayer when he heard the telltale sounds of his oldest grandson walking out onto the porch. He opened his eyes and smiled at Joe as he took a seat on the adjacent rocking chair.

"Good morning, young man."

"Good morning, Grandpa. How did you sleep?"

"Very good, like a rock. You?"

"Eh, not so good."

"Had trouble turning your brain off, huh?" Moses asked.

"Yeah. I just can't believe this day is finally here."

"I know, right? Who would have thought 'No Pepper' would lead to this."

They both laughed.

"Joe, I'm so proud of you for the young man you're becoming and for all that you've done on this adventure. Look at all the new friends you've made and the impact you're having on an entire nation."

"Well, lots of people have helped, especially you. Then there's our ancestor who wrote that note and left it in the trunk, and also made the whole vault thing. If we hadn't found that vault, I'm not sure any of this would be happening right now."

"Providence, young man. Providence. What you said is true, but the key was you finding that old sign. You being curious enough to keep digging for the answers. There's not much for an old man to do with old leather gloves, bats, and baseballs. You studied the old baseball material, and you put life and meaning back into those bats, gloves, and baseballs. You brought the game back, Joe. You resurrected an over one-hundred years dead game and gave it life and meaning again. You did that, not me."

Joe sat and took in his grandpa's words. Everything he had just said was true, but Joe was determined to give credit to others for the rebirth of this grand game, when the time came, and was determined to not let all this go to his head.

⚾ ⚾ ⚾

American News Network President Harry Scully had selected Good Morning USA host Laura Tubman to take part in the first live broadcast of a full baseball game, the first in over one hundred years. As a bonus, it was to be from the same location she had overseen the demonstration of baseball during the Good Morning USA show.

The broadcast crew had arrived three days earlier to set up equipment for the nationally telecasted game. Mr. Scully and the rest of the network bosses knew it was going to be a historic moment for the nation and the world, so they were determined to pull out all the stops to ensure the full game got the big-time broadcast treatment.

The fact that the president of the United States, the first lady, and their twelve-year-old son, Dwight, were attending was sure to boost interest in the game. With Dwight playing in the game, well, sponsors had been falling all over themselves to reach the network to purchase airtime for ad space.

Joining Laura in the booth would be veteran sportscaster Frank Crede, who would call the play-by-play. Scully had made it clear that Laura's role was to provide color commentary. She was beyond excited by the opportunity.

Frank and Laura had arrived in the broadcast booth at 10 AM to prepare for the pre-game show. After going through their notes and speaking with the control room in Boston, as well as the mobile control room beyond the right-field stands, they finally had a few idle minutes before everything got very busy.

"Laura, I can't thank you enough for getting me some of the old DVDs of baseball games from the Scott family. It helped immensely to watch those. It also helped to study the baseball books they loaned out to me as well. So, thank you again."

"Anytime, Frank, anytime. I know you'll call a good game today. I love watching the lacrosse games you call. By the way, how's the family?"

"They're doing great. Thanks for asking. My sons, Mike and Dave, will be here today in the stands with my wife. They've taken a keen interest in checking all this out."

"That's nice. Either of them into sports at all?"

"Neither one of them was ever really all that excited about soccer or lacrosse, although they both enjoy basketball and football in the fall," Frank answered.

"Mmm, okay. Well, it should be a fun afternoon. I'm looking forward to it. I brought my daughter with, and she'll be in the stands as well."

"Is she taking an interest in this, too?"

"Very much so," said Laura. "Very much so."

"You know, I hadn't even thought about crowd size until now. Any ideas at all?"

"Well, for the live demo we had about 800 people show up."

"Wow, really? I'd be happy with that," Frank said. "Plenty of spectators to interview and get their thoughts as the game progresses."

⚾ 🎾 ⚾

McHenry Mayor Vic Meyer and Chief of Police Brandon Thomas had just sat down for the morning's last critical meeting. In attendance, along with local authorities, were members of the White House Advance Team, United States Secret Service, Illinois State Police, McHenry County Sheriff's Department, and American News Network, as well as Mr. Donnerson. The day's agenda was the final logistics review for the game.

The mayor looked around the table and spoke first. "Ladies and gentlemen, thank you all for attending this final meeting. Well, today is the day. I know it's been a whirlwind since all this came together so quickly, and sleep has been a little scarce for some of us. Well, maybe all of us."

Almost everybody in the room laughed, except for the Secret Service agent.

When the laughter died down, the mayor continued. "Chief, what's the latest on crowd estimates?"

"Looks like, from what I am hearing around town, we could have several thousand trying to come and watch this game today," Chief Thomas answered.

"Several thousand?! Fantastic!" Mayor Meyer exclaimed. "I want a full house! Someone tell me again, what's the capacity of the temporary bleachers there?"

Mr. Donnerson jumped on the opportunity to answer. "It's 2,500 down each baseline, 2,000 in the outfield seats, plus 500 standing room, for a grand total of 7,500 fans."

The mayor grinned. "Seven thousand five hundred?! Wow! That'll be something if they all show up."

Tosha Davis, VP of sports for the American News Network, laughed and blurted out, "Don't you worry! We have built this thing up big time. They will come, Mr. Mayor, they will come."

The mayor nodded in approval. "I don't know about all of you, but this is giving me goosebumps. I'm so excited I can hardly stand it. Secret Service, is there anything else you need from us before the gates open at noon?"

United States Secret Service Agent Bill Clemmens answered, "Mayor, Chief Thomas, ladies and gentlemen, it's been very, very smooth coordinating between your teams and ours. I know I speak for, not only myself, but the rest of the agency, the protective detail assigned here today, and POTUS in extending our compliments. We're ready to go."

The mayor turned to the representatives of the Illinois State Police and the McHenry County Sheriff's Department. "State and county all set?"

Both nodded their heads in the affirmative and, in unison, said, "Yes sir."

The Army Corps of Engineers had performed a phenomenal job, at a lightning pace, to reconstruct the old Illinois Rt. 120 bridge over the Fox River. They had, additionally, cleared an area of the woods just west of the ball field site to provide a staging area for the crew that built the ball field, but then hastily converted the space into parking, once it was announced the president was coming to attend the Opening Day game. Lastly, they built a paved helipad 50 yards beyond the left field fence and bleachers, adjacent to a patch of wild feed corn.

Mr. Donnerson stood in the middle of the gravel parking lot, did a 360-degree turn, looked it all over, and smiled widely. "This is all very, very good." He turned to look at Army Corps of Engineers Lieutenant Guillen and shook his hand.

At the far end of the parking lot, Secret Service agents, along with McHenry police, McHenry County sheriffs, and Illinois state troopers raised the gates to let the first cars in, which had parked there very early in the morning the day before.

The agents and the officers could only see a line of cars at the top of the bridge. McHenry City Police Officer Pardue radioed to his fellow officers stationed on the other side of the bridge. "Hey, guys, what are you seeing over there?"

"Buddy, we can't see the end of the line of vehicles. It looks to stretch all the way past Rt. 31 and the firehouse. Standby, while we patch in the live cam from the drone. We just got the bird aloft."

Officer Pardue looked down at his comm screen on his left wrist, and his jaw gaped wide open as the picture came into focus. He turned to the others and smiled. "Looks like this is going to be a full house. They're coming from every corner of the city!"

Air Force One touched down at King Air Force Base in Rockford and rolled to a halt on the tarmac. A hundred yards away was the Marine One Helo-X, capable of holding one hundred passengers and crew. The president's aides deplaned first. After just a few moments, out came the president, the first lady, and their son, Dwight. They were whisked away to Marine One and, within minutes, had lifted off for the short flight over to McHenry.

Back in McHenry, the Secret Service had received word that the president, first family, and entourage were en route aboard Marine One. Overhead, unmanned Secret Service Sentry Drones hovered a safe distance from the concrete helipad.

The Scott family, Mayor Vic Meyer, and a host of other elected officials and dignitaries all waited patiently. Within a few minutes, they heard the telltale sound of a large helo approaching from the west.

Joe looked up at his parents. "Is that the president?"

"Sure sounds like it, son," Mary responded. "Several years ago, I was at an event and saw Marine One come in. Very distinct sound. This sure sounds like it."

A Secret Service agent very near to the Scott's overheard the exchange between mother and son. She leaned over to Joe and whispered, "The president will be here within a minute or two."

Joe just smiled.

Sure enough, 90 seconds later, the enormous bird appeared from the west and came to a halt three hundred feet above the helipad. After just a moment or two, Marine One slowly descended and touched down dead center on the pad. The pilot shut down the engines and rotors.

Once the rotors had come to a full stop, the door opened, and they lowered the ladder to the pad. A moment later, many aides and press staff disembarked. Heading past the receiving line, they stopped, turned, and awaited the president.

At the first sight of the president in the doorway of Marine One, the cue was given, and the McHenry High School Band struck up the familiar "Hail to the Chief."

The president was all smiles and waved at the exuberant, bi-partisan crowd awaiting them down below.

The first lady and Dwight appeared in the doorway, and the crowd erupted even louder. After some more waving from them, the president and first lady disembarked, with each holding a hand of Dwight all the way down to the helipad. The Secret Service detail had already taken up their positions around the large receiving line awaiting the presidential family.

With the three of them all on the ground, the president walked the receiving line and began shaking hands and exchanging pleasantries. First in line was Mayor Vic Meyer, along with his wife Samantha. As president of the McHenry Garden Club, Samantha presented the first lady with a gigantic bouquet of red roses. The first lady, dressed beautifully for the occasion in a pale pink sundress and matching hat, seemed genuinely touched by the gesture.

Next in line were Governor Beckert, Senators Abreu and Baines, Congresswoman Barton, and the rest of the dignitaries. The Scott family was last in line. As the presidential family made their way down the line, Dwight stood close by his mom and had a Secret Service agent right behind him.

The president, first lady, and their son finally reached the end of the line and warmly embraced all the members of the Scott family, including Grandpa Moses. The president leaned down toward Joe. "Joe Scott, we are so excited and honored to be here. We've been looking forward to this all week. I'd like to introduce you again to our son, Dwight Kennedy. I can't thank you enough for extending to him the opportunity to play in today's game. He's so excited to be here today."

Joe blushed and, for just a brief moment, was again at a loss for words in the presence of the president of the United States of America. Regaining his composure, he responded, "Thank you Mr. President for coming out here today. I promise to take good care of your son."

The seriousness in Joe's tone touched the Secret Service agent assigned to Dwight. She rarely broke composure in a line, but she could not help herself. She looked Joe squarely in the eyes and mouthed the words, "Thank you," and smiled at him.

Mrs. Kennedy also thanked Joe for his reassuring words and hugged her oldest son, before he and Joe walked away to prepare for the game. Dwight's Secret Service detail was right behind them — and in front of them.

Sam and Mary were then ushered away for their pre-game interview with Frank and Laura in the press booth.

As Joe walked away with the son of the president and first lady, he took it all in stride.

Dwight seemed to warm up to him right away. "So, Joe, where am I playing today?"

Joe knew that question would be asked. "Well, I'm not exactly sure. How'd you do practicing catch?"

"Actually, pretty good. I practiced a lot catching grounders, pop-ups, and fly balls."

"Really? Wow, that's great! Who helped you?"

"My dad or my Secret Service agent, especially last week. A lot of times, though, I threw a tennis ball against a wall. I got real good at it, Joe. Honest!"

Having seen his other friends learn the game in gradual form, Joe knew the best and safest place for the president's son. "Awesome, good job! How about right field today?"

"That would be cool! I'm ready to play! Thanks, Joe!"

"Maybe later in the game, I'll switch you over to second base. It's really cool you're here."

"You're not just saying that because my dad is president, are you?"

"No. Well, that's a bonus, but what I meant is that you're the first kid from a different part of the country to play this game again in over a hundred years. Think about that. So far, it's just been me, my brother, Austin, my buddy, Ted, and the rest of my friends here in McHenry. I was hoping you could learn the game too, and bring it back to your friends in Washington. Maybe you can help get the game going again back home."

"Hey, I never thought of it that way. That is cool! But we don't have any of the equipment. I was using an oven mitt and a tennis ball to practice!"

"Well, we'll figure something out."

It was sixty seconds to airtime, and Frank was all set. He had copious amounts of notes written down on index cards on the table next to his mic and had watched that old DVD again twice more the day before. He figured he'd watched at least 15 old games by that point.

His earpiece chimed, and Frank heard the producer announce, "Live in five, four, three, two, one."

"Good afternoon, America, from McHenry, Illinois. This is Frank Crede, along with Laura Tubman, your broadcast team today for this nationally telecast, historic event. The first baseball game telecast live in the world in over one hundred years.

"There's an overflow crowd here today with over 7,500 hundred fans here to watch this historic baseball game. That's right, a baseball game. For those of you that missed our pre-game interview with Sam and Mary Scott, most of our viewers have no doubt read the fascinating stories about the tale of their young son, Joe Scott, rediscovering this lost game called baseball and bringing it back to life, here locally in McHenry, Illinois. Then, with the help of Laura Tubman here, a demonstration game on Good Morning USA reintroduced the game to the nation at large. Laura, great to have you here today. Tell us how many innings that demonstration game lasted."

"Thanks, Frank. So happy to be here today for this historic occasion. The demonstration game only lasted a single inning. My daughter watched it that day and instantly fell in love with it. When she heard they paired me up with you for today's telecast, she was emphatic about coming here to take in today's game."

"Well, Laura, a similar story unfolded in the Crede household as well. My sons felt the same way after watching the demo game. Funny you should mention your daughter insisting on being here today. That's exactly what my two sons insisted on too. So, they're both here in the stands today as well.

"For fans needing a primer on the game, go to our website and download the baseball primer file. It's linked clearly in the description heralding today's telecast.

"Of course, adding to the pre-game buzz is the participation of Dwight Kennedy on the field today, with his parents, President and Mrs. Kennedy, in attendance as well.

"Marine One carrying President Kennedy and the first family arrived approximately twenty minutes ago. Dwight was whisked away by Joe Scott, with a Secret Service detail in tow, to have Dwight suit up in preparation to play at this historic event. The president will give remarks before throwing out a ceremonial ball—"

Laura politely interjected. "First pitch, Frank, they called it the first pitch."

"Thank you, Laura. The first pitch to be tossed out by an American president in over one hundred years.

"It looks like the local dignitaries are done addressing the crowd. Let's listen in as the announcer introduces Pastor Graham Black for the invocation."

Pastor Black was the senior pastor of the largest non-denominational church in town. When Mayor Vic Meyer had invited him to give the invocation that day, Pastor Black had insisted that the senior pastors and priests of every church in town be standing next to him, as a sign of unity. The mayor loved the idea, and so, with clergy from 15 churches of all denominations standing next to him, Pastor Black turned to them and smiled, then looked forward toward the mic and bowed his head.

Without prompting, the crowd all hushed, and Pastor Black said a prayer of hope and thankfulness for the continued peace across the country and requested protection for those who had gathered to watch and play in the historic game.

When he had finished, the crowd said, "Amen," and remained on their feet as the president walked out onto the infield, toward the podium. There was loud applause. Then the crowd quieted down as the president stood at the back of the podium, shaking hands with Pastor Black, the other clergy, and assembled dignitaries.

Then the announcer spoke. "Ladies and gentlemen, the president of the United States of America."

The crowd immediately erupted into a tremendous roar, followed by sustained applause for almost a full minute. The high school band played an almost flawless rendition of "Hail to the Chief" again. The president made repeated gestures of thanks to the crowds along both foul lines and turned around to repeat the gesture to the fans in the outfield seats.

With the crowd finally settled down, the president approached the mic. "Thank you very much, Pastor Black, members of the clergy, Mayor Vic Meyer, Governor Beckert, Senators Abreu and Baines, Congresswoman Barton, members of the press, my fellow Americans, and a special thanks to Joe Scott and the entire Scott family.

"Fellow Americans. Five score and seven years ago, the unaltered trajectory of our nation, after decades of division and animosity, met its awful date with destiny, the Second American Civil War. Although no one of that era prayed for it, all paid dearly for it with the staggering loss of lives and culture and of the very fabric of our nation torn asunder.

"It is a scripture verse, cited by Abraham Lincoln over three hundred years ago, in 1858, just before the First Civil War, that best describes the times prior to its second occurrence on our soil. 'A house divided against itself shall not stand.' Divided again we became, and divided again we fell. Only, this second occurrence of civil war was far costlier than the first.

"It has been clear for decades, since that second occurrence on our soil, that the trajectory of our nation prior to that time was, indeed, alterable, and that the war was avoidable. Sadly, that trajectory remained unaltered, and the Second Civil War came in the 60th year of the 21st century.

"Unlike the First Civil War, which, in the era of the 1860s, largely spared civilians, this Second Civil War and its aftermath led to the loss of 90% of our population. In the ensuing years, it has taken America, and indeed, the world, a long time to recover. But recover we have, by the grace of God.

"While the pre-war generations had become soft and co-dependent, the generations after the war went through, not only the crucible of civil war, but also the protracted fight for survival afterwards, where many more millions of lives were lost from famine and pestilence.

As a result, the post-war generation of survivors developed an ingrained resiliency and patriotism, along with a healthy dose of actually living the Golden Rule. This change played a major role in helping us build back and recover as a united nation.

"And so, we are gathered here today, not to dedicate another field to the dead, but rather to the living.

"This baseball field is the very first constructed in well over one hundred years. The story of the rebirth of a game lost long ago, in a time in our nation's history long since passed, is, for many of us, now well known, and it is the reason we here are assembled today.

"We owe a debt of gratitude to so many, but especially to young Joe Scott and his family. In particular, Joe Scott's sense of exploration and inquisitiveness. Joe Scott played a huge role in uncovering, relearning, and reintroducing this game of baseball back to the community here in McHenry and to the rest of the nation and beyond.

"Though I am a man of the Christian faith, I make no profession of being a prophet. However, I have seen God's providential hand in the healing and restoration of our nation. My family and I have basked in the renewed light of liberty for all people. I have seen love and community spirit abound afresh in my lifetime. I have seen justice for all people become the norm, and I have seen an abiding peace continue and strengthen throughout the land.

"Our nation was once steamrolled, almost into oblivion, but here we are still — standing, rebuilding, thriving, even. Those cultural things that were lost so long ago have been, at times, elusive and difficult to recover. But now, we have this back. Baseball is back.

"Today marks another milestone in the cultural restoration of our nation in that, at one time long passed, baseball was once called America's pastime. I am also told they regarded it as being as American as apple pie.

"So, as this game is restored back into America's lexicon and lifeblood, let us here today highly resolve that those who died here on this battlefield so long ago also shall not have died in vain. That, by God's grace, they might be offered a peek out of Heaven's windows to gaze down upon us and again see Americans at peace and rest with one another.

"That they would also see us enjoying this game that some of them, in their younger years, must have enjoyed before that awful war came. A war that extracted from them their last full measure of devotion for the cause of liberty. Again, I am no prophet, but I predict that baseball will again become as American as apple pie and, perhaps, will again become America's pastime.

"As the president of the United States, and by the consent of the local government and, especially, the citizens of McHenry, I hereby declare that this brand-new baseball field will be named Liberty Field. Let the game begin!"

Thunderous applause erupted again, and chants of U-S-A reverberated throughout the stands. Overhead, the president's surprise arrived on cue, as a squadron of ten F-59 fighter drones roared by at high speed, in precise formation, to the sheer delight of the crowd. The president stepped away and approached the pitcher's mound. Joe Scott handed him a brand-new baseball. Teddy Banks was positioned behind home plate and set up to catch the first pitch.

Meanwhile, in the booth, Frank spoke once again. "Would you listen to this crowd, Laura!"

"Frank, I've got goosebumps. Surely that has to be the president's best speech to date! The president steps over to the mound now for some photos before his ceremonial first pitch."

"I have to agree with your comments on the president's speech," Frank said. "I had goosebumps listening to it as well. Okay, the president is almost ready."

"Our White House correspondent tells me that, for the last few weeks, the president has thoroughly enjoyed his sessions of catch with his son, Dwight, whenever he could steal away some time," Laura reported. "Unbeknownst to Dwight, the president had also snuck a peek or two as Dwight used an exterior wall of the White House to hone his catching and throwing skills, using a tennis ball."

"Well, Laura, a big moment for the president is coming up right now."

Out on the mound, the president readied himself. *"I'd better not screw this up,"* he thought to himself. *"Especially on a national telecast."* The president took a deep breath and remembered his son's instructions to relax and not think too hard. Look at the target and throw the ball.

He zeroed in on the catcher's mitt being held up by Ted Lee Banks. He took aim and threw the ball fairly hard. The president watched, in sheer delight, as his pitch sailed in straight toward Ted's outstretched mitt. Ted didn't even have to move. Perfect pitch! The crowd roared with delight. Ted caught the pitch and ran forward, toward the president, to hand him the keepsake ball. They all posed for a photo, after which, the Secret Service escorted the president to his reserved seats along the third baseline.

After he took his seat, Anne Kennedy gave her husband an enormous hug, kissed him, and then said, "Nice job with the pre-game!"

The president smiled widely, then they all stood, hearing the announcer introduce the national anthem.

CHAPTER NINETEEN

Opening Day Part 2: Play Ball!

The umpires for the day's game had been hand-selected by Mr. Donnerson. They had years of experience umpiring multiple sports, but it was their particular experience umpiring cricket games that caught the attention of Mr. Donnerson during his search for a qualified crew.

Although nowhere near as popular as lacrosse and soccer, cricket's old ties to baseball had caught Mr. Donnerson's attention while doing his research. Among the cache of videos from the Dyersville hoard were videos on umpiring baseball. Without those, it would have been almost impossible to prepare for the game. The umpires had studied hard and were ready. They stood at home plate, awaiting the two coaches. Umpiring home plate would be Bill Evans, first base would be Ned Chylak, at second base was Dave Eddings, and August Donatelli was the umpire at third base.

Joe had realized that Ted's acquisition of baseball knowledge was now equal to his own. He had thought about it long and hard, and his mind was made up. To help propagate knowledge of the game to others, Joe and Ted had agreed, earlier the week, that it would be best to move forward with each of them managing separate teams in the new fledgling McHenry Youth Baseball League, organized by Mr. Donnerson.

For the inaugural year of this new league, they were able to recruit enough kids for seven teams.

For the Opening Day game, Joe's team, the White Stockings, consisted of Austin Scott, Billy Cross, Jim Gander, Jeff Gander, Dan Simpson, Norm Gould, Ken Orbison, and Dwight Kennedy.

Ted's team, the Bear Cubs, included Mark Samuelson, Steve Dearing, John Gander, Roy Hobson, Jim Hart, Doug Jeffries, Bill Adams, and Tony Fisk.

Back up in the booth, Frank Crede and Laura Tubman were seated and eager to get the historic game underway. The commercial break had ended, and the cue countdown started. "Five - four - three - two - one," and the "On-Air" light flashed on.

"Good afternoon, everybody. Frank Crede here with my special guest and broadcast partner for today's game, Laura Tubman. We are moments away from the start of this historic and exciting moment in American history. Laura, I have to believe that if there is anyone here that has not had goosebumps at least once today, there must be something wrong with them. Your thoughts?"

"My sentiments exactly, Frank. I thought the pre-game ceremony was fantastic, and of course, highlighted by President Kennedy's speech, as well as his on-target first pitch. What a great day for the president, the first family, and the nation."

"Indeed, Laura, and hopefully their son, Dwight, will have a great day as well. We have just been given the lineups for both teams, so here we go. Ted Lee Banks is managing the Bear Cubs. The lineup is:

"Batting first and playing catcher, Bill Adams.

"Batting second and playing shortstop, Roy Hobson.

"Batting third and playing third base, Steve Dearing.

"Batting fourth and playing first base, John Gander.

"Batting fifth and the starting pitcher, Ted Lee Banks.

"Batting sixth and playing left field, Mark Samuelson.

"Batting seventh and playing center field, Jim Hart.

"Batting eighth and playing second base, Doug Jeffries.

"Batting ninth and playing right field, Tony Fisk.

"The base coaches will be Jerry Banks at third and Tom Banks at first. They are brothers of Ted Lee Banks. They graciously agreed to coach today, rather than take up playing time from the others, unless there is an injury.

"For Joe Scott's team, the White Stockings's line-up:

"Batting first and playing center field, Austin Scott.

"Batting second and playing left field, Billy Cross.

"Batting third and the starting pitcher, Joe Scott.

"Batting fourth and playing third base, Jim Gander.

"Batting fifth and playing shortstop, Jeff Gander.

"Batting sixth and playing second base, Dan Simpson.

"Batting seventh and playing catcher, Norm Gould.

"Batting eighth and playing first base, Ken Orbison.

"And finally, batting ninth and playing right field, the president and Mrs. Kennedy's eldest son, Dwight Kennedy.

"The base coaches will be Eduardo Chavez Jr. and his brother, Louis. Eduardo Jr. was to have played today, but he was recently injured playing lacrosse."

First Inning

"The dimensions of this brand-new baseball field are as follows: 210 ft. from home plate to the yellow foul poles down the third base and first baselines. Straight-away center field is 240 ft.," Frank informed the spectators. "We're told this was a typical distance for this age of players. Laura, quite a story behind the building of this brand-new field for these kids."

"Indeed, Frank. I spoke with Earl Donnerson before the game. He, as we all know, was hugely instrumental in getting this project going and driving it to completion. He's a humble man, though, and was quick to deflect praise outward to all the volunteers who made this field possible."

"Well, the results are quite stunning," Frank said. "Alright, it looks like we're ready to go here in McHenry. Joe Scott has finished his warm-up pitches, as the leadoff batter, Bill Adams, steps up to the plate.

"Bill looks down to catcher Norm Gould and has a friendly word and then steps into the neatly chalked batter's box. Joe steps up to the mound and places his feet onto the pitching rubber and winds up and here is pitch number one! A strike down the middle of the plate. America, that was a hundred years in the making! The crowd, still standing, gives a thunderous round of applause and, as you can see, are now taking their seats to settle in for what we expect to be an exciting eight-inning game today.

"Here comes the second pitch offered by Joe Scott. Adams swings and fouls it off for strike two. Oops, Joe Scott's shoe went flying off after the pitch. Looks like a broken shoelace is the cause, and suddenly we have a shoeless Joe. Joe retrieves his shoe and motions to the dugout as he steps off the mound.

"While we wait, we note that the start of today's historic game will be officially logged as 1:20 this afternoon. Current weather conditions here in beautiful McHenry are a very pleasant 77 degrees, with a gentle breeze blowing out of the southwest, to straight-away centerfield, at five miles per hour. Humidity is low today at 33 percent. The sky is mostly sunny, with sporadic puffy white clouds against a clear blue sky. The sight of the rich green grass, blue sky, and bright, puffy white clouds is a beautiful and calming sight today. Laura, it's a beautiful day for a ballgame."

"Absolutely, Frank. A stunning day here in McHenry. When I left Boston after the show yesterday, it was raining and a little chilly for this time of year."

"Alright, shoelace replaced, and shoeless Joe is no more," Frank announced. "Joe Scott settles back in and asks for just one warm-up pitch, which home plate umpire Bill Evans grants. Joe takes that warm-up pitch and motions for catcher Norm Gould to come out to the mound."

⚾ ⚾ ⚾

"What's up, bro?" Norm asked.

Joe placed his mitt over his mouth. "Remember that game last week when I pitched to Bill Adams? Same sequence of pitches. That time, I got him out on a fastball. I think he'll expect that again. Don't you?

Gould looked at Joe and brought his mitt up too. "Try that slow curveball you've been working on. Ya' fooled me with it a few games ago."

"Ok, let's do it," Joe replied. He put his mitt down and returned to the rubber, while Norm headed back to get in position behind home plate.

⚾ ⚾ ⚾

Back in the booth, Frank resumed his play-by-play. "Adams steps back into the box and settles in, once again, for the pitch. Joe Scott takes the signal from catcher Norm Gould and readies. The windup and the pitch. Strike three! Adams misses by a mile and strikes out as the first batter of the game. Laura, that

215

appeared to be a curveball that broke down and away out of the strike zone.”

“I agree, Frank. Adams simply had zero chances of hitting that pitch.”

⚾ ⚾ ⚾

Mary, Sam, the girls, and Grandpa Moses all jumped out of their seats and cheered after Joe's first strikeout of the game. Sam beamed with pride as all the months his sons spent studying and learning the game bore fruit on a national stage.

⚾ ⚾ ⚾

Back in the booth, Laura said, “Frank, I spoke with Joe before the game and asked what his pitching plan was for today. His answer was ‘just throw strikes and try to keep the hitter off balance.’ He succeeded brilliantly there, getting Bill Adams to go fishing for a pitch that broke out of the strike zone. Folks, out number one of this history-making game is in the books.”

“Indeed. There's a slight delay on the field, as someone walks out toward the mound, where Joe tosses the ball to them. Wait a second. I've just been told that a member of the Smithsonian has just been given the baseball for posterity.”

“As well it should be, Frank. By the way, Bill Adams was hitting the ball pretty hard during batting practice. I was surprised he didn't get a hit his first at-bat.”

“Yes, in batting practice, I watched as Adams crushed a ball to right-center. Obviously, plenty of opportunities for Adams coming up later in this game. Stay tuned.

“Well, everybody, here we go again as the number two batter, shortstop Roy Hobson, steps up and quickly settles in. Joe Scott winds up and delivers. There's a swing and a line drive into the gap between the left and center fielders. Roy Hobson rounds first, while left fielder Billy Cross and center fielder Austin Scott both try to catch up to the ball. Cross catches up to the ball first and fires it to the cutoff man, shortstop Jeff Gander, who quickly relays it to second baseman Dan Simpson. Hobson puts on the brakes and barely makes it back to first base before the relay throw from Simpson to first baseman Ken Orbison. Orbison fakes a tag on Hobson, and the two of them exchange a chuckle. And that, ladies and gentlemen, is the very first hit of the day, here in the first inning of this historic game. A single by Roy Hobson. Fittingly, the crowd gives Hobson a nice round of applause."

"That first hit, Frank, was also a hundred years in the making."

The rest of the Hobson family, all eight of them, were seated with the other players' family members in the special reserved seating area behind the president and Mrs. Kennedy. Martha Hobson could not help but shed a tear of joy at her son's accomplishment. As she looked up at her husband, Rajesh, she saw tears in his eyes too, as all their kids jumped up and down, wildly screaming.

Up in the press box, Mike Drucker knew magic when he saw it. Only two batters into the first game, magic had occurred in his hometown, and the game was just getting started. With a huge grin on his face, he sent a text message to his boss, Khalil, seated down below with his family. *Boss, I've got the lead story. Page one, or I retire! What say ye?"*

He watched his boss look down and read the message and

laugh. Khalil looked up at Mike in the press box and gave a thumbs-up, before turning back toward the field to continue applauding the first hit.

Mike looked left and right at all the reporters assigned to the game. All of them staring down at the field with a look of anticipation. Mike immediately remembered the dream he'd had a few months back. All he could do was smile and laugh, while the goosebumps rose up and down his arms.

"Frank, that was a nice clean hit by Hobson to start the offense off here in the first inning of play. You have to believe, by the crowd's reaction, that they want to see a generous amount of offense here today, and I expect both teams are intent on delivering."

"Laura, in doing my homework on the game, it seems that, historically, some baseball games had what was called a pitcher's duel, when two outstanding pitchers were doing well in a game and getting outs. Typically, those were low-scoring games. Then there were plenty of other games with lots of runs. Time will tell what plays out here today, but I agree. I think the crowd wants to see plenty of action on the base paths.

"Next up is the number three batter, third baseman Steve Dearing. Dearing was also hitting great in batting practice today. Catcher Norm Gould yells out to the mound. What do you suppose that's all about, Laura?"

"Well, I would guess making sure Joe stays calm and focused on throwing strikes after that first hit. After all, this is a national telecast, and I would expect some of these kids might be a little nervous."

"Excellent analysis, Laura. Alright, here's the next pitch, and Dearing swings and misses for strike one. Hobson took a leadoff at first base that looked to be a little risky, but Joe Scott stared him down long enough that Hobson took a half step closer to first base to keep him honest.

"Here's the next pitch. Ball one. Hobson took another decent leadoff, before quickly returning to first base after the pitch.

"Frank, as I understand it, stealing a base, where the runner runs to the next base as the pitcher begins their pitching motion to home plate, had become a lost art in baseball's waning days. Looks like these kids intend to bring it back.

"The complete package, Laura, the complete package. These kids have done their homework and are dead set on not inventing new rules or ignoring old ones. Speaking of which, there goes Hobson for second on Joe Scott's next pitch. Norm Gould jumps up and fires the ball down to second base, where Dan Simpson receives a perfect throw and tags Hobson. Second base umpire Dave Eddings is in perfect view and raises both hands outward — 'safe' is the call!

"Wow, Frank, excellent defensive play, and the crowd again goes wild. Even though Hobson beat the throw, it was sheer artistry watching the play unfold. I'm loving this!

"I concur, Laura, and this is still the first half of the first inning! Alright, Dearing steps back into the batter's box with a count of one ball and two strikes. And the pitch. Dearing hits a sharp ground ball right up the middle. Joe Scott reached for that ball, but it was just past his outstretched mitt. Austin Scott runs straight in quickly to field the ball and tosses it in to second baseman Dan Simpson, who fires the ball home to catcher Norm Gould. Hobson slipped at third base, had trouble getting back on his feet, and then got back to third base. Dearing, seeing an opportunity, raced to second base standing up. Catcher Norm Gould wisely held onto the ball and now signals for a timeout, with runners at third and second and only one out.

"Frank, another nice hit to keep this inning going. I saw

Dearing raise his grip a little higher on the bat to try to poke the ball through. I think the baseball term is to choke up on the bat."

"Exactly, Laura. Alright, the next batter is the first baseman, John Gander. Looks like he will not be allowed to hit, as catcher Gould signals for an intentional walk. For our viewers, an intentional walk is where, instead of pitching to the batter, the defensive team concedes the at-bat, and the batter is automatically awarded first base. This is done to try to force a double-play out, but it can also backfire.

"The next batter is pitcher Ted Lee Banks, and the crowd is on their feet."

"Special moment here, Frank. Two very close friends facing each other on a national telecast. You can't script drama like this!"

"Indeed. Joe Scott tips his hat at his friend, Ted, and the crowd takes notice and applauds again. Catcher Norm Gould yells something out to the mound again. What's he saying now, Laura?"

"Frank, my guess is he is telling Joe to stay calm and coax a pop-up into the infield, or maybe a ground ball, and hopefully get a double-play. A double-play is when the fielders get two outs on the field during the same at-bat."

"Thanks, Laura, for another quick lesson for our fans. Gould settles back into position. Banks steps into the box and readies for the pitch. Joe Scott stares down the catcher's signal and nods his head in agreement and delivers the pitch. Inside and low for ball one."

"Yeah, Ted was sizing up this moment and determined not to swing at that first pitch, Frank."

"The next pitch comes in, and Ted swings and fouls it off. Strike one."

"Frank, that was a dangerous pitch for Joe Scott to throw. That was right down the middle of the plate."

"Laura, I'm going to guess the next pitch will be inside and low again. Here it is. Ball two. That was inside, but higher up in the strike zone. And the count now stands at two balls and one strike."

"Frank, Joe Scott is in a tough position now. He can't afford to get to three and one on the count. He has to throw a strike here, but to what part of the zone?"

"I would think down and in. Here is the pitch. Ted connects! A long fly ball into the gap in right-center field. One run is in, while Austin Scott and Dwight Kennedy go running after the ball that rolls to the fence. Two runs are in! Look at Kennedy go! He catches up to the ball and throws a near-perfect strike to shortstop Jeff Gander, covering second base, while John Gander also crosses the plate with the third run! The roar of the crowd is deafening, as Ted Lee Banks is at second base with a three-run stand-up double!"

⚾ ⚾ ⚾

The Banks family was delirious as they took it all in. Ted's mom, Samantha, made eye contact with Mary Scott. They were both laughing and screaming.

The game progressed, and Joe Scott got Mark Samuelson and Jim Hart to strike out, ending the top half of the first inning.

In the dugout, Joe looked out and waved at his family sitting two rows behind the president and first lady. He yelled, "Grandpa!" to get Moses's attention. Grandpa looked over at Joe, smiled, and gave a thumbs up.

Norm Gould walked up to Joe and said, "Nice pitching those last two outs!"

"Thanks, man! Now let's get some runs!"

In the bottom of the first, Austin Scott and Billy Cross both hit long fly balls for outs. Joe Scott reached first base on a single, and Jim Gander walked. Jeff Gander came up and struck out.

So, at the end of the first inning, the score was Bear Cubs - 3, White Stockings - 0.

Second Inning

In the top half of the second inning, Doug Jeffries singled, followed by Tony Fisk, who did the same. Bill Adams was up again, with the count at three balls and one strike.

"Bill Adams is doing a good job of working the count here," Frank announced. "Here's the pitch. He hits a sharp ground ball up the middle. Jeffries scores, but Fisk is held up at third base by third base coach Jerry Banks."

The next two batters, Roy Hobson and Steve Dearing, flied out. With two outs, John Gander stepped up to the plate.

"John Gander walked in the first inning," Frank reminded the viewers. "Let's see what he does this time. Here's the pitch! Gander hits a long fly ball to deep right-center field. Right fielder Dwight Kennedy took off as soon as the ball was hit. It's gonna be close! He dives for the ball and catches it! Dwight Kennedy makes a spectacular catch of John Gander's well-hit ball to right-center field. The president and Mrs. Kennedy are jumping up and down with elation! The side is retired, and the score is Bear Cubs - 4, White Stockings - 0, as we head into the bottom half of the second inning."

"Frank, that was a thing of beauty to watch!" Laura said. "Dwight got a great jump on that ball as soon as Gander made contact."

In the bottom half of the second, Joe's team, the White Stockings, were again scoreless, with Dan Simpson and Norm Gould striking out, and Ken Orbison grounding out.

And so, going into the third inning, the Bear Cubs had brought their score up to four, while the White Stockings were still at zero.

Third Inning

The Bear Cubs were batting in the top half of the third inning, with one out, one runner on base, and Jim Hart up to bat.

"Hart struck out in the first inning on a full count. He comes up to bat, with Mark Samuelson standing at first base after a one-out single. Scott is ready for pitch number one to Hart. Here it is. Hart drills a line drive down the third-base line! It's rolling all the way to the wall. Samuelson reaches second and is headed for third. Left fielder Billy Cross catches up to the ball and fires it to third baseman Jim Gander. Samuelson slides under the tag. Third base umpire August Donatelli signals 'safe'! Hart is at second base with a stand-up double."

The next two batters, Doug Jeffries and Tony Fisk, grounded out to retire the side.

After a short commercial break, Dwight Kennedy was the leadoff batter for the bottom half of the third inning.

Before Dwight left the on-deck area, Joe walked up to him. "Dwight, when you get up there to bat, block out all the noise. Remember that. It's important. It's just you and the pitcher. Take a deep breath and relax. Have fun up there. Make sure to keep an eye on the ball, from the pitcher's hand all the way to the bat. Ready?"

Dwight looked Joe square in the eyes. "Yep."

⚾ ⚾ ⚾

The president and Mrs. Kennedy were both nervous as their son made his way onto the field. The president had a quiet habit of fidgeting with his wedding ring when he got nervous. When the first lady saw him doing that, she put her hand on his, stared at him, and smiled. It always had a calming effect on him.

⚾ ⚾ ⚾

Back in the booth, Frank got the cue. "And welcome back, everybody, from our commercial break. We begin the bottom half of the third inning with the much-ballyhooed at-bat of Dwight Kennedy, first son of the first family. Laura, I can only imagine what is going through the minds of the president and Mrs. Kennedy at this very moment."

"I'm certain they're no different from any other parent watching their child about to enter the spotlight. A combination of pride, hope, and nerves, I expect," Laura said.

"Indeed, as I know I would be feeling," Frank agreed. "Well, here we go. Banks finishes his warm-up pitches, and Dwight Kennedy slowly walks up to the plate and takes his place in the batter's box as a left-handed batter. Ted walks off the back of the mound, rubs the ball several times, and scans the positions of all his fielders behind him. Satisfied, he returns to the top of the mound and takes his position astride the pitching rubber.

"Kennedy digs his left foot into the dirt and readies himself. Banks zeros in on the call from catcher Bill Adams. Ted nods with approval. Here's the windup and the pitch. Kennedy swings late but makes hard contact. The ball is rocketing out towards left field and curving … curving … fair ball! Dwight Kennedy crushes a ball that winds up landing just short of the fence down the third baseline! Kennedy is headed for second base! The ball takes a funny bounce off the foul pole and careens away from left fielder Mark Samuelson. Kennedy rounds second and is headed for third. Samuelson catches up to the ball, after the weird bounce off the fence, and fires a strike to third baseman Steve Dearing, while Kennedy slides in under the tag. 'Safe' is the call from Donatelli! Dwight Kennedy has hit a lead-off triple in the bottom of the third inning of play here in McHenry! Would you listen to this crowd!"

"Oh my gosh, Frank, the president is jumping up and down with excitement, along with Mrs. Kennedy. There's a photo for the ages!"

"Pandemonium here, as Dwight Kennedy leads off the bottom half of the third inning with a triple! By golly, I'm falling in love with this game fast!"

The inning continued. Austin Scott hit a double and drove in Kennedy. Billy Cross lined out hard to second baseman Doug Jeffries, who doubled up Austin at second base, in an unassisted double-play. Joe Scott struck out to end the inning.

As Joe walked back to the dugout, he made eye contact with Grandpa. No words were exchanged, but Joe could feel his grandpa encouraging him that the best was yet to come.

At the end of the third inning, the Bear Cubs were still up at four, while the White Stockings stood at one.

"My goodness, Laura! I daresay half this crowd may already be hoarse from all the cheering that has gone on here so far. Come to think of it, I'm not detecting the crowd rooting for one team over the other. Everyone here is just cheering everything good and exciting that happens here today."

"You're right, Frank. That's exactly what's happening here. This is sheer magic to be here in person and feel the electricity in this ballpark!"

"Wow. What's next? Well, while we wait for the first batter of the fourth inning, we have our roving reporter, John Staley, with another fan-in-the-stands interview. Johnny, who do you have for us now?"

"Thanks, Frank!" John said. "I'm with Tom and Karen Paulsen, of Wonder Lake, Illinois. Folks, how are you liking the game so far?"

"Oh, I think this is fabulous," Karen Paulsen answered. "When my husband said we were going to go see a baseball game, I wasn't all that excited, to be honest. But, now that we're here, it's been a fabulous time, and an exciting game to watch."

"Your thoughts, Tom?" John asked.

"I'm hooked! Great time today. Can't wait for the next opportunity to see a game."

"Back to you Frank!"

"Alright, John, great feedback from some new fans. We're looking forward to your next report."

Back in the control room in Boston, the rating meter was pegged in record territory. The switchboard lit up as national companies called to inquire when the next televised game would be and when they could book their commercials.

Fourth Inning

Bill Adams and Roy Hobson struck out to start the fourth inning. Then Steve Dearing hit a ground-ball single, just beyond the outstretched mitt of Ken Orbison. With two outs and a man on base, John Gander was up to bat.

"John Gander walked in the first inning," Frank recounted. "Joe Scott has been conferring with catcher Norm Gould and the infielders out on the mound. Home plate umpire Bill Evans had taken about three steps toward the mound, when the confab broke up.

"Catcher Gould is now back behind the plate and giving the signal to Joe Scott. Scott shakes off the first sign and nods in approval for the next. He sets, and the pitch. There's a line drive to right-center field that quickly drops beyond Austin Scott. Steve Dearing is rounding third and headed for home. Austin Scott catches up and throws the ball into second base, where Jeff Gander puts a late tag on his brother, John, who arrived standing up with a double!"

The next batter, Ted Lee Banks, struck out for the third out. After taking one step back toward his dugout, Ted turned and yelled out to Joe, "That ain't happenin' again this game, buddy!"

In the bottom of the fourth inning, the White Stockings were looking to turn things around. Jim Gander started off with a double, and his brother, Jeff, followed with another double, scoring Jim. Dan Simpson hit a single, scoring Jeff. Then Norm Gould reached base with a single. Ken Orbison hit a double, scoring Simpson. But Dwight Kennedy and Austin Scott struck out, while Billy Cross hit a long fly ball out to Mark Samuelson to end the inning.

At the end of the fourth inning, the score stood at Bear Cubs - 5, White Stockings - 4.

Back in the press booth, Mike Drucker was typing copious amounts of notes for his lead story the next day. He had already received confirmation from his boss that they were going to print 25 percent more copies than normal and that many major papers across the nation had stopped their presses and were changing their lead stories to feature the game.

Fifth Inning

In the top of the fifth inning, the Bear Cubs scored two more runs, with doubles by Mark Samuelson and Jim Hart, followed by an RBI single by Doug Jeffries. The next three batters grounded out.

In the bottom of the fifth inning, Jeff Gander drew a two-out walk. Dan Simpson hit a double, but Jeff Gander was held up at third base. Norm Gould reached base on a walk. Then Ken Orbison hit a single, driving in Gander and Simpson. Kennedy grounded out to end the inning.

The Bear Cubs had seven runs, while the White Stockings trailed with six.

Mr. Donnerson's phone lit up with messages from people he knew, and many people he did not know, all asking about joining the new youth baseball league. He also got a message that massive crowds had gathered at the local sports pubs in and around McHenry, as word spread of the game. An enormous crowd, that could not get in for the day's game, was camped outside of the ballpark, watching the game on their comm devices. He was also seeing wire service reports of crowds gathering at sports pubs around the nation.

Sixth Inning

In the sixth inning, the Bear Cubs scored a run with an RBI single by Jim Hart, after Ted Lee Banks and Mark Samuelson each singled, with two outs. Jeffries walked, but was left stranded when Tony Fisk flied out to left.

In the bottom half of the sixth inning, Billy Cross was up to bat, with one out.

"Frank, Cross hit a long fly ball his last at-bat, in the fourth inning. He was also hitting well in batting practice today. Big opportunity for him here, with his team down by two runs."

"Yeah, Laura, I thought that fly-ball he hit was leaving the yard. Well, here we go. Banks settles in. He gets the signal. The pitch. Cross watches that one for strike one."

"Cross clearly waiting for a good pitch. That one was a strike, but low and on the inside part of the strike zone."

"Banks is ready again. The pitch. Strike two! Again, Cross made no attempt to hit that pitch. So, with no balls and two strikes, Cross needs to be ready for this next pitch."

"Wow, nerves of steel there, Frank!"

"You better believe it! Banks steps off the mound and rubs the ball. Removes his cap and wipes the sweat off. Cap on, ball in mitt, Banks returns to the top of the mound. He zeros in on the signal from catcher Bill Adams. Here's the pitch. There's a long drive to straight-away center field. Jim Hart is tracking the ball well … all the way to the wall … gone! Billy Cross has just hit a towering solo home run that cleared the center-field fence with plenty of room to spare!"

The next two batters were retired, and at the end of the sixth inning, the Bear Cubs had eight, to the White Stockings' seven.

Reggie Spalding was hoarse from yelling. He was dying to meet the Scott family at the end of the game. Between innings, he had been busy making calls to the CEOs of the nation's largest sporting goods stores, who all confirmed they were watching the telecast. They had all told him, "We're in."

Seventh Inning

The Bear Cubs went down in order, with Bill Adams striking out, Roy Hobson grounding out, and Steve Dearing popping up.

The White Stockings also went down in order, with Jeff Gander lining out hard, Dan Simpson flying out to left field, and Norm Gould hitting a fly ball to the warning track in right field.

Eighth Inning

"Joe Scott and all the infielders are conferencing on the mound. What a game, Laura, what a game we have witnessed here today, and it's not over yet. We have one out here in the top half of the eighth inning. There's a history behind the number of innings in a baseball game. Laura has more on this."

"Thanks, Frank. History shows game lengths were never measured in elapsed time, unlike most other sports, but in innings played. The baseball history that has been uncovered so far shows most youth baseball games had games that lasted five to nine innings, depending on the age bracket. Today's game is an eight-inning game, which is actually a longer game than kids this age played way back when. I asked Joe Scott about that, and he said he and his buddies had tried different game lengths and were quite happy playing eight-inning and, occasionally, even nine-inning games."

"Thanks, Laura. So here we go. The mound conference has ended, and all players are back in their positions. Ted Lee Banks is up to bat to face his good friend, Joe Scott, again. Ted has gone two for four today, with a double in the first inning and a single in the sixth inning."

"He is having a great day at the plate, for sure, Frank."

"Joe Scott into the wind-up, and the pitch. Ted connects again, and it's a long drive, way back … back … back. Hey, hey! Ted Lee Banks crushes the first pitch deep into the center-field bleachers. I can barely hear myself in my headset, as the crowd's noise is thunderous!"

"Frank, that was the highest and farthest hit ball we've seen today, no question."

"As Banks rounds third, his teammates are waiting for him just outside the first base dugout. He trots in with a gigantic smile on his face and promptly gets mobbed by his teammates! The crowd remains standing, as Mark Samuelson approaches the plate as the next batter.

"Looks like we're going to have a pitching change, as Joe Scott points to his brother, Austin, in center field, to come in and pitch to Mark Samuelson, with the score now 9 - 7, in favor of the Bear Cubs. Austin will, of course, be allowed some time to warm up, while Samuelson steps back away from the plate to wait and also study this new pitcher.

"Now, Laura, while we wait, let's talk about how Banks absolutely crushed that ball!"

"No doubt about it, Frank. I have to believe Banks stepped up to the plate thinking Joe Scott would offer up a fastball as his first pitch. He figured right, and promptly sent that ball out of the ballpark in a hurry."

"While we wait for Austin Scott to warm-up, let's go back down to John Staley with another fan-in-the-stands interview. John?"

"Thanks, Frank and Laura, deafening noise down here, for sure, after Banks's home run! Right now, I have with me Eddie Bennett, who got into the spirit of the occasion today! Eddie, nice uniform and ball cap you have on. You look like you're ready to take to the field and play ball right now! Say, where are you from and where'd you get that pinstripe uniform?"

"Well, um, I was born out on the East Coast. My father gave me the uniform, before I traveled to the game. He made it just for me. I really, really love it!"

"Say, your dad's pretty handy."

"Yeah, he can make anything."

"Well, that's very cool. Say, what do you think of the game so far?"

"It's just like I hoped it would be. You know … uh … oh, never mind."

"It's okay, finish your thought, young man."

"Well, I'm just so happy to see a baseball game. I can't wait to go back home and tell all my friends. They're gonna be so excited to hear the news, especially my pal George."

"Are they watching the telecast right now?"

"Ummm, not sure, there's no TV reception where they live."

"No reception? Well … ok … well, alright then, folks, Eddie Bennett. Enjoy the rest of the game, and your father must be very special indeed. Back to you, Frank and Laura."

As little Eddie Bennett walked away, he smiled and thought to himself, "*You have no idea, mister, no idea.*"

Laura picked up the conversation. "Thanks, John. Frank, when I spoke with Joe before the game, I asked him who his relief pitchers would be today, if he got into trouble. Without hesitation, he named his brother, Austin, as his first choice and said, beyond that, several of the guys were good pitchers in relief. In particular, he mentioned Billy Cross and Jim Gander. Joe said Cross can be a little on the wild side but has a wicked curveball. Jim Gander has a lights-out fastball and an off-speed pitch. Joe said that Austin has learned the craft of pitching well and has a fastball, curve, and off-speed pitch. He's also good at locating his pitches anywhere in the strike zone."

"Well, alright. So, Austin Scott finishes with his warm-up throws, and into the batter's box steps Mark Samuelson. Mark is three for four today, with a single in the third, a double to lead off the fifth, and a single in the sixth.

"Austin gets the signal from Gould. Austin pitches from the stretch, which is to say, no wind-up. Here's the pitch. Ball one, outside."

"Frank, smart move by Samuelson to sit on that first pitch and, hopefully, try to get into Austin's head."

"Samuelson stays in the box and remains ready. Austin Scott readies himself and gets the signal again from Gould. Here's the pitch. Ball two. Samuelson remains stoic and in the batter's box. Austin steps off the rubber to rub the ball and steps back on. He waits for the signal from catcher Norm Gould. Into the stretch he goes, and the pitch. Samuelson swings and misses. Strike one."

"Austin challenged him with a fastball right down the middle of the plate, but Samuelson could not get any wood on that one," Laura commented. "Excellent pitch choice by Austin there."

"I'd have to agree, Laura. He challenged him with that pitch. Austin Scott settles in and waits for the call from Gould. He nods his head and settles in for the next pitch, with the count at two balls and one strike. Here's the pitch. Mark Samuelson hits a screaming line drive down the third baseline. It keeps rising slightly, still going and fast, and just like that, clears the fence with about a foot to go! Home run for Mark Samuelson, and the game score is now 10 - 7, in favor of the Bear Cubs! Pandemonium erupts here again, in magical McHenry!"

"Wow, Ted hit the highest and farthest, but Mark hit that one the fastest. That ball rocketed out of here, Frank! Look at the scene in the dugout."

"Samuelson rounds third, with the second solo home run of the inning, and is mobbed, as well, outside the dugout! Banks walks over and bear-hugs Samuelson, while the rest of the team mobs both of them. How about that?!"

⚾ ⚾ ⚾

Although he was a little shaken by Mark's home run, Austin was able to get the next two batters out and get out of the top half of the eighth inning.

As Joe's team trotted in for what could be their last at-bat, everyone on the team patted Joe on the back.

Mary and Sam looked at each other. Sam had been keeping track, and they both knew there was a chance that Joe could bat in the bottom of the eighth, but he would be the fifth batter of the inning, so at least two batters would need to reach base.

Tabrika and her family were sitting right behind the Scott family. Tabrika leaned over and hugged Mary from behind. Mary turned and smiled and laughed. No words were needed.

Mary looked over at Grandpa Moses, who was sitting there calmly, with a big smile on his face.

"What's that smile for, Dad?"

"Oh, I got a feeling is all."

"I'm a nervous wreck, and you have a feeling? About what?"

"We'll all find out here soon enough, sweetie."

Mary turned and looked at Sam. Sam laughed and threw a peanut at her.

⚾ ⚾ ⚾

In the bottom of the eighth, Ken Orbison lined out hard to shortstop Roy Hobson for out number one. Dwight Kennedy reached base on a walk, and Austin Scott bunted for a single.

"And here is Billy Cross, who has gone one for four today, with a monster of a solo home run in the sixth inning. In looking at both lineups today, a nice note is that every player, on both teams, has had at least one hit, Laura."

"Frank, I'm so happy for these kids. It just makes this day all the more special."

"Indeed, indeed. So, Billy Cross steps into the batter's box. Ted Lee Banks settles in, gets the signal from Adams. Here's the pitch. He looks at strike one on a curveball. Cross stays in the box and readies. Banks steps off the mound, rubs the ball, and steps back on. He readies himself and waits for the sign. Here's the pitch. Cross swings and hits it foul into the stands behind first base. If Cross can reach base safely, Joe Scott will be up next."

"Cross just missed getting some good wood on that one, Frank."

"Nice souvenir for some young gal in the stands. Wait, it looks like Cross may have broken his bat. While we wait on that, Laura has some history on bats."

"When I spoke with Joe earlier today, he brought up that the archives revealed that, at one time, youth baseball used aluminum bats and also carbon fiber bats. Eventually, those were outlawed, and all wood bats became the standard, just like the professional players of that era."

"Alright, we're ready to go again. Billy Cross, with a new bat, settles in again, and Banks delivers. There's a swing, and a sharp single between third baseman Steve Dearing and shortstop Roy Hobson. Kennedy trips and falls at third. Austin pulls up at second base, while Billy Cross pulls up at first."

"Smart base running by Austin Scott," Laura commented. "When he saw Kennedy fall at third base, he had the good sense to pull up at second and not overrun the base."

"Well, everyone, here's a potentially magic moment. The bases are loaded, with just one out. The White Stockings trail the Bear Cubs 10 - 7, and the next batter is none other than Joe Scott! As he walks up to the plate, he represents the winning run. Let's pause here and take this in."

⚾ ⚾ ⚾

Grandpa Moses was feeling sheer delight. Sitting with his friend, Wesley Wainwright, they were having the time of their lives. He looked around and saw everyone on their feet, expectantly. He turned and watched Joe. They made eye contact as Joe slowly walked up to home plate. Moses gave his grandson the thumbs up. Joe acknowledged the gesture with a nod and smiled back at his beloved grandpa.

⚾ ⚾ ⚾

"Speaking of special moments," Frank said. "The applause for Joe Scott has not abated. I'm not sure he was aware of it, at first, until Ted yelled out from the mound and pointed over to the Scott family, sitting by the president. Joe turned to look and acknowledge them, put his right hand over his heart, and seemed to toss it over to where his family was sitting. On seeing the crowd still standing and still in their sustained applause, Joe Scott is removing his hat and tipping it toward the fans along the third baseline, now the first, now the outfield bleachers. He had his hand in motion to put his ball cap back on, but he's now pausing and looking skyward, pointing a finger heavenward. The crowd is finally quieting down and taking their seats.

"Joe takes a huge breath and steps into the batter's box. Mary Scott has remained standing, and now her husband, daughters, and dad stand back up. The president and Mrs. Kennedy stand back up as well. All the fans behind them now stand up again, to see what happens next.

"Banks steps off the mound and rubs the baseball. He steps back onto the mound and places his foot on the pitching rubber. He stares down Kennedy at third and then faces the plate. The windup and the pitch. Joe swings and misses. Strike one! Mary Scott is nervously bouncing up and down on her toes, with both hands over her mouth, as the excitement of this moment becomes heart racing."

"Joe steps out of the batter's box and bends down to grab some dirt and rub it into his hands. He steps back into the box, with the count at no balls and one strike. Ted readies and fires the next pitch. Joe swings and fouls it off, over toward the first-base side. No balls and two strikes is the count. Banks, again, steps off the mound to rub the ball. Stepping back, he gets the signal from Bill Adams. He sets and delivers. Joe Scott stands and watches the ball trail down and away for ball one.

"The count is now one ball and two strikes, with one out. Banks gets the call and doesn't like it. He awaits the second choice from catcher Bill Adams. This time, he tips his head in agreement. He sets for the pitch and delivers. Joe Scott swings and connects! Oh my! That is way high — way higher than Ted's home run — but will this one stay in the park? It's still going … going — gone! It leaves the yard!!! Joe Scott has hit a game-winning, four-run home run that has left the ballpark, over toward where Marine One is parked at the helipad! The White Stockings have come from behind here, down three runs in the bottom of the eighth inning, and have defeated the Bear Cubs 11 - 10! What a magical finish to this incredible day!!"

"Frank, they call that a Grand Slam in baseball lingo."

"Grand indeed! As Joe Scott rounds third base, he has a smile a mile wide, and his teammates await his arrival at home plate. He crosses home plate and is immediately mobbed by all of them and more. His family is now rushing out onto the ball field, and his beloved Grandpa Moses takes a slow walk over toward the raucous scene as well.

"Joe Scott is now overcome with emotion as he sees his Grandpa Moses. He rushes over toward him, and they embrace. They both tap their hearts and point skyward. This crowd has gone absolutely crazy here!"

⚾ ⚾ ⚾

Mary Scott was crying tears of joy while hugging Joe, then her husband, then her dad, and the rest of her kids. The crowd would not stop the celebration. Mary had to yell into the ear of her dad, "Was that what you meant?"

Grandpa Moses moved his head back to see his daughter's face and held her head between his aged hands. With a few tears of his own, he nodded his head, yelling, "Uh-huh!"

They both laughed and cried.

As Joe had crossed home plate, the president and Mrs. Kennedy could not help themselves either. They also ran out after the Scott family did, to embrace their son, Dwight. The Secret Service, somewhat caught by surprise, quickly recovered and went running alongside the president and first lady.

With the celebration showing no sign of abating, Mayor Meyer gave the signal to launch the special surprise he had planned for the end of the game. Beyond the left-field fence, a hundred yards away, was a small wild cornfield that stood high enough to hide his surprise. With the celebration of the game's end at full volume, the Mayor texted the cue, and ten seconds later, a Fourth of July-style fireworks grand finale started. It whipped the crowd into another sustained celebration, as the sky was lit up with a brilliant display for the next ten minutes.

⚾ ⚾ ⚾

The lead Secret Service agent at the helipad looked over toward the fireworks display, back in the wild cornfield. He was taking in the moment, when he noticed a small boy wearing a pinstripe uniform and ball cap. He was standing 50 to 60 yards away, at the edge of the cornfield, and peeking out from between corn stalks. The kid was small enough not to alarm the agent, but even so, he was near a secure area. Curious, the agent decided to check on the boy and investigate. The agent started walking toward the area the boy was peeking out from, but the boy suddenly vanished from view. He ran the remaining 20 yards to the spot where he had seen the young boy, but the young lad had simply vanished. The agent blinked, rubbed his eyes, and chalked the whole thing up to a lack of sleep.

⚾ ⚾ ⚾

Ted Lee Banks and the rest of his team had all run in. They had promised each other that, no matter which team won, the losing team would congratulate the winning team, and eventually, when the commotion calmed down, they posed for a group photo with Joe Scott's team at home plate. A throng of press were there taking photos as well. Among them was Mike Drucker, who was broadly smiling while taking the entire scene in.

There was no trophy, just a bunch of smiling kids and adults. Sam Scott stepped forward with a rusty old sign that he handed to his son, Joe. Joe Scott gazed at it, laughed, and looked back up at his dad and yelled, "Thanks!"

Joe turned and held up the sign to his brother, Austin, Ted, and all the rest of their friends on both teams and yelled, "No Pepper!", as Mike Drucker snapped what would later become the headline photo of the year.

Mr. Spalding had watched the entire game, seven rows behind the president and the Scott family. After finding out where Sam Scott was seated, he planned to introduce himself to Joe Scott's dad immediately after the game. But he was unprepared for the mayhem that erupted with Joe Scott's game-winning, four-run home run, and he lost sight of Sam Scott. So, he entered the field and headed toward home plate. He had to show his credentials when a Secret Service agent spotted him and challenged him. Producing his ID, the agent let him pass after seeing the NSA Class 10 Security Clearance logo. When the commotion on the field had died down, he approached Sam Scott, who was hugging Joe again.

"Excuse me, Mr. Scott, my name is Reggie Spalding. Can we talk?"

CHAPTER TWENTY

Extra Innings!

Meanwhile, up in Heaven, George Herman Ruth, famously known as Babe Ruth, had been enjoying his visit with Lou Gehrig, when they received word to immediately assemble in the Diamond Hall. They both headed over there right away. As they walked through the 15-foot-high diamond-studded doors of the great hall, they stopped dead in their tracks at the sight before them. So many old baseball friends from their playing days, and so many of baseball's greatest players from before and after their time in the game.

Babe turned and looked at his longtime pal. "Wow, Lou, you know anything about this? This is incredible!"

"No, Babe, I'm as shocked as you are."

"Look, Lou, there's Cy, Mel, Tris, Roger. By golly, there's Satchel Paige! Look at 'em all! Look Lou, over there, it's Earle, Mark, Bob, Joe, Dugan, and Pat yacking it up with Huggins!"

They both ran over excitedly to mingle with their 1927 teammates and catch up with the guys. Then they noticed the "Fabulous Six," the first six female players of professional baseball. Babe excused himself and went over and introduced himself and shook their hands. The gals were in awe to see Babe Ruth. Babe looked several feet past the Fabulous Six and saw Shoeless Joe Jackson. Babe excused himself again. He walked over to Joe, and they embraced one another.

The attention chime rang, and the crowd quieted down. In walked number 42, Jackie Robinson, the guy who broke the color barrier in professional baseball. They greeted Jackie with a round of sustained applause. As he made his way forward, up the aisle, he stopped next to Babe, who promptly gave his friend a big bear-hug. After they exchanged a few pleasantries, Jackie broke away and continued down the aisle, hugging and shaking hands with many of baseball's greats, including a prolonged greeting and embrace with Henry Aaron. Next, he stopped for a sustained embrace of his dear friend, Branch Rickey. A few moments later, Jackie finally arrived at the podium.

"Thank you all for that greeting. Thank you. If I could have your attention for a moment, please."

The crowd quieted down for number 42.

"I have been instructed to pass along the following bit of news from the King. I just know it will thrill all of you to hear it. Today, in the city of McHenry, Illinois, in the United States of America, the first telecasted baseball game in over one hundred years was held. That's right everybody, baseball is back! They finally found the old game we so dearly loved down there!"

An instant, deafening roar of the crowd erupted in the giant hall. They all jumped, yelled, whooped, fist-bumped, high-fived, and hugged. In fact, they were all delirious. They had all known of the sad story of the demise of the game and the near total destruction of their old nation, so long ago in earth time.

After several minutes of jubilation, Jackie motioned to the crowd to again quiet down. After they did, Babe interrupted and yelled out, "Who found the old game, Jackie?"

Jackie turned and motioned for his friend, Chuck Hiller, to approach the podium.

"Thanks, Jackie. A thirteen-year-old boy named Joe Scott. He lives in McHenry and had a little help from his grandpa, family, and friends. This is so fantastic! I lived one town over from McHenry, in the village of Johnsburg. That's where I learned to play the game, before I signed up with San Francisco and played in the 1962 Series."

"Ya' don't say! Gee, that's swell! Ya' hear that, boys …" On seeing the Fabulous Six again, out of the corner of his eye, Babe quickly added, "… and ladies!"

The crowded hall erupted in good-natured laughter.

Babe, still exuberant, again yelled out, "Who brought the news up to us, Jackie?"

Jackie, back at the podium, smiled and looked straight at Babe, "Your little buddy, the 1927 batboy, Eddie Bennett."

"Eddie Bennett! Did ya' hear that, Lou?! Eddie Bennett!"

At that, Babe saw his beloved friend, Eddie Bennett, running towards him, and they embraced. "Aww Eddie, I'm so glad to see you again. You have no idea, kid. Say, let me get a good look at you! Look at that, Lou! Eddie's got a pinstripe uniform and a ball cap, just like the ones we wore in '27! Eddie, where'd you get it?"

"The King gave it to me earlier today, before my scouting trip to the game in McHenry! Oh, George, just wait till you see what comes next!"

Then, the Royal Trumpeters immediately appeared behind Jackie and blew the familiar sound. Each one turned and saw the King enter the hall.

As He walked down the aisle, He was, of course, mobbed by many of the players that were near enough to Him. The King was kind and gracious, exchanging hugs and pleasantries all along the walk to the podium.

Once at the podium, the King motioned for the room to

quiet down. He looked out at those assembled, smiled, and then clapped once. Instantly, all in the room were blinded by a brilliant flash of light. While still momentarily blinded, everyone now felt a gentle breeze on their cheeks.

As their eyes all collectively readjusted to the light, their vision quickly returned to them. When it did, an amazing sight greeted them. For they all found themselves on a ball field so gloriously perfect that it took their breath away.

As they looked around, they were astounded to see ballfields as far as the eye could see, and then they noticed that they were all in baseball uniforms from long ago, from their playing days.

Babe turned and looked at Shoeless Joe, who was standing next to him and Lou Gehrig. Babe laughed and quipped, "Joe, this sure ain't Iowa."

Shoeless Joe let out a big laugh as well, looked at Lou Gehrig, and then back at Babe. "No, Babe, this is Heaven."

To a person, they all looked down at their feet and saw their favorite baseball mitts, from their playing days, lying in the grass, just in front of them. In each mitt was a baseball. They all grabbed their mitts and, without a word, began to divide up into teams, and each paired up with another player and started playing catch. The first real baseball game in well over a hundred years had just been played on earth. It was time to play ball in Heaven!

Then, in that supernatural way that only the King could do, each person there saw the King of Kings standing right in front of them, with those eyes gazing deeply into theirs. Those eyes exuding the great love of the Father. Those eyes so filled with love and compassion for His children. In a small, still voice, He said, "Let's play ball!"

THE END

EPILOGUE

Joe Scott was dressed to the nines in his newly purchased suit. Now 14 years old, Mary Scott had taken Joe to the local tailor in town a week earlier, after realizing Joe's winter growth spurt had left his old suit too small.

Now, on May 10th, 2169, at the White House Rose Garden, Joe stood quietly with his parents, siblings, and other honored guests.

As he awaited the start of the ceremony, his thoughts turned to his Grandpa Moses. He sure missed him, and it hurt badly that he was not there to see that day. He felt a tear welling up, but the gentle hand of his mom on his shoulder assuaged the ripple of grief, and he kept his composure.

The hurt of Moses's passing the previous winter was tempered by the very real sense of his presence at the day's ceremony, where Joe, Eduardo Chavez, Laura Tubman, Earl Donnerson, and Mike Drucker were all to receive the Presidential Medal of Freedom, the nation's highest civilian award.

President Kennedy arrived on time and gave an eloquent speech. He spoke at length about Joe's exploits two years earlier and the ensuing ripple effects of his bringing back the game of baseball. How baseball's rebirth had helped bring further healing to a nation that still felt the great wounds of the war that had occurred over a century earlier.

It was as if baseball's return was, in a genuine sense, a missing piece of the puzzle of the nation's recovery. Before Joe brought the game back, the general sense in the nation was that, while America had mostly recovered from the war, some things were missing. Those *things* were intangible, and people struggled to put a name to them.

Judging by the outcome, one big intangible was baseball.

It all seemed surreal as Joe stood listening to the president of the United States speak about him and people he knew.

Joe glanced over at Mr. Chavez, Mrs. Tubman, Mr. Drucker, and Mr. Donnerson and gave each of them a faint smile as, one by one, the president recounted the important part they had each played in the game's resurrection.

Eduardo Chavez had made personal trips to the Library of Congress to oversee their data recovery efforts and had taken a personal interest that no stone was left unturned regarding all thing's baseball.

In addition to his national newspaper articles, Mike Drucker had also written a best-selling novel about Joe's efforts.

Laura Tubman had been influential in taking Good Morning USA to other cities all across America and covering "cultural recovery efforts."

Earl Donnerson had spent enormous sums of money to build youth ball fields all over the northern part of the state of Illinois and was currently working on assembling a team of wealthy investors to start a professional baseball league. He was even exploring building a 40,000-seat stadium to the west of town to house a new professional baseball team, yet to be named.

The president, as expected, saved his best accolades for last. As Sam and Mary Scott listened to the president's gracious and endearing words directed at their older son, Joe, they both subtly reached out, searching for one another's hands, and found them. Grasping Sam's hand gently, Mary too felt a wave of emotion, as her thoughts turned to her dad. *"Oh, that he could have been here for this day,"* she thought.

As the thought lingered, a few tears flowed. Sam, seeing them out of the corner of his eye, squeezed her hand a few times, then gently nudged his side up against hers.

One by one, the president called the names of the recipients and placed the medals around their necks. Sam, Mary, and the kids beamed as the president reached Joe and awarded him his medal.

But Mary was unprepared for what happened next.

"There is one more citizen we need to recognize here today," President Kennedy announced. "Of whom, without his aid, perhaps we might not even be standing here holding this ceremony today.

"Brian Woodbridge, affectionately known as Grandpa Moses. For it was on his farm, in Dyersville, Iowa, that he dug up the huge cache of baseball items that played a key part in all of this. Brian Woodbridge passed away three months ago in his sleep. As you know, Mr. Woodbridge was a member of the Crucible Generation, those Americans born within the first twenty years after the Second Civil War.

"More than any other generation in our nation's history, it was that generation in particular that bore the heaviest burden of keeping the light of liberty alive through so much suffering and darkness.

"I would like to call upon his daughter, Mary Scott, to receive his award, posthumously, on behalf of her father."

As Mary heard all of this, her heart was filled with joy. She stepped forward, and the president placed the medal around her neck. Joe Scott broke rank and stepped over to hug his mom tightly, so very tightly.

The president concluded his remarks, giving an update on the de-radiation efforts ongoing in Chicago, New York, Charlotte, and Atlanta. The massive scientific and military undertaking was ahead of schedule. In another year, perhaps, these vast, former-metropolitan areas would be reopened to allow the long process of clearing, rebuilding, and resettlement.

Toward the back of the audience, Mr. Spalding had been quietly listening and was filled with pride to be an American. At the ceremony's end, he approached the president, as well as the award recipients, and thanked them all, one by one. He was especially diligent to meet Sam and Joe Scott again to update them on the baseball equipment deal. Although they were manufacturing new baseball equipment as fast as they could, they were still unable to keep up with demand.

As Joe listened to his dad and Mr. Spalding talk business, his thoughts again turned to his beloved grandpa. A single word that came to Joe's mind, one that he had heard his grandpa use many times: *Providence*.

About the Author

William R. Douglas is a first-time novelist. After obtaining a Journalism Degree in 1980, his career took a turn down the road of Information Technology. In the IT Field, he was still able to enjoy writing, no matter if it was technical documentation, newsletters or other material. He lives in the small town of McHenry, Illinois, with his wife Laurie and cat Peaches. They enjoy spending time with 6 kids and 8 grandkids and are very active in their local church.